The False Princess

The False Princess

EILIS O'NEAL

SCHOLASTIC INC.
New York Toronto London Auckland
Sydney Mexico City New Delhi Hong Kong

ISBN 978-0-545-46822-0

12 11 10 9 8 7 6 5 4 3   12 13 14 15 16 17/0

Printed in the U.S.A.   40

First Scholastic printing, April 2012

Book design by A. Castanheira

I couldn't choose.

For my mother,
and all the days in the garden.

For my father,
who opened the door to Middle Earth and beyond.

And for Matt,
who, like Kiernan, knew first.

The False Princess

CHAPTER ONE

The day they came to tell me, I was in one of the gardens with Kiernan, trying to decipher a three-hundred-year-old map of the palace grounds. We were sitting on a stone bench, the delicate roll of fabric lying between us. Instead of looking toward the gardens, however, we faced the gray wall that separated the northernmost edge of the palace grounds from the streets of Vivaskari.

"It can't be there," he was saying. "Look, Nalia."

I glanced up from the map to follow Kiernan's finger, which pointed at the expanse of wall in front of us. Once he had my attention, he jumped up from his seat on the bench and strode toward the wall. He rapped his fist against it, then winced comically. I rolled my eyes. "See?" he said. "There's nothing here. Are you sure, oh princess wise and stubborn, that you're reading it properly?"

I sighed in frustration. He was right. We had examined this section of wall for over an hour, searching for any cracks or indentions that might indicate a secret door, all without success.

"We're where it says we should be. At least, where the part that I can read says we should be." I tugged a hand through my hair, pulling a few of the dark brown strands loose so that they trailed against my neck. "It's those markings along the bottom. I've looked and I've looked, but I can't find anything that even comes close to them. They aren't any modern language I know, or even any ancient one." Which was irritating, since I knew four modern languages well, bits and pieces of six others, and enough of five ancient tongues to at least recognize them. But these . . . runes—I could think of no better word to describe the scratchy markings—were completely baffling. Not that I had asked anyone else about them, not even the librarians who should have been the map's keepers. It was a mystery, one Kiernan and I had discovered, and we were determined to figure out the answer by ourselves.

"They could say anything," I continued. "They could say, 'Do the opposite of everything you've just read.' After all, the location of the King Kelman's Door is supposed to be secret."

We had been trying to find King Kelman's Door since the snowstorm last winter that had trapped the entire city indoors for days. Though I would have enjoyed sitting in front of a fire in one of the palace halls with a good book, Kiernan chafed at being kept inside. And since I was his best friend, finding ways to help him expend his boundless energy had generally fallen onto me.

So we had spent most of the four snowbound days exploring the palace, which, being more than six hundred years old, had enough interesting places to keep us busy for forty days. Kiernan liked the armory best, where he could examine the weapons of deceased kings and queens, and where we found a tiny hidden recess in the wall behind the shield of my great-great-grandfather. Inside the recess had lain a dagger, no longer than my hand from wrist to fingertip. It was quite plain and, since we couldn't imagine that anyone had missed it during the past hundred years, Kiernan had kept it.

It was in the library, though, that we made our most exciting discovery. After two days of exploring, I had felt a strong, almost overwhelming need to read something, anything, and I had been determined to spend at least an hour in the palace library. Kiernan, though able enough when it came to books and learning, had little true patience for sitting and reading. Still, he had followed me, protesting all the while. When I told him that he didn't have to come, he only shrugged and came after me anyway. That wasn't strange, though. We were best friends; we did everything together. He dragged me into scrapes that I would never have considered getting into otherwise, pulled me from my shell of shyness and reserve, and for my part, I made sure that he read a book every once in a while.

I had wanted to look at a book on the history of Thorvaldian magic. The particular volume I wanted, which covered a span of some five hundred years but contained magical theories now considered out of date, was shelved in a tiny room in the very back of the library, tossed amid a collection of moldering scrolls and maps. Even though I lacked any magic myself—no member of the royal family had possessed magic for four hundred years— I had always been fascinated with it anyway. Not that I had as much time as I would have liked to devote to it; there were always more pressing things that a princess needed to study. But I read what I could, even when I didn't understand some of it.

I was sitting at a low table placed beneath a window, trying to make out some of the more arcane phrases, when I heard a sudden crash and looked up in time to see a shower of dust waft out of the small room where I had found the book. I glanced around, sure that a librarian would come running to investigate, but none did. So I hurried into the room to see Kiernan standing ankle-deep in a pile of scrolls and books.

"I was just looking," he protested before I could say anything. "They fell on their own!"

Scowling at him, I gestured to the pile. "Help me clean this up before Torvoll gets here." Torvoll was the palace's head librarian, and a man with very particular ideas about the treatment of books, even those no one had touched in years.

We worked quickly, eyes on the door, and had replaced all but three items when I paused. One of the scrolls had fallen open, the brittle string that had held it snapped in its crash to the floor, to reveal a drawing of the palace grounds. At first, I only glanced at the writing surrounding the image, but something in it snagged my eye, and when I looked more closely, I had to gulp to swallow my gasp.

"Put those up," I ordered.

Kiernan, who was holding the last two books, shoved them onto the shelf. "What is it?"

"I'll tell you in a minute," I murmured. My legs felt shaky with the discovery, and I hoped that I'd be able to make it out of the library without falling down or tripping on anything. "Just hurry." Then I tucked the map—drawn on a roll of fabric rather than paper—under my arm and darted out of the tiny room.

"Aren't you going to put that back?" Kiernan asked as we

passed the table where I had been reading, my book still lying on it, but he went silent when I glared at him. We paused behind a shelf near the entrance to let a librarian shuffle past, and then slipped from the room. Kiernan's eyes never left me; unlike me, he hardly even had to concentrate at walking unobtrusively, what with all the tricks he pulled. Finally, when we were three corridors away, he said drolly, "I'd heard that even princesses weren't allowed to take books from the library without Torvoll's permission."

"*You're* really going to bother me about rule breaking?" I asked. My heart was beating fast, both with the excitement of the find and the daring of my actions. He was right, though; I had never instigated something like this. It was always Kiernan who dragged me into mischief. I was a good, quiet, and rule-following girl. The perfect princess, if not for my clumsiness and sometimes painful shyness.

Kiernan grinned, his eyes bright. "So what is it?"

I couldn't help the matching grin that gripped my own face. "I think it's a map of King Kelman's Door."

And so the search had begun. King Kelman, I had explained to Kiernan, had ruled during a tumultuous time in Thorvaldor's history, an era when plots to overthrow his rule had abounded. So he had instructed his best wizard to create a magically hidden door in the palace's outer walls so that he could escape if he was attacked. According to the cryptic writings of that wizard, however, peace had come soon after the door was completed and it had never been used. Still, Kelman remained a suspicious man, and he told few people about the door. After his death, its location had been forgotten.

Now that map, also forgotten for centuries in the stacks of unwanted library materials, was giving me a headache. I closed my eyes against the brightness of the sun. "It's a *really* good secret," I grumbled. "No wonder Kelman didn't mind one of his wizards making a map of it, if he even knew about it. No one can read it, so what's the harm?"

"Maybe it's a code. Or a magic language," Kiernan suggested as he plucked a newly greening blade of grass and twirled it between his fingers. He leaned nonchalantly against the trunk of the huge tree that shaded us, his dark blond hair falling across his face, the very picture of idle nobility.

"Maybe," I conceded.

Kiernan puffed out his cheeks with a breath. "And you're *sure* we're in the right place? Because there's just a city street on the other side of this wall. What's the point of making a magical escape route if you're still going to be inside the city once you go through it?"

"Well, the city was smaller when Kelman was king. There used to be open forest on the other side of this wall. But there was this great expansion effort during the reign of—"

I would have gone on, but I didn't have time to explain it further, because the sound of feet crunching the tiny stones on one of the garden's paths caught my attention.

Glancing over my shoulder, I saw Cornalus, the steward, coming across the garden toward us. Cornalus was an old man, his gray hair trimmed so that it brushed his shoulders in an old-fashioned style. He had been my grandmother's steward as well as my father's. He had always been very kind to me, and one of my earliest memories was of his sneaking me a sweet with a wink during a very dull ceremony.

EILIS O'NEAL

"Good morning, Your Highness," he said formally when he reached us.

I smiled at him. It was a small smile, my lips closed together, not because I didn't like him, but because there were few people other than Kiernan who could elicit a full, toothy grin from me. "Good morning, Cornalus." As I spoke, I casually slid the map until it was hidden behind me so that he wouldn't see what it contained. It was our secret, after all, mine and Kiernan's.

"Your parents are requesting your presence in the Hall of Thorvaldor," he continued. "They've asked that you come immediately."

I frowned, my eyes going to my lap. The sun was warm on my shoulders, I would remember later, the stone bench hard beneath me. A striped insect crawled across the grass, pausing in confusion when it found its path blocked by my left foot.

It was strange, I thought, that my parents should want to see me in the Hall of Thorvaldor before noon, and strange that they should send Cornalus to find me. My parents were usually so busy that I sometimes went several days without seeing them at all, and they rarely asked for me during the middle of the day. They reserved that time for the business of the ruling Thorvaldor, not for chatting with their only daughter.

As I raised my eyes, I realized that both Kiernan and Cornalus were watching me. So I smiled, a little tightly this time, and rose. A quick glance at Kiernan and he was beside the bench, casually rolling the map up. "I don't know how long they'll want me," I said to him. "But I'll find you when we're through."

Kiernan shrugged, grinning. "Don't worry about me," he said, then walked off, a whistled tune floating through the air behind him. He would have no trouble amusing himself during my absence, I knew, whether it took two hours or two days. With his ready smile and quick wit, the Earl of Rithia's son was a palace favorite. No matter the amusement, he was eager to participate and prepared to laugh at himself if he failed, and even his many tricks and practical jokes didn't hurt his reputation. Many of the palace residents, I knew, considered it his greatest feat that he was able to get me, the reclusive princess, to relax in his presence.

I followed Cornalus through the garden, making myself match his slow pace. Before us loomed the palace. The windows on the upper floors glinted in the morning sun. The seat of the Thorvaldian royal family hadn't changed much over the centuries, adding a wing here or a tower there with reluctance. The lack of change had always simultaneously comforted and disturbed me. On one hand, it was nice to think that my ancestors had once slept in the very room I slept in; on the other, couldn't one of them have figured out a way to keep my sitting room a bit warmer in the winter? Still, it was a grand building, one I rarely tired of, and my home.

"Do we have time for me to stop in my rooms?" I asked once we were inside. My hair probably looked like birds had nested in it, since it took only a few minutes of wind to mess it up and I'd been outdoors all morning.

Cornalus looked doubtful. "They mentioned that they wanted you as soon as possible, Your Highness."

I bit the inside of my cheek, then nodded. "All right." After a moment, I let myself fall a few steps behind Cornalus, then ran my hands through my hair when he wasn't looking. Without a mirror, I had no way of knowing if I had made it better or worse;

EILIS O'NEAL

I could only hope that it was lying flat instead of standing out like a nimbus around my head.

"Wait, please," I said softly when we reached the huge oaken doors that led to the Hall of Thorvaldor. Taking a deep breath, I smoothed my hands down the front of my dress, adjusted the belt made from silver links against my narrow hips, and patted my hair down one last time. The Hall of Thorvaldor was the hall of state, where coronations and public hearings and all sorts of official business took place. It was large enough to hold hundreds of people on the ground floor, and it had a balcony as well. If my parents wanted to see me there, it must be something important. Maybe some diplomat from Farvasee or Wenth had unexpectedly brought a son or daughter who needed entertaining, or maybe it had to do with the current feud between two noble houses over who owned the rights to several northern mines. More than ever, I wished I had been able to stop to make myself presentable.

I blew out the breath I had been holding. No matter. I couldn't do anything about my appearance now, so I would just have to make sure I didn't trip walking across the long, smooth floor that led to the two thrones at the end of the hall. I nodded to the guards standing on either side of the great doors, and they reached forward at precisely the same time to reveal the hall.

The Hall of Thorvaldor was long, high-ceilinged, and lined with tall windows. Unlike the Great Hall, where feasts took place, or the Hall of Fires, where the palace residents might go to read or listen to the latest songs or poems, the Hall of Thorvaldor rarely felt warm. White columns set at intervals created a wide pathway that led across the marble floor to a dais, where two large thrones sat. Without waiting, I raised my chin and walked toward them. Behind me, I heard the doors shut with a thud, and then the slow steps of Cornalus following.

The prickles on my neck started as soon as the doors shut. At the end of the hall, my parents sat on their thrones, wearing their heavy crowns of state. Two other people stood at the base of the dais. There was no one else in the room.

I swallowed. Something was going on.

I recognized the others as I neared the dais. The older man was Neomar Ostralus, the head of the wizards' college in Vivaskari and my father's chief advisor in magical matters. He looked exactly as you would expect one of the most powerful wizards in the country to look, with his white-flecked beard; sharp, dark eyes; and haughty movements. Beside him, tall and straight-backed, her dark, lustrous hair swept up and pinned like a crown on her head, was Melaina Harandron. Melaina was considered to be Neomar's most probable successor, both as the college's head and as my father's wizardly councillor. She was also a noblewoman, the Baroness of Saremarch, and very beautiful. Both wore black robes, the indicators of master wizards.

I had never had much contact with either of them, though Melaina lived in the palace some of the year and Neomar visited it almost every day. Neomar stayed busy as the college's head and my father's advisor, which made him brisk in his dealings with nearly everyone. I always felt that I was taking too much of his time when I talked to him, as if, even though I was the princess, I wasn't quite important enough for him. And Melaina had a way of looking at me that made me think she could see into my head, a steady, unblinking gaze that unnerved me a bit. She was lovely, her graceful movements so deceptively languid, which made me feel all the more clumsy in her presence. Still, they were important people, and seeing them there made the prickles on my neck sharpen.

I nodded to both of them as I passed and, out of the corner of my eye, saw that Cornalus had gone to stand with them, but then directed all my attention to my parents. "Your Highnesses," I said formally as I stopped a few feet from the dais. Then: "Mother, Father."

"Nalia," my mother said. She didn't smile as she said it, though, and I thought I heard a catch somewhere in the back of her throat, though it was gone so quickly I couldn't be sure. "We have something to tell you."

She cast a glance at my father, a movement so sharp that it made me blink. My mother was light and a little winsome, not at all quick or hard. My father looked down, as if steeling himself for something, and when he looked up, he was wearing the face of the king, strong and steady, and cold.

"You know," he said, "that when every son or daughter of the royal house is born, the oracle at Isidros makes a prophecy about that baby."

I nodded slowly. Of course I knew—everyone knew. The oracle at Isidros was the conduit of foretelling from the Nameless God. People from across Thorvaldor and even beyond sought out the oracle for guidance; sometimes, if the God decreed it, they received an answer. But for a child of the royal family, the Nameless God always sent a prophecy before the baby's birth. Sometimes they were specific, telling the manner of the child's death or of a particular triumph of war, but usually they were very general so that the meaning was debated for years.

"Can you tell us the prophecy given for you?"

Again, I nodded; I knew the words by heart. "Long and well shall she rule. War shall not touch her, nor famine, nor plague."

My father smiled, but it was a brittle smile, without even comfort in it. "A fine prophecy," he said. "But it was a false one."

"What?" My prophecy was false? Was this what they had called me to say?

I could hear the slightest of tremors in his voice now, but he continued without stopping. "Before the birth, when the queen was still well enough to travel, we journeyed to the oracle, and she gave us the God's prophecy. But it was not the prophecy you just recited. The true prophecy was one of blood."

My heart thumped in my chest, and I could barely hear my father over the rushing in my ears.

"According to the oracle, there was a chance the princess could die, murdered, before her sixteenth birthday. It was not certain, but the chance was great enough that, when she sought the foretelling, all the oracle saw was blood, and the princess dead in this room."

But I am sixteen, I thought hazily, even though I couldn't seem to speak. *Is that what they want to tell me, that I'm safe now?*

My father went on, gaining speed as he spoke. "It had been a . . . difficult conception, and an even more difficult birth. The physicians had told us that it was unlikely that the queen would bear another child. The princess was the only heir. We had to keep her safe, no matter what the cost. We formed a plan."

I wanted to rub my head with my hand, but I managed to

keep it at my side. Why did he keep saying that? *The princess.* As if I wasn't there. And if I were safe now, why did he look so grim?

"After the birth, we put our plan into action. Only a few people had seen the baby, and one infant looks so much like another."

He stopped short, his eyes fixed on mine. When he spoke again, he sounded tired, like a man at the end of a long journey. "We hid the princess away so that she would be safe until after her sixteenth birthday. And we replaced her with another baby, a false princess. You."

I swayed. The Hall of Thorvaldor tilted, the light from the windows becoming hard and glittering, blinding me. I squinted against the sudden brightness, and as I did, the room seemed to change, its familiar shape shifting until I wasn't sure I knew it anymore.

"What?" I gasped. My throat was too small, not enough air getting through it, and I couldn't breathe. "How? I don't— I don't—"

The queen had hidden her face in her hands, and the king placed one hand on her shoulders. "We couldn't just send the princess away, because then whatever malice had been foreseen could just go looking for her. We had to make it seem that she was here, living in the palace. There was a spell," he explained, "to make you appear to be the princess to any eyes, magical or otherwise. You had been picked because it seemed likely that you would resemble her as you grew. But the spell gave you her birthmark, and a glamour that would make any probing wizard think you were of royal blood. Our daughter. It was strong magic, wrought by the strongest wizards living then. But now it is time for it to be removed."

Neomar stepped forward, his hand upraised. He didn't speak to me as he held his palm up over my forehead, his intense, black eyes fixed on my face.

Stop, I wanted to say, but Neomar was already muttering something under his breath. A spell, I realized, and a difficult one, for sweat had beaded on his wrinkled forehead.

A golden haze blossomed around me, making it hard to see. I tried to say no, but the word wouldn't come. The golden haze brightened suddenly, and something inside me, something I hadn't even known was there, fell away, like a cloak slipping onto the floor. Then the golden haze faded, and Neomar stepped back, his hands pressed against his chest.

Trembling, I held out my left arm, turning it so that my palm faced upward.

I had had the birthmark for as long as I could remember. Three small reddish dots shaped almost like a triangle on my inner arm, just below the bend of my elbow. As I watched, the marks faded, slowly dwindling until nothing but unblemished skin remained.

"It's a trick," I said, but faintly.

"Yes, it was," said the king. "But a trick to fool the world. And so it had to fool you, too." His face softened for a moment, and I had the urge to run to him, as I had as a child. But then it closed, became the king's face, and not my father's.

"Who knew?" I asked dully.

"As few people as possible." He gestured to the two wizards. Neomar was still breathing heavily, Melaina holding his arm

EILIS O'NEAL

with concern, but he looked up at the king's words. "We went to Neomar, but it was Melaina's plan. She was a talent even then. They and Flavian, the college's head librarian and a great wizard in his own right, created the spell and cast it. One of them renewed the spell every few years when it grew weaker, and then removed your memory of the renewal. Since Flavian died seven years ago, Neomar and Melaina are the only ones who knew, until now. Even Cornalus has found out just today."

"And the—" I broke off, unable to finish the sentence, to utter the name that I had thought was mine.

The king seemed to know what I had been going say. "Nalia has been raised in a convent some distance from here—Melaina took her there a few days after her birth. She has believed that she is an orphan, but one with a noble patron. None of the sisters at the convent know any differently. She has been given a noble's education, taught as well as a princess should be. She was told that one day she would come to court, as her patron wanted. It was safer for her not to know."

"Have you seen her? Do you visit her?"

The king closed his eyes. "No. Melaina and Neomar, they have seen her a few times. Every few years, one of them had to go to the convent, disguised by magic, to renew the spell on her and then erase her memory. But we have not seen our daughter since her birth."

Our daughter, I thought. And then: *He called her Nalia.*

I felt tired, more tired than I had ever been in my life, so it was hard to hold my head up and even harder to ask my next question. "Who am I? If I'm not her, then who am I?"

"Melaina found you. She scryed for a day, searching for the

right baby. Your father was a weaver in the city. We summoned him, told him our plan. He gave you to us willingly, and then Neomar altered his memory, making it seem to him that his baby had died." At my exhalation of shock, he said, a little defensively, "It was safer. The fewer people who knew . . ."

"And my mother?" The question was small and quiet. "Did she give me up as well?"

The king shook his head. "He did not mention his wife."

I clenched my gown's skirts in my hands. It was too much, too much to comprehend. "Is he still alive?"

Again, that flash of sadness across the king's face. "No. He died some years ago, in his sister's house in Treb."

The light from the windows pressed against me, as bright and sharp as diamonds. *I am alone,* I thought as I gazed around the hall. *All of this, all my life, it was a dream. And it is ending.*

"What is my name?" I asked.

For the first time, the queen stirred, raising her head to looked at me. "Sinda," she said, her voice thin. "He said your name was Sinda."

"Sinda," I whispered. I waited for the word to have some meaning, to fill the empty place left when the golden haze had receded.

But the name just faded away, filling nothing, lost in the high-ceilinged Hall of Thorvaldor.

CHAPTER TWO

I stood at the window of the room that was no longer mine. Below me, two of the queen's ladies walked through one of the formal gardens, their three children scampering back and forth across the paths. One of the ladies stopped to speak to a young man dressed in the green robes of a novice wizard—perhaps a noble student at the college come to visit his parents. It was still pleasant outside, I knew. If I pressed my hand against the window's pane, I could feel the warmth seeping through the glass. But inside, I was cold, so cold I thought I might shatter if I moved too quickly.

There had been a council meeting, with all of the king's councillors and all of the high-ranking nobles who were currently at the palace. I had stood beside the king as he explained the true prophecy to the people gathered in the hall. I had held out my arm to show the vanished birthmark, and heard myself say that I was not the princess amid gasps of shock. Then I had been excused. I had heard the king say, as I left the room, that Nalia would be arriving that afternoon.

It had hurt; that had surprised me. I had thought, in the hour or so it took to gather the council and the nobles in the hall for the revelation, that I could not possibly hurt any more than I already did. My chest had felt tight, as if it were being crushed between two giant hands, and my eyes had burned with unshed tears. Surely nothing could make me feel worse, more lost and alone, than I already did. But it had hurt even more when I stood before that crowd and heard the man I had thought my father unname me.

Outside, the lady speaking to the green-robed wizard laughed. I couldn't hear it, but I could imagine how light and carefree she sounded. By now, the pain I had felt in the hall had faded to a muffled dullness, so that I might have been moving through the world while encased in thick wool. *I will never stand here again,* I thought. *I will never walk in the gardens, or eat at the table with Kiernan, or sleep in my bed.*

I had to leave. My father—no, the king, I reminded myself— had explained that there must be no confusion when Nalia arrived. So I must go. My aunt was still alive in Treb, and I could be taken to her. It would be swift, like the severing of a limb, so that the injury would heal more quickly, he had said.

There was a knock on the door, and I started, one hand flying out and banging into the stone windowsill. "Come in," I called once I had ungritted my teeth, and a moment later two serving women whom I barely recognized entered the room.

"We're to help you pack, my lady," said the first. She was the older of the two, her black hair streaked with gray, and she spoke matter-of-factly. The second, younger, goggled at me with wide eyes. Normally, my own ladies-in-waiting would have helped me prepare for a journey. But nothing was normal, not now, and they were probably readying themselves for the real Nalia's arrival.

"I'm no one's lady," I said. "Not anymore."

The first woman nodded, though a concerned look passed over her face. "As you please, miss." She glanced meaningfully at the younger woman, and the two went to work, gathering some of my plainer clothes and folding them into a small trunk.

My hand was still smarting, I realized as I watched, and I lifted the other to massage the soreness out. *I never was much like a real princess,* I thought. I had always been too shy, too clumsy, too unpolished. More comfortable in the library than at a feast, so likely to trip coming down the stairs or bang my shins when getting out of a chair. My hair always messy and in my eyes, and my fingers always covered in ink. *A real princess wouldn't be like that. I should have known. I should have guessed.*

It took surprisingly little time for them to pack the things I would be allowed to take. When they had finished, the women lifted the trunk, nodded to me, and left. Since they had not indicated that I should follow them, I stayed where I was, looking out the window. After a time, there was another knock on the door. When I went to open it, I was surprised to find Cornalus there.

"It's time to go," he said simply. He leaned on a tall stick, one he had not been using when he had come to fetch me from the garden that morning.

I nodded, took a final look at my room, and stepped out into the corridor.

I had known that rumor traveled quickly in the palace, but I had not realized just how quickly. It had been Kiernan, before, who trailed rumors behind him, not me. But there was no one, it seemed, who did not know that I was no longer their princess. Every pair of eyes locked onto me as I approached, and once I was past, the whispering began. It made my face burn, but I lifted my chin, jaw tight, and marched on with Cornalus.

It was only when we passed a window that looked out onto the grand entrance to the palace that I faltered. As we walked by, I glanced outside for one last look at the great stone causeway that led past the gates and up to the wide stairs at the palace door. At the bottom of the steps, the king and queen waited. As I watched, an elegant carriage drawn by four white horses approached. The driver reined the animals in, and then a footman stepped forward to open the carriage doors.

A girl emerged. She was dressed in a red gown, and her dark hair fell unbound down her back. She moved smoothly, gracefully, like a deer stepping from the forest. She paused for a moment, and the king and queen came toward her, hands outstretched. She turned to offer them her own hands, and I caught a glimpse of her face.

She looks like me, I thought. Then Nalia smiled at something the queen had said. It was an easy smile, one given often, simply because it made her happy to do so. At the window, I curled my own lips inward, my hand going instinctively toward my mouth.

No. I *look like* her.

Outside, the king and queen ushered Nalia toward the palace doors, where they disappeared from sight. The carriage drove off, leaving the space where the family had stood empty. The pain

EILIS O'NEAL

in my chest started throbbing again, slowly, but with growing intensity, spreading from my chest throughout my body. Only when Cornalus touched me gently on the arm did I move away.

My own carriage waited by the palace stables. It was a simple conveyance, clean and practical, not at all like the gilded one that had brought the princess from her convent home. The trunk of my things had been tied to the back.

"My lady," Cornulas said, and even through the rushing in my ears I could hear how it shook. "I am sorry, so sorry. I had no idea, and it has all happened too quickly for an old man like me. I wish . . ." He swallowed. "I have been asked to give you this," he said, and then handed me a small velvet bag that clinked when I took it. "And this is for your aunt." A letter written on thick paper and sealed with the king's signet; I fumbled to take it as well.

"The queen, she asked me to tell you . . ." He seemed to be searching for the words, his eyes filled with pity. "She will pray for you to the Nameless God. Every day."

I pictured, for a moment, the queen kneeling before the little altar in her quarters, as I had seen her many times. But the image was immediately replaced by the sight of her welcoming Nalia on the palace steps, and I couldn't reply for the thickness that suddenly choked my throat.

He shook his head hard. "I have a granddaughter your age. She's never been to court, but you have always reminded me of her. If I had only known, I would have tried to spare you this pain," he said. "Somehow . . ."

The barest strand of comfort, and part of me wanted to grab on to it as hard as I could, but it was too little, and too late. I only turned my face away from Cornalus, not wanting him to see my reaction.

I should be crying, I thought as I gazed up at the palace. The wind picked up, whipping my skirts against my legs and blowing my hair into my eyes. Clouds scuttled across the sky, obscuring the bright light of the sun.

For a long moment I stood there, waiting, though I didn't know what I waited for. To burst into tears, maybe, or to wake up from the horrible dream that clung to me. But I remained unawakened and dry cheeked, just a girl standing in the shadow of an immense palace.

There was nothing else to do. I nodded to Cornalus and accepted his hand into the carriage. "Take her to Treb," I heard him tell the driver as I arranged myself gingerly on the seat. "Her aunt is a dyer there." There was a pause and then, "Keep her safe."

The driver flicked the reins, and the carriage lurched forward. Pressing my face as close to the glass window as I could, I readied myself for one last look at my home. Just as I did so, I heard a familiar voice yelling, "Nalia! Nalia!"

Kiernan came dashing around the side of the stable, running as fast as he could, his arms waving to stop the carriage. But the horses had already begun to trot, and even his long legs couldn't keep up with them. As I watched, he stumbled to a stop, breathing hard, his hands braced on his knees. "Nalia," he called one last time, but the carriage did not halt.

I raised my hand to pound on the window and insist the driver stop, but just before my hand hit the glass, I let it drop. He had been calling to Nalia, to the girl who had thought herself the princess.

I never was Nalia. They just called me by her name.

I fell back against the seat, heavy and tired. The carriage passed through the outer palace wall into Vivaskari, and it was only then that I began to cry.

It was full night by the time we arrived in Treb, and with my eyes used to the city lights of Vivaskari, I could make out little of my new home as the carriage pulled into the tiny village.

I had stopped crying soon after leaving the palace. I had never been much for weeping, not since I was a little girl. A princess, I had thought, needed to remain composed. In fact, I doubted there was anyone besides Kiernan who had seen me cry since I was seven years old.

My stomach clenched as I remembered the way I had last seen Kiernan, his hands braced on his knees, his face red from running. Then I shoved the thought away, my throat closing.

I had tried to pray when the crying was over, but my thoughts kept straying from the Nameless God to Kiernan, or my once-parents, or just to a sort of blank nothingness.

Finally, however, the carriage halted, breaking through my tangled thoughts, and I heard the driver say, "Is this Treb?"

"Aye." The voice came from the right side of the carriage, and I slid across the seat to peer out the window. The owner of the voice was an old man with a pipe, leaning against the wall of what might have been a smithy.

"We're looking for the dyer's house. Can you direct us?"

The man tilted his head to indicate that we should keep going. "Same as I told that courier this afternoon. The Azaway house is on the left, flower garden in front." He took a puff on his pipe, then added, "Bit strange, so many fancy folk come to see Varil in one day."

The driver flipped a coin at the man, who reached out with surprising agility to catch it. As the carriage began to move, I sat back, my heart thudding. Varil. That must be my . . . aunt's name. It felt strange to think about having an aunt, for neither the king nor the queen had any living siblings. She must be expecting me; the old man had mentioned a courier, who could have reached Treb long before the carriage.

I barely had time to reach a fretful hand to my hair before the carriage stopped again, this time in front of a small house. I heard the footman on the back of the carriage hop down, then saw him make his way up the short path that cut through the garden growing around the front of the house. He had gone only a few steps, though, when the door of the cottage opened and a woman appeared, a lantern in her hand. The footman stopped, apparently taken aback, then hurried back to the carriage. My heartbeat sped up, if that was possible, as he reached for the handle on the carriage door.

"Your High—" He faltered, reddening enough that I could see it in the dim light. "I mean, my lady, we're here."

"Thank you," I said as I stepped down from the carriage. The weight of the darkness seemed to press on me, and though part of me longed to run toward the light of the cottage, part of me also wanted to run as fast as I could in the other direction. But I sucked in a breath and imagined myself walking through not the Hall of Thorvaldor—that hurt too much—but the Great Hall, the eyes of all the people in it upon me. That allowed me to raise my head and slowly set one foot in front of the other to walk down the path toward the cottage.

My aunt was a tall, thin woman with an angular set to her bones. Her hair was light brown, with strands of gray running through it, and her nose was long and sharp. I didn't see much of myself in her. We studied each other for a moment, and then she exhaled a puff of breath through her nose.

"You look like her," she said. "Your mother."

In my mind, I saw the queen, who was all softness and grace, whereas I had always been small and dark.

As if she could see my thought, my aunt pursed her lips. "I mean your real mother." It was a dry voice; it reminded me of reeds clacking together.

"I hope . . ." I licked my lips to wet them. "I hope that I have not inconvenienced you too much. It seems that you are my only living relative, and they could not think where else to send me."

My aunt looked at me for a long time, then barked at the footman, "Bring her things in, if she has any." Then, to me: "Well, you might as well come inside, too."

She turned, the light from the lantern suddenly hidden behind her body, and I followed, wanting whatever scrap of brightness I could find to push back the dark.

I awoke the next morning knowing exactly where I was. No moment of confusion, no thought that I was still in my bed in the palace. Even before I opened my eyes, I knew what had happened and where I was. What I didn't know was who I was.

Sinda, I thought into the darkness behind my closed eyes. It sounded hard inside my head, without the fluidity of my . . . of the princess's name. But it was mine now, the only name I had, I reminded myself before grinding my teeth together and opening my eyes.

I was lying on a narrow bed on a faded mattress stuffed with straw, a brilliantly dyed red blanket above me. Aside from the bed, the tiny room contained only a battered-looking stool with a shallow bowl of water perched on it. The trunk that held my things sat in the corner, my dress from the night before heaped on top of it. Long lines of light seeped in through the slats of the small shuttered window. I stood, rubbing my eyes, and stumbled over to my trunk. The dress I had worn the day before wasn't dirty, so I struggled to pull it on over my shift. It was one of the simplest dresses I owned—or had owned—but I had rarely dressed without the help of at least one of my ladies, and it took some time to arrange it properly. Luckily, the shoes I had worn were thin slippers, with no buckles or ties, and I simply shoved my feet into them. I straightened up, not sure whether I felt proud or frustrated by my ability to dress myself, when I noticed something else sitting atop the trunk.

It was the small bag Cornalus had given me the day before, lying beside the letter for my aunt; I hadn't looked inside it all the way from Vivaskari to Treb. Now, putting the letter aside on the bed, I reached down and picked the bag up, weighing it in my hand before pulling open the ties that closed it.

Gold. A small pile of gold coins winked back at me from inside the bag.

My chest constricted suddenly, as if the phantom hands from yesterday were squeezing me hard around my middle. I stared at the coins for a moment longer as I tried to remember how to breathe, before throwing my trunk open and shoving the bag into the deepest corner. I slammed the top shut and whirled away from the trunk, my arms around myself.

Conflicting emotions tore at me, so that I didn't know what to feel. Anger, that they had seen fit to pay me for my "service" to the crown. Humiliation, that they had viewed sixteen years of my life as worth so little. For it wasn't much, the money that filled that bag. Enough to impress a common woman, perhaps, but I had been a princess once, and I thought I knew how far that money might go. It would have given me enough to live on for a year, if my aunt hadn't taken me, enough to keep me in food but not enough that I could have caused trouble, if I had wanted to.

It was that thought that cleared my head. I knew the problems a pretender to the crown could cause. Thorvaldor had been nearly torn apart by war four generations ago when one royal son decided he was a better candidate for the throne than his older sister. If my once-parents felt the need to protect their real daughter by making sure that I did not have the funds to start a rebellion, I could understand that. I might have done the same, if I still lived in the palace. It still hurt, but perhaps it was only meant to save Nalia from danger, and not to injure Sinda. Yes. I forced myself to breathe calmly. That was what I would think.

I wavered then, wondering if I should give the money to my aunt. She had taken me in, after all, when she might have turned me away. And from what I had seen of Treb last night, even that much money would be a generous gift indeed. But something stopped me from going over to the trunk and taking out the bag of coins. I still had the letter from the king, and who knew what that said. Perhaps it was a gift for her, something to make up for dumping an unknown and unlooked-for relative on her doorstep last night. I stared at the trunk, twisting my hands together, before taking up the letter and opening the door to the rest of the house.

I had gathered, even in my dazed state last night, that there were three tiny rooms to the house—the main room, mostly taken up by the hearth and kitchen, and two other rooms. Aunt Varil was not in the main room, and the room I had not slept in was shut tight. I didn't have the courage to sneak a look inside it. Kiernan would have, of course.

No. I shook my head, wrapping my arms around myself. I would not think of Kiernan.

So I was standing there, unsure of what to do, when the front door opened and Aunt Varil entered, her arms green up to the elbow.

"I've been working around back," she said by way of a greeting. She went over to the hearth, where a large bowl of water stood, and plunged her arms into it, scrubbing them furiously, though when she removed them, I couldn't tell if the color had actually faded.

She studied me for a moment, her sharp eyes flicking over everything from my shoes to my face. I glanced down, cheeks hot, and remembered the letter in my hand. "This is for you," I managed, and held it out.

Aunt Varil took it in a greenish hand and broke the seal. She stood while she read, then tossed the paper down on the table. "Do you know what it says?" she asked.

I shook my head.

"The king has granted me the right to come to the Royal Forest five days out of each year, to search for any plants I might not have access to. In exchange for taking you on, I suppose."

I flushed harder and made myself meet her eyes. A thank-you, or a guilt gift, like the money they had given me? Payment, for the burden that had been dropped on her lap? It made me want to shrink with embarrassment. Still, I would try to put a happy face on it, as I had my own "gift." After all, the Royal Forest, which lay to the north of Vivaskari, was reserved for the royal family alone. No one else could hunt any animals or gather any plants there. "That's kind of them, isn't it?"

Aunt Varil snorted. "It might be, if I had the funds to get to the capital even one day a year. Which I don't. Or if I thought there would be any plants there that don't grow here. Which I also don't." She shrugged with a sigh. "No matter. I don't expect that kings know much about what will help common folk like me. Nor do they much care."

I wanted to protest, to say that the king and queen did care, but the words wouldn't come—just the thought of them sending their own baby away and accepting another, common one to perhaps die in its place. That, and a niggling, uncomfortable sensation that perhaps, on some level, my aunt was right.

"I expect you're hungry," she said abruptly, and I could tell the matter of the gift had been dropped. "It won't be what you're used to, but there's some bread and cheese on the table."

She was right; it was not what I was used to. But I smiled gingerly—my face didn't quite remember how to complete the motion—and nodded. "Thank you. I am hungry."

There were two chairs set around the small table, and we settled ourselves into them. As I began to eat, Aunt Varil watched me like someone observing a strange, newly uncaged animal.

"We'll have to see if anyone has a bed to spare," she said. "Alva Mastrom might. Her daughter's just moved to Greenwater with her new husband."

Startled, I glanced involuntarily at the door to the other room, which I had assumed was Aunt Varil's bedroom. But then my eye caught sight of the blanket folded on a chair beside the hearth. I could feel heat suffusing my face and knew I must be going red again. I had slept in Aunt Varil's bed last night, I realized with shame, and she had slept on the floor.

"It'll be tight in there with two beds, but I don't think we'll both fit in the one," she continued. "Though we might be able to find a larger one, of course. And some clothes, boots. You won't be able to do much in those."

Now my gaze fell onto my lap and the blue fabric of my dress. I had thought it plain just a few moments before, but now, comparing it to the dress my aunt wore, I realized it must seem extravagant.

Aunt Varil was still peering at me with great intensity. "Which brings us to the question. What can you do?"

I chewed the piece of cheese in my mouth, trying to think. "I can speak four languages," I said slowly. "I can sew some embroidery and I can paint. I'm well versed in Thorvaldian history and custom, and mathematics and theories of war. My tutors said I write a fair hand . . ." I trailed off. There were other things, but I doubted that knowing the intricacies of Wenthi greetings or a dozen Farvaseean dance styles would be much use here. "I'm willing to learn," I said finally. "I don't . . . I don't know about dyeing or cooking, but I can learn."

"You'll have to," Aunt Varil said without any mirth. "Summer's coming, and that's the busiest time for me, what with everything growing. I have to harvest enough materials to keep me busy for the winter. You're too old to be an apprentice, but there's nothing to do about that. You'll have to earn your keep. I can't feed someone who doesn't work."

"I'll do my best," I said, a little stiffly.

"Good," she said. "Then let's walk down to Alva's and see if her daughter left any clothes behind."

The village was exactly as small and humble as it had seemed from the carriage window the night before. A single dirt lane cut through the center of town and then meandered off toward the great road some distance away that led back to Vivaskari. Treb consisted of perhaps twenty houses, an inn with two rooms for rent to passing travelers, a tiny temple to the Nameless God, and one small shop that sold the few things not made among the village's inhabitants or brought in by traveling tinkers. An apartment, larger than many of the houses, sat over the shop, and I assumed the owners lived there. A few outlying farms could be seen in the distance, backed up against the looming forest, though all of the village's small houses had their own tiny gardens or pens for goats or pigs.

Like Aunt Varil, the people of Treb seemed to have been up for hours. I could hear the clank of metal on metal coming from the blacksmith's house, and most of the gardens had women bent over in them, pulling weeds or tending plants. Several children darted out in front of us as Aunt Varil and I left the garden that encircled the front and sides of her house. Three of them would have run by without even looking at us, but one, a little blonde girl with a dirty face, slowed to give a wave to Aunt Varil. When she caught sight of me, however, she stumbled to a stop so quickly that one of her friends collided with her.

The girl stared at us, then suddenly whirled around and ran

down the street with the others trailing after her. "Mama!" she screamed. "Mama! There's a girl at Mistress Azaway's house!"

Aunt Varil frowned. "Well, that's that," she said. "The whole village'll know you're here by noon." She sighed heavily.

"Is that bad?" I asked tentatively.

She looked at me down her long nose. "It's talk," she said finally. "I don't like talk. There was enough of it after your father ran—" She broke off then and shook her head slightly, like she was rebuking herself.

I couldn't help it. "After my father what?" I felt a sick yearning inside me, a desire to know something, anything, about the man who had given me up. And yet I also wanted nothing to do with him, as if by pushing away such knowledge I could remain myself, the self I had been, a little longer.

"Never mind," Aunt Varil said, an edge in her voice. She pursed her lips together and marched off down the road so quickly that I had to hurry to catch up. As we walked, I could feel eyes on me as people paused to stare. Whispers followed as we marched past, making my cheeks go hot, but Varil only raised her chin and ignored them. That gesture, at least, I recognized.

Alva's house stood several properties down from Aunt Varil's own cottage. Aunt Varil didn't bother knocking on the door, but strode assuredly around the house toward a small vegetable garden, where a woman was attacking the ground with a hoe.

"Morning, Alva," Aunt Varil called.

The woman stopped what she was doing and leaned against the hoe. "Morning, Varil. What brings . . . ?" She trailed off as she saw me, her eyes widening as they swept over my dress. "Who's this?" she asked.

EILIS O'NEAL

"My niece."

Alva licked her lips. "Ardin said that a fancy carriage came through last night, looking for your house. I thought he might have gotten into too many cups at the Hollyhock. But here she is, and us never knowing you even had a niece."

Aunt Varil looked even more forbidding than usual as she said, "It's a long story, and gossip travels fast. I'm sure you'll hear it soon enough. But for now, the girl's come . . . from the capital. We're looking for an extra bed, and some other things. She's not used to country living, and her clothes . . ." She trailed off again. "I don't suppose your daughter left anything behind when she married. I think they might be of a size."

Alva's eyes traveled over me again, but with a calculating look this time. "They might be. And Saree's husband's family, well, they own that tailor shop in Greenwater. They gave her four new dresses as wedding gifts, so she did leave some old things here when she went. I've been meaning to cut them down for Neda's girl, but if you need them . . ." She paused, as if uncomfortable. "Of course," she said to me, "they're nothing like what you've got on now. Plain, if you know what I mean."

I wasn't sure I did, but I nodded anyway. My own clothes were apparently so outlandish here that they stopped children in the street; I wouldn't care if Alva gave me a potato sack to wear, so long as it stopped the staring.

The dresses were as plain as she said—one a faded blue and the other something that might have been green once. They had obviously been much mended. But they wouldn't call attention to themselves, and that was all I cared about as I struggled into the blue one. We left Alva's house with a piece of my past trailing over my arm, and when we got home, I folded my old gown into my trunk of belongings.

As I smoothed the fabric down, I could feel panic building in me, my throat tightening so that I had to struggle to swallow. When I closed the trunk, it would be real. I would be Sinda Azaway, in all the ways that eyes could see. But what did I know about being Sinda, except that she lived in a tiny, nowhere village and wore someone else's dresses?

My hand hovered over the trunk's lid, and I could see it shaking. For a wild moment, I thought about running away, just so that closing the lid would mean something else—the beginning of something, instead of the end. But where would I go, and what would I do when I got there?

I closed my eyes and, a few tears leaking out onto my cheeks, blindly pushed the lid shut.

I would stay in Treb, I knew, with Aunt Varil. I would try to make a life here. After all, what was the use of running away when what I really wanted to run away from was myself?

CHAPTER THREE

So began my life in Treb—a life that, in most ways, I was completely unprepared to live.

The first days passed in a haze as I tried to fight my way through the blur of exhaustion and shock that dogged me from waking to falling asleep. I rose in the morning, pushing myself up from the narrow bed we had procured and squeezed into the bedroom beside Aunt Varil's, then ate a simple breakfast with her. We then, depending on the weather and her mood, went into the woods in search of dye plants, weeded her own garden, or settled ourselves behind her house to actually begin the dyeing process. I dreaded whatever task she chose for us, because Aunt Varil's scattered teaching methods made learning almost impossible.

"There's agrimony in this part of the forest," she might say. "Fill this basket with the leaves and stalks. Yellow flowers, saw-edged leaves. It's hard to miss. I'll be by that pond when you're done," she would add before striding off, leaving me holding the basket and staring around in confusion. It did no good to ask her to find one of the plants and show it to me before setting off, I quickly learned. All that would gain me was a deep sigh and a sharp shake of her head, as if I were the dullest creature she had ever seen. So I would wander through the forest, basket in hand, looking anxiously over my shoulder at every crack of a twig or rustle of the leaves. The few times I managed to find the plant she wanted, it was not due to my aunt's teaching but to my recollection of conversations I had had with the gardeners in the palace.

Searching for plants in the forest, however, sometimes seemed like a gift when compared to the dyeing itself. In the forest, at least, I was often alone, something I preferred during the first days of my exile. It was infinitely worse to sit under Aunt Varil's watchful gaze as she tried to impart the secrets of creating clear, strong colors. To her dismay and, I had to admit, to my own, I appeared to have little aptitude for dyeing. While I could easily remember the amount of mordent to use with black willow bark or the steps involved in transforming ragwort into the deep yellow liquor of dye, I had no eye for telling when the ingredients had steeped long enough or if the color seemed fast in the wool. I was used to quickly learning almost anything my tutors cared to teach me, and this new limitation frustrated me. It also made Aunt Varil sigh even more often.

In the evening, we returned to the house for supper. After we ate, Aunt Varil taught me one of the innumerable tasks that kept a household going when that household did not employ hundreds of servants. My hands, already chapped and discolored from the dye baths, were soon aching and covered in blisters. I learned to sew more than pretty embroideries, to chop wood and move it from the pile behind the house to the hearth, to scour pots and pans, to keep the fire in the hearth burning evenly, to arrange the skeins of wool in the small storage room off the main room, and much more as Aunt Varil worked me to exhaustion each night. That she did as much as I did and more did not make me feel better. I collapsed on my bed—procured with some difficulty from Alva's cousin—each night and slept deeply until morning, when the calls of country animals would wake me.

In some ways, though, perhaps such a grueling schedule was better than the alternative, because, if my body ached and my head spun with the efforts of remembering how to prepare a stew or porridge, at least I had little time for dwelling on the life I no longer had. It was strange to me, how much of my mind I could fix on the mundane tasks I performed, so that whenever I began to drift into remembrances of Kiernan or the king and queen, I could force myself to concentrate on the pot or ax in my hand. But no matter how hard I tried, I could never quite fill the emptiness inside me. Sometimes, I found myself rubbing at the empty place on my inner arm, just below the crook of my elbow, where my birthmark had been. I wondered if Nalia looked at that spot, too, if the birthmark had appeared on her when it vanished from me, or if the wizards had allowed it to remain on her even through her disguise. I wondered if I would ever stop missing it, missing my life.

It might have been easier to accept my new situation if I had felt any bond with my aunt. Aunt Varil, I soon realized, was not a warm woman. She greeted the other villagers politely enough and offered aid if it was asked, but she had no particular friends, and she never went down to the inn to sit in the common room and chat as so many others did. She remained aloof, content with her own company and suffering mine.

During the first few days, I hoped that, once she was used to me, she might grow to like me. I knew that I was not Kiernan, whom it was almost impossible not to like, but I thought that she might eventually come to view me fondly, once she had adjusted to my presence in her life. But a week passed, then another, and another, all without change. She was not cruel, but neither was she kind. Occasionally, as we sat in the main room at night, I caught her staring at me with a pinched look on her face, as if I were something that had been dropped on her doorstep and of which she wished she could rid herself. In many ways, I suppose I was just that. I did not hold any illusions of being truly helpful to her—my skills at dyeing, cooking, and cleaning were mediocre at best. Still, I knew I was polite, quiet, and generally inoffensive, so, for a while, I continued to hope that she might someday find me agreeable.

But it was only when I asked her about my parents that I understood that her apparent dislike of me ran further than my abysmal cooking or tendency to break dishes while I was trying to wash them. We were inside, hanging plants from the rafters of the storage room to dry. As I reached up to hang some sweet gale, I noticed a carving on the wood of the rafter: a picture of a cat, all curled up in a ball, its tail curved around its front.

"Did you carve this?" I asked, pointing.

Her back was to me, but I could see her stiffen. She didn't answer, only reached out to arrange some skeins of pale blue wool on their shelves.

"The cat?" I added, but quietly, so that even I could hardly hear the *t* in the word.

"Your father carved it," Aunt Varil said in a clipped sort of way. "This was our room, when we were children. Our parents slept in the other."

I wasn't able to stop myself from sucking in a breath at her words. She had not spoken of my father, not even once, since I had arrived. She had offered no stories of their childhood, or any explanations of why he might have given me up. And I had not, until now, had the courage to ask.

"What was he like?"

Again, I saw that stiffening in her shoulders, but she didn't turn around. "He was . . . quiet. Serious. He knew he wanted to be a weaver from the time he was six years old. He always wanted to believe the best of people." Something in her voice darkened. "That's why I worried about him when he went off to apprentice in Vivaskari. He was too trusting, and I was scared he would come to ill because of it."

My mouth was dry. Something inside me didn't want me to ask the next question, but I couldn't help it. "And my mother? Did you know her?"

This time, Aunt Varil did turn. She whirled around so quickly that I had to stop myself from taking a step backward. Her face grew tighter, her eyes narrowed.

"It was your mother who was his ruin."

"What?" In my head, I heard the king's words. *He did not mention his wife.*

Aunt Varil smiled, but it was a bitter expression, one full of old wishes and hurts. "He met her in the city. She was passing through, and she came into his shop by mistake. Her name was Ilania. They were married in the city, almost at once, and he brought her back here afterward, to visit."

Aunt Varil paused, not looking at me, her eyes fixed on something from the past, something only she could see. "She was quite beautiful. She had dark hair that fell in these loose waves down her back. She refused to pin it up. You take after your father," she added after a moment, "except that she was just as small as you, and you have her nose, and the color of her hair. I noticed it, that first night you came. But she was . . . charming. Always moving, always talking, always looking for the next thing to make her laugh. He was completely in love with her. He couldn't keep his eyes off her.

"You were born two years later, in the city. They came to visit me just after they found she was with child. I thought that she seemed restless then, like she wanted to be somewhere else, not like a woman who'd soon be having a baby. But your father was so happy that I didn't mention it to him. I just watched her, and wondered. And five days after you were born, she was gone. Left a note, saying that she wouldn't be coming back, that she didn't want him anymore."

I swallowed, but I couldn't find anything to say. Aunt Varil's face was like stone, so hard and cold I thought it wouldn't feel like flesh if I touched it.

"It broke him. He was never the same afterward. He closed his shop in the city after a year and came here. He died when a fever came through, and the last thing he said was her name." She sighed. "That's the other way you seem to take after him. You're both a little too . . . accepting. You do what other people want without fighting."

It caught me off guard. "What do you mean?" I managed.

Aunt Varil gestured toward the north, the direction of

Vivaskari. "You left without so much as a peep. Didn't even complain when they put you in that carriage and sent you off. He let her go, didn't try to look for her or bring her back. He just gave up, came here, and let himself die."

Ice seemed to have crystallized under my skin; a particularly large piece had lodged itself in my heart. For a long time, I couldn't speak, and when I did, it was only a croak. "He thought I was dead, didn't he? They said they had altered his memory so he wouldn't remember giving me up."

Aunt Varil nodded. "That's what he told me. And I thought, 'Well, it might be for the best. At least he won't have something to remind him of her every day.' But it didn't matter. He never stopped thinking of her, even without you. It was heartache that weakened him; he didn't even care when he caught the fever."

The ice had grown colder, sharper, and I heard myself saying, quite evenly, without any tone, "That's why you hate me, then. Because of her."

For the first time, a crease formed between my aunt's eyes, breaking the stone that had hardened her face. She gazed at me thoughtfully, one corner of her mouth pinched in, and then said, "I don't hate you, Sinda. I just don't know what to do with you. Look at you. Sixteen, so old someone should be courting you. But what man would have you, with no skills to bring to his house? It isn't your fault, I know, but you don't know anything that's useful here. And I'm used to being alone. I never counted on a niece."

I opened my mouth to say, "I'm trying," but Aunt Varil had already brushed past me to go outside. I didn't follow her. That night we were silently polite with each other, and we didn't speak of my parents again.

One of the other things she had said bothered me almost as much as the description of my parents, however. Had I given up too easily? Had I let myself be evicted from my life when I could have fought to keep some part of it? I had never been one for argument, had always shrunk from confrontation. But should I have stood my ground, demanded something in exchange for the sixteen years I had given the crown?

No, I told myself. *When the king said you had to go, you went. I wasn't a princess, or even a noblewoman; I had no power. There was nothing I could have done to change what had happened.*

I repeated that to myself, but even then, a small part of me seemed to shake its head, unbelieving.

With the distance between my aunt and myself, I suppose I might have looked to the other people in Treb for companionship. But I found no solace there either. With all of Aunt Varil's lessons, I had little time to myself, and certainly not enough to spend wandering the village in search of friends. And besides, the three girls my age were quite busy themselves; two were already engaged to be married, one to a boy from Treb and the other to a carpenter in Hathings. Yet it wasn't this that kept me from doing more than nodding at them when I passed them on the street.

They knew the story. It had arrived just two days after I had, brought by a traveling tinker who had been in Vivaskari when the true princess returned. The king and queen had sent out banns to be proclaimed in every major city, and those too small to have messengers sent to them learned the news the way Treb did. The romance of it, of the princess hidden away with no idea of her true identity, had set fire to the country. In most places, I guessed that to be what the rumors focused on—Nalia, the true Nalia. In Treb, however, they had something else to consider, something almost forgotten elsewhere. Me: the false princess.

Perhaps if I had been another type of girl, I could have made friends because of it. If I had been willing to pour out my heartache at being abandoned, or staunch enough to claim pride at having done the crown such a service, I might have gained many people's sympathy. But I was as I had always been, quiet and reserved, worried about tripping over my own feet if people were watching. The few souls who gathered the courage to approach me about it gained only a close-lipped smile and a shake of my head.

"I'd rather not talk about it," I would say. I could always see the disappointment in their eyes, the reproachfulness, as if I had an obligation to answer their questions. But it was too new, too raw inside me, and even saying that much left me shaking as I walked away.

Only two things broke the pattern of my days in Treb. The first was . . . I didn't know what it was. Something without a name. Not anything I could lay my hand on, or point to and say, "Ah. This is what has been bothering me." It was only a feeling, one that came about a few weeks after my arrival.

It started with a sort of tightness in my chest, like when you need to cry and don't let yourself. At first, I ignored it; it didn't seem odd to feel that way, not after what had happened. But it changed, after a time, growing and shifting until I sometimes felt truly strange, like I had something hot and fizzy inside me that wanted to get out. My hands and arms seemed to tingle, or shimmer, or pulse, even though they did none of those things. At times, without warning, I had an almost overwhelming urge to do . . . *something*. But I never knew what, and after a few uncomfortable moments, the feelings would pass.

I didn't tell anyone. There was no one to tell, besides Aunt Varil. So at night when I had nothing else to think about, I privately worried that I might be going mad. What else could cause me to feel as though I had fire in my veins, fire that wanted to get out through my hands or my mouth or my eyes? I doubted very much that Aunt Varil would appreciate being told about these feelings. Having a previously unknown niece dumped on you was one thing, but a previously unknown, *mad* niece was something else entirely. So I worried, which provided a nice distraction from my misery, and didn't mention it.

The second distraction was quite different, however. It came about one day as I was walking down the dusty main street, a basket of nettle tops in my arms. Aunt Varil and I had gone in search of nettles in the hedgerows that lined the road as it made its way south. I had, for once, filled my basket first, and she had given me permission to go home and begin the dye bath for them.

It was a bright day, so hot that the hair escaping my braid stuck to the back of my neck. My dress felt wet across my back, and my arms stung where the gloves Aunt Varil had given me didn't cover them. Shifting the basket against my hip, I paused to let one of the village children herd several loose goats across the road and back into their pen. Two of the girls my age—Calla and Renata—were standing outside Calla's house, their heads together. I tried to make myself small and invisible, as if I could blend into my surroundings like a tiny sparrow. While they had never been rude to my face, there were always a lot of murmurs whenever I passed those two, and I hoped they wouldn't notice me. As I started out again, though, the toe of my boot caught on a stone protruding from the road. I stumbled, the nettle heads flying out of the basket as I fell to one knee. Across the road, I heard laughter ring out.

Red-faced, I scrambled to recover the nettle heads as quickly as possible, but they had flown in all directions. Keeping my head down, my ears buzzing with embarrassment, I turned to look behind me only to see a young man crouching there, a nettle head in his hand.

"I think this is yours," he said with a slow smile.

"Be careful," I said as I reached out to take it from him. "They . . . That will sting."

"It's not so bad," he said as he dropped another in the basket. He didn't say anything else as we gathered the plants, though he smiled at me whenever I glanced at him. Even compared to all the people I had seen at court, I had to admit that this boy was very handsome. Black hair framed bright blue eyes, and I could see the evenness of his teeth whenever he smiled at me. The laughter across the street, I noticed dimly, had stopped.

When we had found all of the nettle heads, he offered me a hand up. A slight rash had already sprung up on his fingers and palm.

"That was a bad fall," he said. "Are you hurt?"

I shook my head, suddenly aware of how dusty and sweaty

I was. "My body's used to how clumsy I am," I said ruefully. "I don't hurt easily."

"I'm Tyr Varanday. My father owns the shop," he said, pointing at the only general store in Treb. "I've been visiting some friends in the city. I only just got back today."

"I'm . . . S-Sinda Azaway," I said, stumbling slightly over my name. Normally I would have flushed even harder, but he was gazing at me with such a friendly expression that I felt myself smiling back at him instead. "I've come to live with my Aunt Varil."

"That explains the nettles then," he said with a laugh. "But I didn't know Mistress Azaway had a niece."

"She didn't know," I said. "My father died without telling her about me, and I . . . I lived in the city until recently."

His eyes swept over my face, and I saw something register behind them. If he had been in the city, he would have heard the rumors of the false princess and where she had gone. He might have even heard my real name. But he only shook his head and held a hand out toward the main street. "This must be a shock, then, if you lived in the city. We're a little . . . rustic here."

Relief ran through me. For once, here was someone who was not pestering me about my past, not hoping to hear tales of what being a princess had been like. "It's not so bad," I found myself saying, but Tyr only laughed.

"I think you're lying," he said, but lightly. "Treb doesn't have much to offer anyone who knows what the world is like. I've been trying to tell my father that we should rent a place in Vivaskari and set up shop there, but he doesn't see things my way."

He glanced down into my basket, then said, "Your nettles

EILIS O'NEAL

are wilting a little. And if I know Mistress Azaway, she won't be happy if the sun ruins them." He paused, frowning slightly, as if he were nervous. "I don't suppose you think she might let me call on you? I know I said Treb was a backwater, but you might as well get to know it as well as you can. I could show you around."

"That would be nice," I said.

His eyes seemed to sparkle in the sunlight. "Then I'll see you soon," he said, before turning and walking off toward father's shop, whistling.

The next day, as I was clearing my bowl from the table after supper, there was a knock on the cottage door. Aunt Varil, who had been slowly spooning through my attempt at stew, flicked her eyes at me, then nodded at the door. I hurried over, trying to keep from biting my lip in anticipation.

"Hello, Miss Azaway," Tyr said as I opened the door. His voice reminded me of warm honey.

"Who is it, Sinda?" Aunt Varil called, but before I could answer, she had pushed her chair back from the table and come across the room to the door. I thought I heard a pause in her step, the slightest hesitation, but then she was beside me, looking at Tyr with her lips pursed tight.

"Hello, Tyr," she said. "I've told your mother that I won't have that yellow wool ready for another three days."

I knew that I tended to shrink a bit when Aunt Varil stared at me so intently, but Tyr only shook his head easily. "I'm not here for my mother, Mistress Azaway. I met your niece yesterday, and I thought she might like to take a walk around the village with me."

Aunt Varil snorted. "She's seen all there is to see of the village, Tyr."

My heart, which had been hammering high in my chest, dropped suddenly toward my stomach. I had been hugging so tightly to the idea of maybe—finally—having a friend in Treb that I hadn't realized how much I had counted on it until it threatened to disappear.

Aunt Varil looked from Tyr to me and back again. I knew that a pleading expression must be filling my eyes, that the dull ache of wanting must be visible in every line of my body, because she sighed and said, "Fine. But just in town, Tyr. No farther. I won't have people talking."

"Of course not," Tyr said with a smile. Then he held out an arm, gesturing into the day's fading light. "Miss Azaway."

It was still fine, though a hint of coolness hovered in the air. The trees and houses cast long shadows across the road, making everything soft and dim. At the end of the road, I could see Ardin, the blacksmith, standing outside his shop, a pipe in his mouth, but otherwise, we were alone. We didn't speak until we were two houses down from my aunt's. Then, without warning, Tyr let out a breath. "I've always thought your aunt was a hard one, but is she always so strict with you?"

Warmth was seeping through me, like water through the tiny cracks in a stone wall, filling me with something like hope. Still, I tried to keep my face fixed as I said, "She's very . . . well, *strict* is the right word, I suppose." A few steps later, I mumbled, "She doesn't like me very much."

Tyr stopped so suddenly that I tripped over nothing. Throwing an arm out, he caught me by the shoulders. For a

EILIS O'NEAL

moment, we stood like that, his hands pressing against me, and I felt something race up my spine and back down it. *Stop it,* I thought. *He's just being polite.*

"Careful," he said with a tiny laugh. "You know, I'm starting to think that you're a danger to yourself."

The hazy feeling, the little thrill in my bones, vanished. I knew my expression must have changed, because Tyr's lazy half smile was replaced by a frown of concern, and his hands were abruptly at his sides.

"Thank you," I said stiffly.

He shook his head. "It's nothing. Did I say something wrong?"

I bit the inside of my cheek, not sure what I should say. How was Tyr supposed to know that Kiernan had always teased me with just those words? How was I supposed to explain the way that Kiernan's face had seemed to replace Tyr's own, and that, in that brief instant, I had missed my friend so much that my stomach had hurt? Or that, for reasons I didn't understand, I felt strangely guilty about the warmth I had felt when Tyr touched me?

But Kiernan and I weren't like that, I thought. We were just . . . friends, even if we had been friends so long that neither of us could remember a time when we weren't. Even if we were so close we could sometimes finish each other's sentences or say a joke in the instant before the other did. Even if, every time I thought of living my life without him, it was like stepping off into darkness with no lantern and no chance of ever finding one again.

That hard knot in my stomach clenched again, and I realized that Tyr was staring at me.

"I'm sorry," he said, eyes wide. "We don't have to talk about it if you don't want to. I was just . . . surprised." A tentative smile. "You seem very likable to me."

With a huge effort, I forced my thoughts about Kiernan away. They wouldn't do me any good here, and I wasn't going to scare this potential friend—my first potential friend in Treb—away. I would be happy—I would make friends with Tyr if it killed me.

"It's just—" I said haltingly as I tried to recall what we had been talking about. Oh yes. Aunt Varil. I started walking again, heading out toward the end of town, and Tyr quickly kept pace with me. "She didn't like my mother. She left my father, you see, right after I was born. It broke his heart, and Aunt Varil says he was never the same. She thinks he was sad enough that he let himself die when a fever came." I swallowed. "That's why he gave me up, when the king and queen asked him to. Because he didn't want to be reminded of her. They changed his memory so he thought I'd died, and that's what he told Aunt Varil. She didn't know any differently until just before I was sent here.

"Mostly, I think she wishes I weren't here. I remind her of my mother, of what she did to my father, and I don't think she can forgive me for that."

We had passed the blacksmith's house. Before us now lay only fields of crops that slowly gave way to forest. Tyr stopped again, though I didn't trip this time. Turning to face me, he said, "Well, if that's how she feels, Varil Azaway is colder that I ever thought. I think it would be almost impossible not to be charmed by you."

I snorted. "You'd be surprised then. I've never been popular, not even back at—" I faltered, then forced myself to finish. "At court. Everyone thought I was a strange. Too quiet, too serious. I only had one really good friend there. Kiernan Dulchessy." There he was again. No matter which way I turned, all my thoughts seemed to lead back to Kiernan.

Tyr puffed out his chest comically, shaking his head so that his shiny black hair flew around his face. "Well, I don't know anything about this Kiernan, but I can only say that I'll try to match him. That way, it won't feel so odd, being here." His face softened then, and he reached out to take my hand. Again, tiny bolts of lightning shot through me, though I struggled not to show it. "I do want to be your friend, Sinda," he said seriously. "I want it very much."

His face was so handsome in the deepening dark that I could feel heat spreading across my cheeks. My heart was racing now, but for entirely different reasons.

"I'm glad, Tyr," I said. "I'm glad."

CHAPTER FOUR

Not everyone was as happy about Tyr as I was, however. When I returned from our walk later that night, I found Aunt Varil sitting in the main room, a lamp beside her and a pile of clothes to be mended on the table in front of her, but the needle still in her hand. She watched me close the door, her eyes bright and hawklike.

We gazed at each other for a minute, and then I said carefully, "If you don't need me for anything, I think I'll go to bed."

Full dark had fallen outside, and the flickering of the fire in the hearth made shadows dance around the room. Aunt Varil's mouth worked, like she was sucking on a piece of sour fruit, and then she said, "Tyr Varanday is trouble."

I had felt light and airy, happy for the first time in weeks, but I was on the ground in a flash.

"His mother's never liked living here. She's from Vivaskari and thinks she's too good for a little town like this. She's given him ideas. And those relatives she's got in the city give him more when he's there. That he's better than other people, that he deserves things they don't. He likes to push things. Likes to get his own way, too."

Most of the warmth Tyr had brought had been blown out of me, but a stubborn bit remained. "Just because someone's from Vivaskari doesn't mean they're trouble," I said.

Aunt Varil sniffed, then exhaled loudly. "Didn't say it did. But being above yourself often does. And Tyr Varanday is above himself—always has been."

This is what she thinks of me, I realized. As someone who was "above herself." A common girl with a princess's airs. Well, I was trying to get rid of them, to learn how to be a normal person. I was trying my best, but it was hard to undo sixteen years of thinking you were someone—something—else.

"It makes him restless," she continued, "and that's led to—"

I was suddenly angry, tired of listening to her, and I flung out my hand. "Enough," I snapped. "He wants to be my friend. He's the only person in this town who's even cared to try and get to know me instead of whispering about me behind my back or telling me I'm not good enough." Aunt Varil opened her mouth, the line between her eyes long and deep, but I only said, "I'm going to bed. Good night, Aunt."

I stalked from the room, simmering with indignation. Was this just another way to show how much she disapproved of me? A way to make sure that my life here was as dull and cold as hers? I flung myself down on my narrow bed, which was squeezed in between the window and Aunt Varil's. For some reason, I had an almost overwhelming urge to go over to my chest and take out one of my dresses. I hadn't even opened the chest in weeks, hadn't worn anything but Alva's daughter's left-behind things since I arrived here. But now I wanted, desperately, to hold something from a time when I had been happy, when I had had a friend, when I had known who I was.

The urge beat at me, but I clenched my jaw and shut my eyes so tightly my eyelids hurt. No. There was no use holding on to the past. Kiernan's face wafted in front of my closed eyes, but I deliberately replaced it with Tyr's. Grabbing a handful of the blanket upon which I lay, I pinched it between my fingers. This was what I had now. Just this.

I had to make it enough.

After that, Aunt Varil didn't say anything else about my friendship with Tyr. She allowed me to go walking with him, let us sit in the garden, and even, on rainy nights, let him come inside and set up a chessboard for us to play. She was polite to him, but I knew from the set of her mouth that she was no happier with the situation than she had been that first night.

I, on the other hand, was happier than I had been since I came to Treb. It might not have been much of a measure, considering the loneliness I had been enduring, but at least it was progress. A week passed, then two, and I saw Tyr almost every day. I hurried through my chores so that I could present myself to Aunt Varil at the end of the day, skeins of wool dyed, shirt mended as best I could, garden weeded, and be allowed to go and find my friend.

Our activities varied. Sometimes we simply sat outside Aunt Varil's house or in the garden behind this parents' shop and talked. He told me about his relatives in the city, and the various plays and musical performances he attended when he visited them. I had sometimes seen the troupes he spoke of, and though

EILIS O'NEAL

I felt a twinge of homesickness when he mentioned them, I found that I could talk about them without too much unhappiness. Our chess matches sometimes went on long enough that we had to declare a truce because of the hour. I showed him the tiny pond I had found in the woods behind our cottage, where, if you waited at dusk, you could nearly always see deer coming down to drink. We walked up and down the main street of Treb, sometimes stopping at the Hollyhock to sit and drink a mug of last year's cider. Occasionally some of the other girls or boys our age would try to join us, but Tyr always managed to steer them away without making it look like he was being unsociable. Sometimes I wished that he was not so apt at it; it would have been nice to get to know them, and I was too shy to approach them on my own. But mostly I simply reveled in having one friend, one bit of happiness.

I thought about telling Tyr about the strange feeling inside me, the feeling of something trapped and trying to get out. The sensation had worsened with time, until I sometimes imagined I could see heat radiating off my skin. When Tyr looked at me with his clear eyes and smiled, I thought he might understand.

But I hesitated, unwilling to weigh down our time together with fears about something that might or might not be real. Whatever the feeling was, it seemed to do me no harm, except for causing worry, and so I kept silent.

I tried not to think about what Aunt Varil had said about him. She never stopped me from going with him, but her glower couldn't help but give me pause whenever I asked permission to leave the house. It was that expression that came back to me whenever Tyr made a snide joke about some aspect of Treb, or when he tried to get Tabithan to lower the price of our ciders at the Hollyhock. It haunted me whenever Calla threw an especially hurt look at Tyr when she saw him with me, a look that seemed to speak of something torn away without warning. But I usually managed to shake off those momentary flashes of disquiet, because in just the next moment Tyr would look at me with such a friendly smile that I thought surely I had imagined the supercilious tone in his voice.

I tried not to think about Kiernan. I tried not to compare his easy, jovial wit to Tyr's unruffled smoothness and silky smile. I tried not to wish, sometimes, that it was Kiernan sitting across from me at the table. I forced myself not to imagine the way he would have had everyone, from Ardin, the taciturn blacksmith, to Tabithan, the jolly red-cheeked innkeeper, under his spell. I hummed to myself or tried to recount the steps needed to ready tansy for dyeing whenever I began to think about the jokes he would have made about the village animals or the conversations we would have about Aunt Varil. I told myself I did not miss him.

And then came the day when Tyr kissed me, and everything else was pushed out of my head.

We were out in the forest when it happened. I wasn't supposed to have Tyr with me when I gathered plants for Aunt Varil, but he had spotted me trudging up into the woods that afternoon and followed. I had thought about telling him that he should go, just in case Aunt Varil came looking for me, but when I started to suggest it, such a long look came over his face that I let the matter drop.

"Well, you'll have to work then," I had laughed. "You can help me look for the meadowsweet."

The frothy plant tops filled my basket by the time the shadows of the forest had lengthened. We walked back toward the village slowly. I knew that Aunt Varil would be wondering where I was, perhaps even holding supper for me, but I couldn't seem to make myself go any faster. As we reached the tree line, however, I turned to Tyr with a sigh.

"You'd better not come out of the woods with me," I said. "Aunt Varil wouldn't like it if she saw. She'd think we were doing something we shouldn't."

Tyr was gazing at me with an odd, sleepy look in his eyes. "Really?" he asked. "Well, if she frets about it that much, maybe we ought to give her a reason for her worries."

And in one effortless motion, he leaned forward and kissed me.

I had never been kissed before. As a princess, it was simply not part of my experience. I knew some of the other girls at court, and many of the boys, had kissed or been kissed. Kiernan used to regale me with tales of kisses that he had stolen or tried to steal in the dark corners of various palace rooms. But no one had ever tried to kiss me, not even the Wenthi archduke's very forward son, the one with the hand that had always roamed a bit too low during our dances.

So while I had at least some theoretical idea of what a kiss should be like, I had absolutely no practical knowledge. In the last second before his lips touched mine, I saw that his eyes were closed, so I hastily closed mine as well. His lips moved, carefully and gently, and it felt warm, and soft, and nice. He pulled back for a moment, and I wondered if perhaps I hadn't done it right, but then he was kissing me again, one arm going around my waist and pulling me closer to him. My basket was still propped up against one hip, though I put my free hand gingerly against his arm. I could taste something sweet in his mouth, maybe the lingering flavor of the tiny wild strawberries we had found and eaten earlier that day.

The kiss went on for what seemed like a long time, until I felt dizzy behind my eyes. I stepped back, and the cool evening air washed between the space where our bodies had been pressed together.

"Is that all right?" Tyr asked. He was looking at me with a glimmer in his eyes, and his face seemed a little feverish.

Honestly, I wasn't sure. Myriad thoughts jostled for attention inside me. How I liked Tyr, liked the way my stomach knotted up a little whenever I saw him approaching. How, though I had never been kissed, I had somehow imagined it feeling different, less simply nice and more . . . rapturous. How I was scared that, if I let Tyr kiss me again, or if I didn't, I might lose the one friend I had in Treb. How, for just an instant, Kiernan's face had swum before my closed eyes, his brows pinched with something like disappointment.

I felt all these things at once, so that I hardly knew what to say. But I nodded, a little hesitantly, and when his face flushed with pleasure, I knew I had made the right answer.

"I think I can see your aunt standing in front of your cottage," he said. "You go and I'll wait until you've gone inside." He caught me by the arm. "I'm going into the city for my cousin's wedding tomorrow. I'll be gone three days, but I'll come to see you as soon as I get back. I'll miss you."

"I'll miss you," I repeated. Then I turned, my heart racing, and hurried down out of the forest to where Aunt Varil was waiting for me.

The next few days passed in a blur. Aunt Varil chastised me continually for woolgathering, and I almost stepped out in front of a cart full of chicken coops going down the main street of town.

I wasn't dreaming about Tyr, though, not in the fanciful ways I knew that girls dreamed about boys they liked. No, I was worrying about him, and about me. What would it mean, to be with him like this? Was it what I wanted? Would people talk, like Aunt Varil seemed to think they would? Did it matter if they did? What if it ruined our friendship?

Why, why had I thought of Kiernan in the moment when Tyr had kissed me?

Thoughts like this swirled around in my head, making me so clumsy that I soon had bruises up and down my legs. When I broke three plates in two days, Aunt Varil snapped at me and then banned me from helping with supper until I could do it without mishap. None of this helped my mood, which became blacker and more anxiety-filled by the day.

On the third day since the kiss, I was in the yard behind the house, trying desperately to salvage a vat of purple dye. Aunt Varil had gone looking for willow bark in the woods and left me in charge of the dye bath. "You've helped me enough now," she said as she stomped off, basket on her hip. "It's time you learned to manage it by yourself."

It had been going well until, for some inexplicable reason, the waters turned from a pale violet to a muddy, dark brown.

I was frantic, trying desperately to remember a way to correct the problem and simultaneously wondering if I could run fast enough to find Aunt Varil before the dye became irretrievable. Finally, I decided to remove the plants from the water early and, in my muddled state, plunged my hands directly into the dye bath instead of reaching for the strainer. Grabbing at the floating bits of leaves, I was flinging them out into the ground when I heard someone rap loudly on the door to the house and call, "Hello? Is anyone here?"

I froze with my arms in the vat up to my elbows. I knew that voice so well it might have been my own.

"Hello?" The person had given up on anyone answering the door and was coming closer.

I lurched up, flinging brown water into the air and onto myself, just in time to see Kiernan come around the side of the cottage.

He was dressed in a fine blue tunic and dark riding breeches. His dark blond hair had been swept back from his face and tangled by the wind. He looked hesitant as he peered around the corner of the cottage, but as he caught sight of me his face lit up so brightly I thought it might catch fire. Then he was bounding forward, his long legs carrying him across the distance between us in a few steps. He caught me up in a hug as fierce as the grin on his face and twirled me around, heedless of the dye on my arms or the water that had slopped down the front of my dress. He was laughing in my ear, and I felt a smile burn across my own face.

It was like breathing again after almost drowning, like being given water after crawling through a desert. All the worries that had assailed me had vanished, so that I felt loose-limbed and truly alive for the first time since I had stepped into the carriage

EILIS O'NEAL

beside the stables and ridden away from the palace. He was my best friend, and he had come to find me.

Finally, he set me down and put his hands on my shoulders, holding me back to look at me. "Nameless God, I've missed you, Nalia," he breathed.

And my heart, which had shot toward the sky, which had been as light and dancing as a leaf flying on the wind, suddenly plunged toward my stomach.

Kiernan heard his mistake right away. "I'm sorry. I'm sorry— I just— I forgot. Seeing you, I just forgot. Sinda. It's Sinda now, right?"

Slowly, my head so heavy it felt like a boulder on my shoulders, I nodded. I looked down, away, anywhere but at Kiernan. My arms, I noticed, were completely covered in the mucky brown color of the ruined dye, so that I looked like I had been playing in mud. The front of my dress—no, Alva's daughter's dress—was dark with the water I had managed to get on it, but that didn't disguise how old the faded, thinning material was. A bug flew past and I swatted at it with my hand, grazing my cheek with my thumb as I did so. I could feel the wetness on my face and knew I had probably just wiped a brown stain across my cheek.

And somehow, standing there, all the joy that had been held inside me so long with no reason to come out, that had bubbled to the surface at seeing Kiernan, suddenly turned sour and dark. I was ashamed, of how I looked and what I was doing and how I had made a mess of it. In a flash, I hated him for seeing me like this, for coming in and reminding me of who I no longer was. And I knew that, as soon as I opened my mouth, whatever came out of it would be horrible, as mean and sharp as I could make it. I even knew that I should stop myself, that I would regret it later, but in that moment, with my dirty cheeks flaming, I didn't care.

"What are you doing here, Kiernan?" I asked dully.

His eyes crinkled up for a second in surprise at my tone. "I came to see you. I know it's been too long, that I took too long, but . . ." Two spots of color blossomed on his cheeks, like he didn't want to go on, but then he forged ahead. "But there were all sorts of ceremonies and things, to welcome her. Everyone was called to court. They even made sure that the Baroness of Mossfeld came," he added with a puff of laughter and a hopeful glance at me. The holdings of Mossfeld were in the most northern reaches of Thorvaldor and the woman who held them was so eccentric that she had not been seen in court since the crowning of the king. Kiernan and I had spent many hours lying on the grass of the palace gardens, wondering exactly what she was like and what she did with herself stuck out on the boggy, sodden land that was Mossfeld.

But I didn't smile, and I saw Kiernan swallow before he continued. "Anyway, I couldn't leave. My father, he said that it would be an insult to—to Nalia—if I left to find you while they were still welcoming her. He finally gave me permission yesterday, and I started out this morning."

"I see that. But why?" I asked. There was a tone in my voice I didn't recognize, as two-edged and keen as a sword blade. It would cut Kiernan, yes, but it would also cut me where I held it.

I didn't care.

"This," I said, throwing my arm out to indicate the cottage and the tub of dye, "isn't exactly what you're used to." He glanced to where I had gestured, blinking and off balance. I shook my head. "No. You're all fun, all froth and silliness and jokes." He blanched, hurt, and I almost did myself. It wasn't true; there was more to Kiernan than that, and we both knew it. Still, I didn't stop.

"There aren't any pretty women to kiss here, Kiernan, or games to play or pranks to set. No plays to see, no music halls to go to. There aren't even any libraries for you to run away from." I laughed, and it was a high, shrill sound, one I didn't recognize. "Oh, don't worry. It's not just you. Look around. There's nothing here anyone sane would want anything to do with."

"There's you," he said quietly. "I came here to find you. I would have gone anywhere," he added more stridently. "To Two Copper district in Vivaskari or the boggy reaches of Mossfeld or the Nameless God's frozen hell. You're my friend. I came to find you."

Part of me wanted to grab his arm and beg him to forgive me for the things I'd said. Part of me wanted to close my eyes and pretend that we were standing in the gardens of the palace, that nothing had changed. Part of me wanted to sit down on the ground with him and talk until my lips went numb, to tell him about my life here. The deer at the pond, my confusion about Tyr, the strain in my relationship with Aunt Varil, my fears about the bizarre, something-trapped-inside-me feeling that had dogged me since I arrived.

Part of me wanted it. But the rest of me was too ashamed at being caught unawares, all dirty and wet and poor. And I was too proud to take my words back.

"I'm not Nalia anymore," I said, so coldly that Kiernan rocked back on his heels. Taking a handful of my skirts in my fist, I shook them at him. "Look at me, Kiernan. Take a good look. This is what I am now. I'm the niece of a dyer in a backward little town, one who doesn't even have any clothes to call her own. I clean house and I make supper and I dye things. And I'm not even any good at it."

"I don't care," he growled. His eyes were flashing and his fists were clenched white with the fervor in those words. "I wouldn't care if you were the princess or a fishmonger's daughter or a traveling gypsy. That's not why I'm your friend."

Almost, almost it swayed me. But I had gone too far already. I heard myself insisting, "You were friends with Nalia. Well, the real Nalia's back at the palace. Maybe your father was right. You should make friends with her."

Kiernan shook his head so strongly it must have hurt. "No. Sinda, listen to me—"

It was hearing him call me by my name—the name I didn't want—that broke me. "Stop it," I hissed. "You've come, you've checked up on me. You've done your duty. It's no good, Kiernan. Just go away."

With that, I turned away, my back as straight as Aunt Varil's. I could feel hot, prickly tears gathering in my eyes, but I couldn't make myself face him. There was a long silence and then he said, "I brought you something. King Kelman's map. You— You left it with me, that day. I thought you might, well, be able to work on it. Decipher it."

"And what library would I use?" I asked bitterly. "What books would I scour to find the answers to a puzzle no one's cared about in three hundred years?"

"I just thought you'd like it," he said. I had never heard Kiernan sound so quiet, so defeated.

"Well, you thought wrong," I said recklessly, my back still turned. "I have friends here, Kiernan. They keep me busy. I don't need your pity or your gifts."

EILIS O'NEAL

Another long pause. Whole civilizations could have risen up and died back to the ground during that pause. Then he said, with all the stiff courtesy of an earl's son, "I'll go then. I'm sorry to have troubled you. Good-bye, Sinda."

I was truly crying then, huge fat tears dripping down my face while I ground my teeth together so hard my jaw ached. If I had opened my mouth, I would have wailed, so I didn't say anything. A moment later, I heard the sounds of a horse galloping out of Treb as fast as its rider could make it go.

It was only then that I turned around. Lying there, on the stump I sometimes sat on while I stirred the dye bath, was a roll of ancient fabric tied with a blue ribbon. With trembling fingers, I pulled the knot apart and gently smoothed the fabric out to reveal a map of the palace grounds. How carefully must he have carried it to get it here unscathed?

I was moaning, I realized, a keening sound like the kind animals make when they're hurt. I let the map go; it hung over the stump, the ribbon beneath it trailing limply downward. Then I was on the ground, my knees up against my chest and my arms wrapped around them.

I had hurt him intentionally, sliced into the core of our friendship with my words. I had known I was doing it, and, in my pride, I had done it anyway.

I lowered my forehead to rest against my knees, my sobs coming harder. I would never see him again. I had forced away my one true friend, my best companion in the world.

"Please," I whispered. "Please, come back."

There was no one there to hear me.

CHAPTER FIVE

A long time later, I pushed myself up from the ground. I was shaking as if I hadn't eaten in two days, my face puffy and sore from crying. Dusk was falling, and Aunt Varil had still not returned. I should try to see if there was anything I could do to save the dye, I knew, or go inside and start supper. I stared at the tub of water for a moment, then walked away without touching it. After a second thought, I went back for King Kelman's map.

Once inside, I walked straight into the bedroom, opened my trunk, and put King Kelman's map on top, where it wouldn't be crushed by my things. The trunk had no lock. I worried about that for a moment, but then decided that there was no one in Treb who would realize how valuable the map was, so I gently closed the lid. There was still water in the bowl by my bed; I had used it to wash my face that morning. Dipping my hands in it, I splashed my face and scrubbed halfheartedly at my arms, though little of the dye came off. I pulled the soiled dress off and dropped it at the bottom of my bed before putting on my other one.

I was in a sort of frenzy, I realized, moving as quickly as I could so that I wouldn't have to think about what I had done. In fact, the only thought I allowed myself was: *Tyr*. I would find Tyr. He was supposed to be back tonight, and I would go and find him. He was my friend now, my only friend, the one from whom I should be seeking comfort. Never mind that my heart seemed to be calling out another name in slow, aching beats; never mind that I knew, deep down inside, that seeing Tyr could never heal the hurt I had dealt myself. I pushed the thoughts away and, when I finally thought I was presentable, left the house and started down the street to Tyr's family's shop.

Few people meandered about Treb that night. Tomorrow was the Nameless God's day, and most people would be preparing for the large family meal they would eat after visiting the God at his temple. So there was no one to see as I knocked on the main door and, getting no answer, slipped around toward the back entrance that led to the family quarters above the shop.

As I reached the corner of the building, however, I stopped, hearing voices coming from the small garden where Tyr's mother kept plants that Aunt Varil called "decorative nonsense." I waited, listening, before recognizing Tyr's voice, along with those of Renthen and Jorry, two other village boys our age. But I still hesitated. I didn't know Renthen or Jorry very well, and I didn't want to air my troubles in front of them.

I had almost decided to go back home when I heard my name.

". . . finally getting there," Tyr said.

"What, with Sinda?" That was either Renthen or Jorry. Whoever it had been, something in the tone of the voice made me catch my breath.

"Naturally. I told you that it wouldn't take long."

One of the others snorted. "I'd say it's been long enough."

Tyr's voice was scornful. "Don't be stupid. She's like a mouse. I couldn't scare her off. But now . . ." He laughed, and it wasn't like his usual laugh. "Now I have her. You should have seen her when I kissed her. So soft, so willing. It won't be long now."

My heart was beating fast and so loudly I wondered why they didn't hear.

"I don't care, Tyr. I'm not sure anything's worth kissing someone like that. She's so . . . skinny and dark. And there's not even a mouthful to her bosom."

There was a sound of scuffling, as if Tyr had shoved the speaker. "I said, don't be stupid. What does that matter when I'll be able to say I've bedded the girl who was the princess?"

I couldn't breathe. Air was entering my mouth but it didn't seem to be getting to my lungs, and my legs were suddenly too weak to hold me up. I felt myself sag against the wall of the shop and I reached out to grab on to anything that might keep me from falling. A vine, heavy with purple flowers, snaked up the side of the building, and it was onto it that my fingers closed.

I have friends, I heard myself telling Kiernan. But I didn't. All Tyr wanted was to be able to say he'd conquered a princess. I saw Tyr's face in my mind, laughing and full of pride, and Kiernan's, pained and shocked as I had hurled my poisoned words at him. I was the one who had been stupid. I had no one now. No one at all.

The piece of vine that I was holding on to crumbled into black dust in my hand.

The entire vine held for a moment, made of fine black ash, and then it began to fall like snow. I stared upward, shocked and horrified, before I heard a sound like something sizzling in a fire. By the time I looked down, the grass around my feet had turned brown and wilted. The very air around me seemed to warp and twist, filled with heat. And suddenly the feeling, the trapped sensation that had been in my chest all these weeks, was loosed. It broke free from inside me, coiling around me like a snake as it dissipated into the night, and hissed *yes*.

Magic. What I had been feeling all along had been magic, magic that I had not known I had.

I ran. I ran all the way back to Aunt Varil's, not caring if Tyr heard me or anyone else saw me. I ran with my arms pumping and my legs trembling as they carried me, my hair whipping free of its braid. Only when I had reached the cottage and rushed around the corner to hide did I stop, panting, to think.

I had done that. Somehow, I had killed the plant, changing it from something living into ash in an instant. I had charred the grass where I had stood. The only way to do things like that was by magic. But I didn't have any magic, no one in the royal family did. It was a well-known fact that there hadn't been magical king or queen for hundreds of years.

I put one hand to my chest and the other to the cottage wall, suddenly realizing my error. I wasn't royal, so there might be magic in my family after all. But why had I never known it before? Why had nothing like this ever happened before?

My mind immediately began whirling, trying to find an answer, but I forced it to slow. No. As tempting as it was to fall back into the realm of academics, to ponder the reasons that the magic should have remained hidden all these years, there was another question I had to ask first.

Aunt Varil was pacing across the floor of the main room when I entered. She stopped with a stamp of her foot as I came in.

"Sinda!" she barked. "Where have you been? The dye was ruined, and you weren't anywhere to be found. This isn't—"

"Where does it come from?" I interrupted. I felt raw, scraped down to the bone. First Kiernan's disastrous visit, then Tyr's betrayal, and now this. It was too much; I was as tightly drawn as a bowstring ready to be shot. I didn't feel shy or quiet right then. I just felt angry and sick at heart.

"Where does what come from?"

"The magic."

Aunt Varil's eyes widened and her hand went to the base of her throat. Not in shock, but like someone who has just received news that she has been waiting for, and dreading.

"You knew," I said, though I didn't want to believe it. "You knew this might happen, what I've been feeling, and you didn't warn me."

"I didn't know. You didn't tell me. And I hoped . . ." For the first time since I had known her, she looked lost, unsure of herself. "I hoped that it would pass you by. That you wouldn't inherit it."

"Well, I just killed a plant by touching it," I said. "So it looks like I did." The door was still standing open, and I closed it with a bang. My legs were shaking, but I didn't think I wanted to sit down. "Where does it come from? My father or my mother?"

Aunt Varil's eyes flicked downward as she muttered, "Your mother."

EILIS O'NEAL

My mother, the one who had abandoned me, who had sent my father into deep enough grief that he had willingly given me up. I had hoped, a little, that it would have been my father. At least then my aunt might have known something about magic. But in this, I was alone.

I looked up toward the ceiling as my throat tightened. Alone. Always alone. No matter what I did, I was doomed to end up alone, without anyone to turn to for comfort. And why? Because of a prophecy that had nothing to do with me, because I happened to be born at just the right time to a man too unhappy to want to care for me. Just for that, I would never—

"Sinda!"

Aunt Varil's rapier voice yanked me out of the morass of feelings engulfing me. It was only then that I saw the wind swirling through the house, pulling Aunt Varil's skirts, my hair, the bunches of herbs scattered across the table.

More magic. But I didn't know how to control it, how to stop it. I kept very still, hardly breathing in my shock, and gradually the tight feeling of magic in my chest eased again as it flowed out of me. Slowly, the wind died down, and when it had disappeared altogether, I sagged into the nearest chair.

Nameless God, I was a danger to myself and to everyone around me. Just look what I had done in a few moments of hurt and anger. Would I set fire to the house by accident next time I lost my temper? With that thought, I swallowed hastily. What if I did it now? It seemed unlikely; I felt spent, as worn out as if I had run to Vivaskari and back. But I had no one who could tell me what to expect, no one who could help me control myself.

Aunt Varil cleared her throat. "As I was saying, Ilania, your mother, had some power. Mostly, from what I saw, she used it to ensnare people, to get them to do what she wanted. It's one of the reasons I . . . disliked her. I always thought that she had used some magic on your father, to make him fall in love with her."

I didn't look up from my lap. "Was she trained?"

I felt, rather than saw, Aunt Varil shrug. "Not by the college in Vivaskari. She claimed to have studied with a Farvaseean mage during her travels. She said the folk there stood on less ceremony than the ones here."

Which was true, from what I knew of Farvaseean magical practices. They had no college there; instead, those with an aptitude for magic simply found a wizard who would take them on as an apprentice. The wizards in Vivaskari had always put their noses up at such an idea, saying that it was an undisciplined approach and the reason there hadn't been a truly famous Farvaseean wizard in two centuries. Either way, it didn't help me.

"You should have told me," I said wearily. "I'm . . . I'm dangerous now. I killed a whole flowering vine. It just went to ash in my hand. I almost started a windstorm in here without meaning to. If you had told me . . ." I trailed off, uncertain. What then? I still would have had no one to turn to. There wasn't even a village hedge witch in Treb. "You just should have told me."

"I don't like magic," Aunt Varil answered.

I looked up at her. I had never heard someone say such a thing. You didn't like or dislike magic. It was like saying you didn't like air; it was something that was here, something you couldn't do anything about. Some people had it and some people didn't, like red hair or poor eyesight.

EILIS O'NEAL

"I don't like it. I haven't, not since your mother. So I didn't tell you. I guess I hoped that, if I didn't, it would stay away."

A crooked, mirthless smile twisted my mouth. "Well, it's here." I stood up slowly. I didn't know what to do, but I knew that I couldn't think about anything else tonight. "I'm going to sleep. I'll figure out what to do in the morning, assuming I don't set fire to the beds while I'm dreaming."

Aunt Varil didn't even nod. She just watched as, magic thrumming under my skin, I went into the bedroom, lay down on the bed, and fell asleep.

The next morning, I rose knowing what I had to do. I had been confused the night before, but when I woke everything seemed . . . not clearer, but sharper. So many things had collided in one night, and they jostled with one another so that I hardly had any room to breathe. There were edges all around me now, a hedge of thorn-tipped bushes that would snag me if I went the wrong way, and only one path seemed free of them.

Aunt Varil had already left her bed, or perhaps she had not even slept there last night. I had crawled under the blanket, still in my dress. Now I pushed myself up and went over to the chest sitting in the corner. A lump the size of a fist caught in my throat at the sight of King Kelman's map perched on top of the other things inside, but I removed it with only slightly shaking fingers. Near the bottom of the trunk I found what I was looking for: a dark green dress I had brought with me from the palace and the thin, flat slippers that went with it. As I pulled them from the chest, my hand brushed against the small bag of gold wedged in the corner. A flutter of guilt rustled in me. Maybe I should have offered it to my aunt when I arrived, or maybe I should offer it now. Then I shook my head and folded one of the other dresses so that it covered the bag. No, I would need it for what I was about to do.

It wasn't long before I was dressed, but I dithered about, brushing my hair and washing my face even after I knew both were presentable. After all, knowing what you have to do and doing it are two different things. But I finally forced myself to stop, to straighten my shoulders, and go in search of Aunt Varil.

I found her outside behind the house. A tub of water sat before her, along with several baskets of plants and a pile of wool skeins, but she had apparently not touched any of them since placing them there. She was staring off into the woods and looked around only when I cleared my throat loudly.

"Sinda," she said without looking at me. Her voice sounded creaky, and I couldn't tell if she had slept. "I've been thinking. About what you said last night. And I think that you're right. It wasn't fair of me to just hope that you wouldn't have any magic." She spoke in her particular clipped way, with little in her tone to tell me this was an apology. "There's a woman in Widevale, a hedge witch. I bought some remedies from her when your father was sick. They didn't work as well as I had hoped, but they seemed to give him a little relief. If we went to her, she might agree to teach you." Brushing some invisible dust off her dress, she stood up briskly. "Now, there's a cart going that way tomorrow, and—"

She had continued to speak as she rose, but she stopped suddenly when she caught sight of me. Her eyes flitted from my slippered feet to my hair, which I had braided and then looped around my head. Her tongue darted between her lips, and I saw her throat flash as she swallowed.

"But you aren't staying, are you?"

I had prepared a speech, a long explanation that I thought I would need when I confronted her. It fell away now, and I was left searching for words. So I only nodded.

"You're going back to the city?" Another nod. "Today, if you can?" Nod. "I assume you have some sort of money to pay a carriage if one comes through?"

It was only then that I seemed to remember how to speak. "I'm sorry. They gave it to me when I left. For my 'service to the crown.' I should have given it to you, I know, but I thought . . ." I held out my hands and shrugged. "I thought I might need it."

Aunt Varil only jerked her head, but I couldn't tell whether it was a nod or not. "Understandable. And it's yours. After all, I didn't spend my whole life standing in to be killed in someone else's place."

I blanched at the directness of her words, even as I knew they were fair. "But you took me in."

She shrugged her thin shoulders. "Only because you had nowhere else to go. And because I knew my brother would have wanted it." She sat back down on the stump where Kiernan had placed the map yesterday. "I have not been warm with you, Sinda. I have not comforted you, or tried to make your adjustment easier, or even liked your friends."

"He wasn't truly my friend," I said quickly, my cheeks going red.

She blinked then, looking almost as though she would ask me about it, but she just continued, "I am sorry if I made things harder for you. I can only say that I wasn't expecting you. I was used to my life as it was, and I resented the intrusion. Still, I've wronged you twice now. I didn't welcome you, even when I knew you were barely getting by, and I let you stumble into your magic instead of warning you it might be there. I'm sorry for it."

I didn't know what to say. There was too much distance between us, so much that I thought I would never be able to cross it to reach her. But she was my only living relative, and I felt a dark well deep inside me, empty, where it might have been full. If only things had been different, if *we* had been different.

"Thank you," I said finally. "I'm sorry, too, that I couldn't make myself fit in here."

Aunt Varil snorted without warning. "Don't be silly. You don't belong here. You never did. They ruined you for a normal life, but that's not your fault. There was nothing you could do about it." She sighed, like someone rolling into bed for the first time in weeks. "You'll be better off in Vivaskari. But what will you do there?"

I shook my head. "I don't know. I think I'll go to the wizards' college and see what you have to do to be admitted. If they won't take me, well . . ." The fear I had been trying to squash grappled at my throat so that I couldn't speak for a moment. "I'll figure out something. I know the city; I'll be more at home there."

Aunt Varil's eyes were dark when she looked at me. Maybe it was the newly discovered magic running through me, or maybe it was just that she thought it hard enough that anyone would have seen it on her face, but I could hear the words she didn't say. I looked away, north, toward Vivaskari.

EILIS O'NEAL

There might be nowhere I would be at home. I might always be straddling two worlds, and finding solace in neither.

A day later, I was back in Vivaskari.

As the hired carriage clattered into South Gate district, I was unable to stop myself from twisting my neck to look up at the city walls stretching overhead. Luckily, my fellow travelers—a skinny woman from a village south of Treb and her equally thin husband—were also staring out the windows and so didn't see my bumpkinlike reaction. I managed to restrain myself from any more displays as we rolled through South Gate into Flower Basket, where we left the husband and wife, and on into Guildhall district, but I couldn't stop the thumping of my heart. *Home, home, home,* it seemed to beat. Luckily, it seemed that only negative emotions caused the magic inside me to seep out, because the air did not warp or heat even as my heart sped up. I could still feel it, though, now that I knew it was there. The magic felt like a tiny sun inside me, but a sun with an . . . awareness. It wanted to get out; I knew that somehow. I just had to keep it inside long enough to be trained in its use.

The driver left me in front of the Cat's Paw, an inn in Guildhall where he claimed he would leave his own daughter, if he had one. I knew little about accommodations in the city, aside from several expensive taverns in Sapphire district that Kiernan had sometimes gone with other boys from the palace. I knew I could not afford those, and I merely hoped the Cat's Paw would prove to be as clean and as relatively cheap as the driver had promised.

It did, and I was soon ensconced in a room with a window

overlooking Scribe Guild's Hall. The only slippery part of the transaction had occurred when the matronly-looking owner had fixed me with a hard glance and asked, "How old're you anyway?"

"Eighteen," I had lied, trying not to blink. Though she had pursed her mouth in suspicion, the woman had finally nodded and accepted one of my coins. From the widening of her eyes, I guessed that most of her patrons didn't pay in gold, and I vowed to hide the small bag of golden coins tonight, then get them changed to silver and copper as quickly as possible.

Night had fallen by the time I was settled in my room with a tray for supper—I had not wanted to stay downstairs to eat my meal. Though I had rarely strayed outside the upper districts of Vivaskari, I worried that someone might still recognize me as the false princess. After Tyr's ploys of friendship, which I couldn't think about without unhappy rumblings in my stomach, I felt inclined to view almost everyone with suspicion and distrust.

Those feelings extended, strangely, to myself as well. I had changed once again from the person I thought I was. And I didn't trust this new person, this magic-filled self. I had kept my hands clenched in my lap for the entire carriage ride to the city, fearful that I would unleash power that I couldn't control.

All my hope now rested on attending the wizards' college. Surely they would see that I was a danger to myself and those around me and take me in. And if that did not sway them, I could pay with the bag of gold hidden at the bottom of my trunk.

It seemed a long time before I managed to quiet my spinning thoughts, but I finally fell asleep that night. Tomorrow, I told myself as I drifted off, I would begin to pull my life into order.

CHAPTER SIX

"I am sorry, but there's really nothing I can do."

The blue-robed Initiate stared at me, lidded eyes heavy, then looked down and deliberately shuffled through several papers on the desk in front of him. A moment later, he glanced back up and seemed surprised to find me still sitting there.

I hadn't moved because I was in shock. That morning, I had dressed as carefully as I could, choosing the best of the dresses I had been allowed to take from the palace: a red one with long, bell-like sleeves. I had carefully braided my hair around my head and then covered it with a dark veil. Not to keep out the wind—even a breath of breeze sent strands hovering about my face—but as an attempt at a small disguise. I had then walked from the Cat's Paw to the wizards' college and asked to speak to someone about admission there.

Now I found myself pulling fretfully at the veil as I said, "You're sure? I mean, I know I'm a bit old, but I just recently found out that I have magic. I turned a plant into ash and scorched all this grass—"

"So you said," interrupted the Initiate in his drawling voice, "Miss—"

"Azaway," I reminded him.

"However, Miss Azaway, we do have strict policies—very old—about the admission of students to the college. Since you are not of noble birth, you really must be able to pay the yearly fees to be admitted. And, as you've told me, you cannot." His tone trailed up at the end, as if he were waiting for me to correct him. When I didn't, he shrugged. "Well then, you must see that there's nothing I can do."

My chest felt tight, as if iron bands were squeezing it. "But surely there's some way. I have some money—it's not enough for a whole year, but I'll give it all to you. And I could— I could work . . ." I cast around for something else. "I can promise to pay the fees later."

This time he laughed. "Really, we cannot take such promises from every person who traipses in here. We have quite enough wizards to perform all the magical tasks to keep the college running, and enough servants for the rest. As for paying your fees later, you might achieve whatever rank you could"—his tone made it quite clear that he thought I would never rise past Novice, in any case—"and then simply vanish."

"But I wouldn't. Please, I have to learn how to control it."

The Initiate fixed me with a cold stare and said, his drawling tone firming icily, "Then I suggest you go to Wenth or Farvasee. I understand they are not nearly as selective about their students there. Good day."

"Please, is there anyone else I can talk to?"

"There is not. I'm very busy, so I'm going to have to ask you to leave."

EILIS O'NEAL

I stood shakily, nodded at him, and pushed open the door into the hall, nearly bumping into three young Novices in the process. One of the girls sniffed as she picked her way around me, but I hardly noticed. I walked blindly, my body remembering the turns I had made to find the Initiate's office even as my mind froze. After a time, I found myself in the large courtyard that served as the entrance to the college. A fountain in its center sent streams of water into the air that then splashed down into a large, clear basin. It was made of the same white stone as the college's many buildings and towers and had a thick rim all around it. Though wizards in green, blue, purple, and even a few black robes, as well regular people, stood talking in the courtyard or strode across it to one of the many buildings encircling it, no one was sitting on the fountain's rim. Feeling like my legs wouldn't hold me up much longer, I lowered myself onto the rim and let one hand trail in the cool water. To my relief, no one called out or even seemed to notice me at all.

What was I going to do now? Though I had told Aunt Varil that I would figure something out if the wizards' college rejected me, I had never truly believed that they would. It had seemed so simple a few nights ago. After all, I had magic, and I needed instruction on how to control it. It had been a relief to realize that there was someplace I could go, someplace where I would perhaps fit in. I had, in the few days since my magic surfaced, started to view the college as a sort of safe haven, the place I was supposed to be, now that I was not the princess.

What I had not counted on were the rules and regulations governing the admittance of wizards. How had I never realized that only those of noble birth could enter the college freely? That everyone else had to pay an exorbitant yearly fee, one much greater than the amount in the bag in my trunk. It seemed wrong that the crown had never thought to make the college accept anyone not noble or rich.

Think, I told myself. *Think! There must be something you can do, someone else you can talk to.* But the thoughts were as slippery as fish, with nothing for me to hold on to, and they kept sliding away as I remembered the lazy coldness of the Initiate. Was this what Aunt Varil had meant when she said I gave up too easily? Was there something I could do, some action I could take that I was too timid to consider? I couldn't think of anything, but maybe that only meant I really was as malleable as she had said.

As I stared blankly around the courtyard, a quick movement suddenly caught my eye. A woman dressed in the black robes of a Master was walking briskly toward the fountain. Even in my current state, I blanched, nausea rising in my throat when I recognized her as Melaina Harandron. The last time I had seen her, she had been standing with Neomar, watching calmly as he undid the spell they had cast on me to make me appear to be Nalia.

She would recognize me if she saw me. I had known her, distantly at least, from my childhood on. And I did not want to be recognized. Perhaps I wouldn't have cared if I had been sitting on the fountain rim basking in the knowledge that I would soon be taking my place at the college, secure in the thought that I had a place in life. But now, with things the way they were, I cared deeply. I didn't want to be seen as the foundering, lost person I was on my way to becoming.

The veil that I had used to cover my hair was already hanging askew because of my nervous tugging in the Initiate's office. I let it fall forward to obscure my profile and bowed my head as she walked past. Still, I could not keep from lifting my eyes to watch her, my heart pounding as I waited for her to recognize me.

But nothing happened. Her eyes wandered over me and away as if I were part of the fountain. She lifted her hand in greeting to someone across the courtyard, and then moved away.

I should have been relieved, but, somehow, it only made me feel worse.

It was the same problem: Melaina's scant notice of me and the college's casual dismissal. Without a noble's title or money to make up for the lack of it, I was nothing. I had no rank and no chance of getting one. I had thought that the wizards' college would allow me to attain a place in the world, no matter what station I had been born into. But now, as I sat in the courtyard, unnoticed by everyone, I realized that I had never heard a Thorvaldian wizard with the accent of someone born into the lower classes, had never heard of a student taken in on scholarship. I had simply never thought about it before, just as the people around me did not think of it now. But surely that was madness, to leave people with untamed magic inside them, just because they were not nobles or born into wealth? Surely the king and queen would have seen that and ordered the college to change their rules?

No, whispered a tiny voice in my head. *Why should they care if a poor man hurts himself or his family with magic he can't control? After all, they were willing to let a weaver's daughter be killed so that the true princess would live. And happy enough to send her packing when they were done with her.*

The thought lanced through me, awakening the old hurts. And at just that moment, the fountain started to boil.

The water bubbled and roiled around my fingertips, spreading out in waves toward the other side of the fountain. Frightened and shocked, I snatched my arm back with such fervor that I fell off the fountain's rim and landed with a thud on the stone surface of the courtyard. There was rushing in my ears and lightning racing through my muscles. I *was* going to hurt myself—it was the third time in three days that I had done magic accidentally—I would probably kill myself before I could find a Farvaseean wizard who would train me—

"Well now, that was impressive, yes, impressive."

The words cut through my jumbled thoughts, and I looked up to see a figure standing over me.

The person clucked at me. "Really, you shouldn't sit in the dirt any longer than you have to. I can't abide dirt or dirty people. Clutter, yes—and cluttery people—but never dirt. Unless I've been looking for plants, and then it can't be helped."

Perplexed, I pushed myself up from the ground and stood to face the woman in front of me, trying to wipe the back of my dress surreptitiously.

She was a thin woman, perhaps half a head shorter than me, with tangled brown and gray hair that looked as if she had tried to put it up that morning without much success. Half of it hovered like a bird's nest on top of her head, while the rest trailed partway down her back. She was older than Aunt Varil by perhaps ten years. Wrinkles etched her brow and around her eyes, which were a startling shade of green, as sharp as pine needles.

She was peering at me as if I were a scroll written in a strange hand that she nonetheless had to read. "But," she continued, "did you do it on purpose?"

For a moment I thought she was wondering if I fell on purpose, and I opened my mouth to protest, but before I could speak she added, "If you did, it was a stunning use of Syrendal's principle. Very impressive. Of course, if you didn't, and since you're not wearing robes, I think I can say with some degree of certainty that you are not a member of the college, then it means you have a great deal of untrained magic inside you, and you're really quite dangerous to be around at all."

I knew I was gaping at her, but I couldn't help myself. I felt like I was in the middle of a flock of sparrows, being battered by wings and beaks and birdcalls all at once. "You're not wearing robes either," was all I could think to say. She wasn't; instead, she wore a dark dress with a divided skirt, as if she had been riding.

She shook her head so quickly I wondered that it didn't hurt and exhaled loudly. "Those robes, can't abide them either. So long . . . They get in the way. But about that trick you just performed . . . Did you, in fact, intend to prepare the fountain for tea making?"

I swallowed. "No, I didn't. I've only just discovered that I have magic, and I—I came to see if the college would admit me." I could feel my shoulders sag a little. "But they wouldn't. I'm not noble, and I don't have enough money."

Without warning, the woman reached out and grabbed my wrist. There was surprising strength in her bony grip, and after pulling my hand flat, she laid her other hand atop it. As she gazed into my eyes, something warm slid through me, like a cat slipping into a sunbeam. Then she dropped my hand, a scowl pinching her face.

"Stupid ordinances. If I've told Neomar once . . . Well, I shall have to take it up again, not that it will do any good," she muttered to herself. She shook her head and stamped one foot, then said to me, "I can inform you, my dear, that you are positively bursting with magic. In fact, I'm quite confused as to how it could have gone so long without making itself known. Of course, if you were starved as a child, or very, very sick, that might have repressed it some, but . . . No matter, the point is that you have it now, and it can't wait to work its way out of you. What's your name?"

The abruptness of her question made me hesitate.

"Speak up, speak up. You do know your name, don't you?"

Sometimes, I thought ruefully. "Sinda," I said out loud. "Sinda Azaway."

Probably most people didn't know, or if they had heard the name of the false princess, they had forgotten it. But the woman in front of me narrowed her eyes, apparently thinking. "Sinda," she said, looking away, "Where have I heard that . . . Ah."

She tapped her chin, surveying me. "I saw you once, when you were a little girl. I'd come to the palace to ask permission to harvest some blood orchid from the gardens for one of my experiments. There's nowhere else in this part of Thorvaldor that has the plant, very difficult to cultivate . . . You were playing, with a boy, I think it was. You told me where the orchid was in the garden."

She glanced back at the building I had left and shook her head again. "I don't much care for their rules, never have," she said suddenly. "So I'll teach you."

"You'll teach me what?" I asked.

"Magic," she snapped. "Unless I was mistaken and you're as

slow as you seem right now. I may not look it, but I am a Master, if that means anything to you. It means something to everyone else, when they bother to remember, so it probably does to you, too. But not for free. I need a scribe. I suppose you learned how to write a fair hand up there in the palace?"

I nodded.

"And you'll have to be able to do research as well."

"I can do both," I said dazedly.

"Good. I'm very busy with my experiments, so I won't have a great deal of time for you, but it will be better than letting your magic kill you. I'm Philantha, by the way. I don't live at the college. There's a house in Goldhorn that's been in my family for years, and I've found there's nothing worse that living elbow to toe with a bunch of other wizards."

Philantha gave another birdlike shake of her head and was suddenly walking away across the courtyard. I stood, unable to fully understand what had just transpired.

I didn't have long to consider the whirlwind that had just descended on me, however. "Are you coming, Sinda Azaway?" she called impatiently over her shoulder.

This time I didn't hesitate. "Yes," I called, and hurried to follow.

And that was how I came to live in Vivaskari a second time. In exchange for my duties as scribe—and, in fact, assistant researcher, partial librarian, and general fetcher of whatever Philantha wanted at that moment—I was given lodging, magic lessons, and a salary of two silver pieces a week. It was not what a true scribe would have earned, but then most scribes were not receiving magic lessons as well. Besides, I had never earned my own money, and even those two silver pieces made me feel almost heady with wealth honestly earned.

Philantha's house was in Goldhorn district, which lay nestled beside the palace walls and Sapphire district, and was the province of wealthy merchants and those come lately into money but without titles of nobility. It was not as grand as Sapphire, but considerably more dignified than Guildhall or South Gate.

The house itself contained three floors. The first was where Philantha met with friends and the various wizards willing to tolerate her eccentricities. She was not, I discovered, altogether well thought of at the college, but there were at least a handful of wizards who did not look down on her, and they sometimes came to talk magic with her. The second floor was reserved for her workings, and housed her study and various experimentation rooms. The third floor was where her staff, including me, lived. My room was not large, but it was bigger than the cramped room I had shared with Aunt Varil, and it was my own. In addition to me, Philantha employed a cook, a butler, one stable boy to look after her two horses, and two maids. I, however, was the only magical member of the household besides Philantha.

My first lesson in magic came two days after my arrival. I was sitting in the library, bent over a brittle old scroll that detailed, in tiny, feathered handwriting, the uses of common Thorvaldian herbs in magic. I was supposed to be copying the information into a new blank journal, but the process had not been easy. The handwriting was small enough, and the language archaic enough, that a headache was growing between my eyebrows when the door to the corridor thumped open behind me.

I jumped and just barely managed to avoid crushing the scroll with my elbow, which would have surely made at least part of it crumble to dust. I hardly had time to collect myself before Philantha was standing in front of me.

"I thought about sending Briath, but then I thought that by the time I called her into my study—all the maids are just terrified of my study, I'm not sure why—and told her what I needed, it would be easier to do it myself." She paused expectantly, and I realized I was supposed to make some sort of response.

"You thought about sending Briath to . . ." I started hesitantly.

"To get you," Philantha answered as if it were quite obvious.

"Oh!" I pushed back my chair with a clatter and stood up as quickly as I could. "Do you need me?"

"I thought we could begin your lessons. But it would be better to start them in my study. I expect I would be put out if you managed to set fire to the books here, even if half of them are too moldy to read." With that, she turned and left the library without a glance to make sure I was following.

Philantha's study was on the same floor as the library, though several doors down. As we entered, I couldn't help but stop. With so much to look at, I threatened to trip over my own feet if I tried to walk and inspect the room at the same time.

It had once been the house's master bedchamber, of that I felt certain. Philantha must sleep elsewhere, though, because there wasn't room for even the smallest pallet now. Books littered the many tables and stools, as did tall glass vials, mortars and pestles of various sizes, and fat-bottomed bowls. Dried plants hung from the ceiling, a loom with a half-finished weaving on it stood in the corner, and what looked like tools for silversmithing lay forgotten on a desk, surrounded by necklaces both completed and in pieces. A large mirror was propped against the north wall, but it would have been impossible to see yourself in it because of the many symbols painted in red on its surface. Two doors were thrown open to reveal a small balcony that must overlook the tiny walled garden behind the house. The balcony teemed with pots overflowing with herbs and flowers. The room smelled strangely spicy, but also slightly charred, like things were burned here regularly.

"Come in, come in," Philantha called from behind one of the tables. She shoved several books off a stool and gestured me toward it. "Now," she said when I was nervously seated, "what do you know about magic?"

"Only that I have it," I answered without thinking. "Otherwise, only what anyone else would know of it." It wasn't quite true, because I had spent an awful lot of time reading about magic in the palace, but I didn't want to give Philantha the wrong impression of my knowledge.

"Well then, I suppose it's time for a lecture. I used to give them, you know, when I lived at the college, which was longer ago than I think I will admit. But where to start, where to start?" She blew a breath upward, so that it ruffled the hair on her forehead, then said, "Magic is a talent, like being able to sing or learn languages quickly. Some people have it, and most people don't. And some of the people have more of it than others, just as some singers are better than others."

Perhaps because she viewed this as a lecture, Philantha had left off her usual breathless way of speaking. Her explanation was, so far, quite clear, and I let out a sigh of relief.

"The analogy only goes so far, however, because magic, unlike singing ability, has a sort of . . . awareness. Now, you'll find that not everyone agrees with me on this point, but I feel quite adamant about it. I did several studies on the subject when I taught at the college, and it seems to me that many wizards, particularly the more powerful ones, experience a similar feeling when they access their magic. They feel as if the magic *wants* to be used, as if it *needs* to be used."

She paused, and I, remembering the feelings I had been having for weeks, of something wanting to escape me, said, "What happens if you don't use it?"

Philantha folded her arms across her chest, frowning. "The magic will force its own way out. Particularly when the wizard is experiencing strong emotions, and usually in a very primitive way. You might set something on fire, for instance. The magic wants to be used, you see, and if you don't use it voluntarily, it will make you use it. Thus, my feelings that it is . . . different from other talents."

I didn't know what sort of feelings the other wizards at the college got from their magic, but Philantha's ideas made sense to me. And they confirmed my fears that, if I had not left Aunt Varil's, I would have become dangerous very quickly.

"Still, those are conversations for another day. At its heart, magic is simply the ability to take your will and use it on the world around you. You want something to happen, and if you want it badly enough, and you have enough power, it happens. You can use things," she added with a gesture around her study, "like potions or herbs or scrying dishes, to help you focus your energy." She fixed me with an impatient look. "You do know what a scrying dish is, don't you?" I tried to nod quickly, not wanting her to think me completely muddled, but she had already gone on. "It's a dish—very shallow—that holds water. You look into it and, if you have the talent, you see things that will be, or have been, or might be. Touchy magic, I don't do a lot of it myself. The principles remain the same, though, no matter if you're using anything to aid you or not. With all magic, in the end, it all comes down to whether or not you have the power and experience to do what you want to do."

She paused, looking around the room with those quick, birdlike movements of her head, before seeming to find what she was looking for. A silver goblet stood on a nearby table and, picking it up, she placed it on the floor in front of my stool. Water filled it halfway to the brim.

"Now, it's easiest to do things that are natural. Well, that's not exactly true. It's easiest, of course, to cast a spell on yourself. You know yourself, inside and out, even if you don't know that you do. It's other people, of course, always other people who make it hard, because you don't know them, not the way you know yourself. But still, even with yourself, it's easier to do things that are natural. Things that, in the right circumstances, might happen on their own.

"So it would be hard to turn the water into a bird, because, on its own, water will never turn into a bird. But water will freeze, if it's cold enough." She jabbed a finger toward the goblet. "By rights, I should have you start with a spell on yourself, you know. Make you change your hair color or speak in a language you don't know. But I think you're up to a challenge, so try this. Try to freeze the water. Look at it, and *want* it to be frozen."

EILIS O'NEAL

Part of me longed to protest that I wasn't ready, that I didn't know what I was doing. I remembered the way the vine had turned to ash in my hand, and it scared me. But the rest of me felt a charge of excitement, of daring. This was something that could belong to me alone, something that wouldn't remind me of my former life.

I glowered at the goblet. *Freeze,* I thought. *Freeze.* But nothing happened. I glanced at Philantha, but she only gazed back at me without comment. I turned my eyes to the goblet again. Since thinking the word at it wasn't helping, I would have to try something else. But what? Philantha hadn't been particularly specific about how I should do it. I glared at the goblet, and still nothing happened.

I could feel frustration hardening my shoulders. Outside, wind stirred the plants on the balcony, and I realized that it was stuffy in the study. The fire in the fireplace had been allowed to burn too high for the late spring, and a few pieces of hair that had escaped my braid were sticking to the back of my neck. Involuntarily, my thoughts turned to the coolness, to the idea of icy wind against my skin. I thought about the way the fountains in the palace gardens had frozen in winter, about the smooth ice under my fingers, about the icicles that formed on the statues in their centers, hanging down like jagged capes. Kiernan had broken one off for me once, and I recalled the way it had burned my palm with its coldness.

My eyes, which had been wandering, snapped to the goblet. With the thoughts of winter, of snow and ice crackling in my mind, I pointed at the goblet. There was a tiny clank, the sound of something hard hitting metal. As I dropped my hand, suddenly fatigued, I saw that the goblet was covered in tiny frost crystals.

Smiling, Philantha took up a piece of cloth, it wrapped it around her hand, and picked up the goblet. "Completely frozen," she pronounced. "I don't think there's a drop of liquid water in there, which is better than I did my first time—there was still a bit of water on the rim, you see." She set the goblet down, then said, all business again, "And now you see what it feels like to control your magic. Keep that in mind. I don't want you charring my things in a fit of pique. Now, if you aren't too tired, let's talk about other sorts of transformations."

CHAPTER SEVEN

I left the workroom that day feeling buoyant, but if I had thought that the rest of my lessons would be as relatively easy as that first had been, I was mistaken. For one thing, it took more of me than I had thought it would; every spell, even the tiny ones, sapped my energy. Philantha said that I would grow stronger as I practiced and tried harder spells, just as a person's arms grow stronger from lifting heavier and heavier loads.

"Everything has a price," she said airily. "Magic is just like everything else—you have to give something to see a result. In this case, it's a bit of your own energy with each spell. But less and less, as you get better. All that it means—well, perhaps not all, but quite a lot of what it means—is that you have to practice more."

So I practiced. I froze and unfroze water, lit fires by staring at the hearth, and called up wind to float feathers around the study. I ground out potions of clear-sightedness, tried a dismal hand at scrying, and went on long walks with Philantha in the countryside around Vivaskari to collect herbs and plants for her experiments. And it was not all practical study. She set me to reading, and sometimes copying, long passages from books and scrolls of magic. Her library was well stocked with such books, as well as books on the history of magic in Thorvaldor and the countries surrounding it. She also gave me books on the runes used by wizards in older times. They had fallen out of favor in the last hundred years, she told me, but a wizard should be able to read them, as so many older texts employed them.

It would have been easier, I think, if I had had a more conventional teacher. But Philantha's lessons, like everything else about her, were haphazard and often unconnected, so that we went from spells of transformation to spells of strengthening to spells of mind control and back without plan or reason. Once fixed on a topic she was clear and precise, but her tendency to change subjects without warning often left me three steps behind her.

It would also have been easier if I had been better at magic.

It was strange. There had been few things in my life that dealt with learning that I had not grasped quickly and easily. Dyeing, yes, but little else. But after that first triumph of freezing the goblet, I struggled for every bit of progress I made. Spells backfired or simply didn't work. And to my increasing dismay, magic continue to leak out of me whenever I was upset, just as it had outside Tyr's house and at the college's fountain.

"It really would be easier," Philantha said one day after I had accidentally blasted a leg off one of the study's tables, "if you had *less* magic, you know."

"Less magic?" I asked incredulously. "I can barely work any spells now."

"But it's not the amount of magic in you that's the problem,

EILIS O'NEAL

you see," Philantha corrected. "It's just as I said at the college: you're positively bursting with magic. So much that it's trying to all come out at once every time you do a spell, and sometimes it just decides to come out all on its own, regardless of whether you called it. I've rarely seen so much, in fact. And because there's so much, you're choking it off in an attempt to control it." She shook her head as she gazed at me. "I'm surprised, really, that it didn't show itself before now—usually wizards with as much potential as you show it when they're children. I can only assume it was that spell they used, the one to make everyone think you were the princess. Very clever, and very strong, that spell. It kept your magic from showing at all, and tamped it down enough to keep it from surfacing until long after the spell was removed. Which was, frankly, a feat, because there's so much of it."

It scared me, to feel so out of control of something so potentially deadly inside me. To compensate for this fear, I found myself seeking not merely to control my magic but to capture it in a stranglehold. Slowly, things stopped exploding so often. Which was good, except that I kept such a tight grip on my magic that, more and more often, my spells simply failed.

"You have to work *with* the magic," Philantha repeated so often that I went to bed with the refrain jangling in my head. "You're trying too much to control it. Let it flow through you. Pretend you are a riverbed. Don't dam up the water, but don't let it overflow your banks either. Trust the magic, and trust yourself. Let go a little, Sinda."

It frustrated me, to wonder if I would ever gain a true measure of competence. I was used to being good at learning; I wanted to be good at magic. I pushed myself more relentlessly than Philantha did, even while I knew that I was still holding back in some vital way, unwilling to let go of my magic and see what happened. This constant push and pull made me edgy whenever we went to start a lesson, and left me jittery for hours afterward.

And yet, through it all, I felt more peaceful than I had since leaving the palace. I had an identity now. I was a member of Philantha's household. The shopkeepers and families around the house knew me as Philantha's scribe, and they seemed to look no harder than that. And even if no one but Philantha, her servants, and I knew it, I was a budding wizard. I felt, for the first time since I had left the palace, almost whole. I was good at being a scribe, and if I wasn't yet good at magic, Philantha assured me that I would be one day.

I did not have all the pieces of myself intact, but the shattered ones lay quieter than they had in Treb, gradually being smoothed over so that they no longer cut me as often.

As the weeks passed, however, there was one piece of my newly developing self that would not fall into place. At first, I tried to ignore it. But as time went on, instead of improving at my lessons, I got worse and worse. Philantha had to chastise me to make me pay attention some afternoons. I accidentally left scorch marks on the cover of a book I was copying in the library, and caused a windstorm in my bedroom that nearly blew my bed out the window. Eventually I couldn't sleep at night, but lay awake, miserable under the warm blankets.

I knew the cause, though I tried to ignore it. But it was like trying to ignore a wound that wouldn't stop bleeding, like

EILIS O'NEAL

trying to ignore the breaking of your own heart. Even with my relief at finding a place with Philantha, the world began to seem drab and lifeless, lacking in color and sound. I pushed through it, stubbornly, for weeks, telling myself that I was happy, but eventually I had to admit the truth. No matter how comfortable I became in Philantha's house, no matter how much magic I learned, none of it would matter until I had put things right with Kiernan.

Finally, three weeks after I arrived in the city, I went to Philantha to ask for an afternoon off. I was surprised, however, and almost went away again, when I found her ensconced in her workshop with Neomar Ostralus, the head of the wizards' college, and the man who had once helped cast a spell on me to make me seem to be the princess.

"Oh, I'm sorry," I said as I entered the room and saw them sitting with their heads together, bent over a tattered old scroll. Philantha looked up and smiled, though Neomar scowled a little at the interruption. "I didn't know—"

"That anyone so illustrious ever came to visit me?" Philantha finished.

"No," I said, shaking my head. "That you were busy." Of course, I hadn't known the other, either. So far, my experience with Philantha had taught me that most of the wizards at the college had little use for her, with her odd ways and general flouting of convention.

She wagged a finger at me. "No point denying it. I'm usually surprised myself when he deigns to call on me, but we *did* start at the college in the same year, and even his prestige hasn't stopped us being friends. He's just come to ask my opinion of this spell they found in the archives—hasn't been seen for, oh, two hundred years—and, of course, it's easer to find me here than at the college."

Neomar had looked up from the scroll by then and fixed his dark eyes on me. I couldn't help remembering the last time I had seen him, and my stomach twisted. But I managed a stiff smile. "My lord," I said.

"Miss Azaway," he said, seeming equally stiff. He frowned and swallowed, giving the neck of his black robes an almost nervous tug. Maybe he, too, was remembering our last encounter.

I expected him to continue, but he only watched me with an expression of irritation, so I turned to Philantha.

"I have . . . business I need to tend to," I told her, and though her sharp eyes brightened with interest, Philantha only nodded. "In the city. I was hoping, if there's a time that you won't need me . . ."

"Take tomorrow," she said. "A friend of mine—a Wenthi wizard—is coming to visit, so I won't be able to give you a lesson. Just make sure that you copy down the notes I took yesterday. I spilled tea on them, so it will give you chance to practice vanishing spells if you aren't able to make out the words, and with the amount of tea on the papers, I expect you won't. Just try not to vanish words instead of the tea."

I nodded to her, then gave a little head bob to Neomar, and slipped from the room. As I was leaving, however, I heard Neomar say with a huff, "I had no idea you were teaching her, of all people, Philantha. It's very unorthodox."

"Well, you might have had her yourself, if it weren't for those archaic rules at your college," Philantha answer snappishly. "If

I've told you once, I've told you a hundred times . . . And there's talent there, quite a bit of it, even if it is erratic right now. No, don't look at me like that. I won't be dissuaded, no matter what you say."

A long sigh, one that I could hear even in the hall. "Then I at least ask you to keep me apprised of her progress," he said. "It could be important . . . to the crown, that is."

I was eavesdropping, I realized, and with their being wizards they might realize it. I hurried away, wondering why Neomar though it important to know the strides I made with my magic. Perhaps the king and queen would worry I was trying to gain back the power I had lost. But I wasn't, I reminded myself, and if Neomar watched, he would see that. And besides, I had more pressing matters to worry about, so I put it out of my head.

The next day I rose and went to the library right away, without visiting the kitchen for breakfast. My stomach was doing a country dance inside me, and I thought that if I ate anything I would see it again shortly afterward. It took me four tries to vanish the tea stains on Philantha's papers, and halfway through I managed to blotch enough ink onto my copy that I had to start over again. By the time I finished at noon, I was trembling visibly, my hand jerking as I took up a clean sheet of paper to pen my own note.

I am in the city. Please meet me in the Goldhorn Gardens this afternoon.

I paused, the pen hovering dangerously over the paper. There was so much I wanted to write, in case he refused to see me, but at the last moment my courage failed, and I only scratched: *Your friend, S.*

I folded the paper, dripped wax across the opening and sealed it with Philantha's seal, then wrote *Kiernan Dulchessy* on the outer fold. I stared at the words for a moment, my mouth dry, before grabbing it and leaving the library.

All the way to the palace, I thought that I might be sick at any moment, regardless of not having eaten breakfast or lunch. What if Kiernan wasn't there, or was too busy to come to find me? Or worse, what if he was there and simply wouldn't meet me? I had said such horrible things to him in Treb, things that some people would say were unforgivable.

But I needed him. I had lived my life without him for almost a season now. I had tried, in Treb, to replace him. While I might have fooled myself at the time, looking back I saw how hard I had had to work to convince myself that I cared for Tyr the way I cared for Kiernan. In Vivaskari, I had tried not to think about him, trained my eyes not to look north toward the hill on which the palace stood. Neither tactic had worked, and I quailed at the thought of going through even one more day feeling as empty as I felt without him. Even so, walking toward the palace, I trembled even more at the thought of his turning away from me, telling me that I should go . . .

No. I stopped the thoughts with a hard shake of my head. I had to try—he was my best friend, and I had to try.

The palace walls stretched across the upper end of Goldhorn without a break, so I had to go into Sapphire to reach the gates. The people walking the streets here might actually recognize me if they looked closely enough, so I ducked my head whenever anyone passed until I realized such suspicious behavior might draw other sorts of attention. After that, I forced myself to keep my head level but straight ahead, never making eye contact, wishing all the while I had already learned the spells to alter my own appearance. Not that I could have performed them successfully in my state; I probably would have ended up looking like a bearded man for the rest of my life. Even without the spells, however, I reached the palace without incident. Two guards dressed in deep red, the color of the royal family, stood at attention before the gates.

I didn't recognize either of them, so I put on a meek face and walked toward the gate.

"Your business?" the guard on the right asked in a bored voice.

"I've come with a message for the Earl of Rithia's son," I said. "From the house of Master Wizard Philantha Sovrit." That was the truth; I was part of her house now. "I—I don't need to deliver it myself, though."

The guard nodded and snapped his fingers at the door to the guardhouse just inside the gate. "Selic," he called. A young page burst out of the building at a jog, his yellow hair flapping on his forehead. "Run this woman's message to Kiernan Dulchessy. You'll probably find him in his rooms. He hardly leaves them until evening these days."

The page nodded and held out his hand for my message. My throat was thick as I laid it in his hand. Then he was gone, hurrying off toward the palace. I smiled weakly at the guards, bobbed my head in thanks, and lurched back toward Goldhorn district.

The Goldhorn Gardens were public gardens, kept up by the donations of the residents of the district in their hopes of someday surpassing the gardens of Sapphire. They were not crowded, for it was midday and growing hotter. As I entered them, I cast around for someplace to sit, someplace where I might see Kiernan coming before he saw me. A bench set just in front of a tall weeping willow looked like a good spot, so I settled myself down to wait. And wait, and wait.

I sat. The sun moved slowly across the sky as I waited; sometimes a cloud obscured it, but mostly it just drifted implacably westward, shining off the water in a nearby pond and hurting my eyes. My bottom grew numb from the stone bench, but I had endured long years of sitting through lengthy affairs of state, and I hardly even shifted to make myself more comfortable. At first, I wondered about Kiernan and what the guard had said. Kiernan had never been one to lock himself up in his rooms; he thrived on conversation and company. Perhaps he was ill. Perhaps he had taken a lover and was staying up until all hours with her. Both thoughts made my empty stomach flip over weakly. But even my worries died away, replaced by a sense of growing internal numbness, as I sat there longer and longer without seeing his figure coming toward me.

I had resolved, the night before, to wait until dark, but now that seemed like a feat worthy of song. Maybe I should get up and walk around. Maybe Kiernan had come but was waiting in another part of the garden, and if I didn't find him quickly, he would leave. Yes, I decided, I would go and look for him. But as I put my hands against the bench to push myself up, I saw him.

He was moving slowly, glancing to his right and left and sometimes behind himself. A fancy green tunic that I recognized as one his parents had given him for his last birthday covered light brown hose. His hair was dark with water, as if it had just

EILIS O'NEAL

been washed, and it was pushed back from his face, though it was already starting to wave slightly around his ears.

It was then that he saw me, ridiculous looking as I half crouched to rise. He started to take a step toward me, but then hesitated, and that hesitation nearly snapped my heart in two. Before I knew what I was doing, I had flung myself from the bench and was stumbling across the grass toward him.

I was breathing hard when I reached him, but from nerves rather than the distance. We stared at each other, silent, and then I gasped, "I'm so sorry. Nameless God, I'm sorry, Kiernan. I—"

I didn't get any more words out, because he had caught me up in a ferocious hug that lifted me to my toes. All the air was crushed out of me, and my face pressed against his shoulder. To my dismay, I even snuffled a bit into the shoulder. We stood like that for a long moment, pressed together, before propriety forced itself into my brain. "You shouldn't be seen hugging random girls off the street," I mumbled.

"Let the king and queen see. I don't care," he hissed fiercely over my head.

But I pushed back, and he let me go reluctantly. "Well, I do." I tried a shaky laugh. "One of us still has a reputation to maintain, after all."

Kiernan looked ready to argue, so I shook my head. "I came to apologize, not fight again. So will you let me?"

This time Kiernan smiled. "Only if I get to apologize, too. I've been sick ever since that day. It was so stupid, my riding in like that. I should have warned you I was coming. I was asking to get my head bitten off." He raised one eyebrow. "Though, I have to say, you bit harder than I would have imagined possible."

I flushed to the roots of my hair. "I am sorry," I said. "I knew when I was saying those things that I shouldn't. I couldn't seem to stop myself. But I didn't mean them."

"And I'm sorry, too, for sneaking up on you like that. Friends?" he asked.

"Yes," I said, letting out a huge breath.

We grinned at each other—silly, happy grins—and then began to walk slowly down one of the gravel paths, past shady stands of trees and several more formal collections of flowers and bushes. I felt . . . loose, like a string that has been tied in a knot and finally unwound. I was still smiling so hard that my face hurt, and my feet wanted to skip instead of walk.

"Are you here, then?" Kiernan asked finally. "In the city, I mean. Speak carefully, though!" he warned. "You'll crush my heartfelt dreams of the past . . . afternoon . . . if you say no."

"You don't need to worry," I confirmed. "I am living in the city."

"You left your aunt?" Kiernan's brow wrinkled in concern. "Or is she here, too?"

"No, she's still in Treb. I'm the one who left."

Kiernan seemed to consider before he said carefully, "What about your friends there?"

A huge familiar hand gripped my chest as I said, "There was only one friend, really. And he turned out to be . . . false." Kiernan didn't ask, but I found myself saying, "He was only pretending to be my friend. He really wanted . . . that is . . . he wanted to say he had . . . with me . . ."

I was stuttering and blushing, but Kiernan seemed to have understood me. His eyes widened as he asked slowly, "Well, did he?"

EILIS O'NEAL

"No!" I stopped and stamped my foot at him. "Who do you take me for? I didn't lose my brains when I lost my title." Kiernan had the good sense to look abashed, so I continued, in a low voice, "But who knows? I let him kiss me, and I was lonely. I might have, if I had gotten lonely enough . . ."

Kiernan's face had gone white, and his jaw was so tight it looked like rock. "He kissed you? A piece of dirt like that?"

"I doubt I'm the only one who's been kissed these last few months," I said with feigned lightness. I didn't want to talk about Tyr anymore, not when I was finally back with Kiernan. "You were pursuing Lady Vivia when I left. I'm sure you've kissed her by now."

My ploy worked. Kiernan launched into a story involving a feast, a loose dog, and the comforting arm he had had to wrap around Lady Vivia, and had both of us laughing. And if some of the laughter on both sides was a little forced, neither of us mentioned it. Afterward, we walked a little farther in silence, and then Kiernan said, "So where are you living?"

I started to answer, and then realized that I had a whole story to tell myself. "I'm scribe to Philantha Sovrit," I said slowly. "I live in her house."

"Philantha?" Kiernan sounded shocked. "The crazy wizard?"

I puffed up like an angry cat. "She's not crazy! She's a Master, and she's just . . . different. She does all sorts of experiments and new sorts of spells. She just doesn't like the college, that's all."

Kiernan raised his hands in mock surrender. "I'm sorry, I'm sorry! Please," he said with a bow, "let me not offend Mistress Sinda so that she attacks me with magic no doubt learned from the veritable Philantha." He grinned at me as he raised his head, but I didn't say anything. Slowly, the grin dwindled. "What?" he asked.

"I—I—well, look." Holding out one hand, I narrowed my eyes in concentration. I could feel sweat under my arms. *Please,* I thought. *Nameless God, don't let me fail in front of him.* Slowly, there appeared a tiny spark, and then a ball of weak blue-white light hovered above my hand. I glanced from my palm to Kiernan, whose mouth was hanging open.

"It's not a hard spell," I said, and as I spoke, the light vanished. "And see? I'm not really any good at all. There's no need to look like that over it."

Still, Kiernan stared at the spot where the light had been until I dropped my hand. "How did you do that?" he asked, gaping. "You don't have magic, no one in your family—" Understanding lit his eyes. "Your real family. They were . . . wizards?"

I shrugged, embarrassed now. "My mother was, not my father. And I don't think she was a wizard, just . . . someone with power. She was always on the move—I don't think she would have gone to the college, even if she had had the money or title to get in." I ran a hand through my hair to tuck an errant strand back behind my ear. "I tried to get into the wizards' college, but they wouldn't have me. Philantha found me there, and she offered to teach me as part of my payment for being her scribe. She says that the spell they put on me to make me seem to be the princess must have . . . pushed it down. Kept the magic from surfacing. And that it took a while after the spell was gone to reassert itself.

"I'm really hopeless, though. Philantha says that there's too much magic in me, that I didn't use it early enough and now it's trying to get out all at once. Sometimes things happen without my meaning them to when I'm upset. Or sometimes I can't get even tiny spells to work at all. I'm sort of . . . dangerous, I think."

I had worried that he might think of me differently, once he learned about my new powers. That the thought of being accidentally roasted alive if I got angry with him might send him running back to the palace.

I shouldn't have bothered. Kiernan's tongue was poking between his lips. I had seen that look a hundred times, usually just before a stunt that would have him, or both of us, in trouble. "Magic," he murmured. "You, a wizard. A dangerous one." His eyes swept over me, then landed on my face. "Do you have any idea how much fun this could be?"

Once I had Kiernan back, I began to think that, perhaps, my life was finally beginning to come around. It might not have been the life I had once thought I would have, but it was not a bad one. I did the work Philantha needed: copying tattered books and scrolls, translating her experiment notes into a legible script, visiting the shops of Vivaskari in search of ingredients not found in the surrounding countryside, and helping her with her experiments. She was so scattered that, on many days, she did not bother to think ahead to my next task, so I was left alone to study magic. Not that it seemed to make much difference sometimes. I still struggled to control my magic, and sometimes despaired of ever learning enough to call myself a true wizard.

I had rare success, however, with a message spell. It took me two days to get it right, but eventually I could conjure up a tiny ball of green light that, after I spoke to it, would convey a short message to whomever I wished. It was handier and quicker than letters, and it allowed me to tell Kiernan immediately whenever I had an evening free.

"What are you telling them?" I asked during our fourth visit. We were sitting at a table in a tavern in Guildhall, one that Kiernan had apparently been coming to for some years whenever he felt tired of the fancy spots in Sapphire. I had been to so few taverns that I couldn't help staring covertly at every new person who came through the door. I felt rather daring for just being there, though I tried to look unmoved by the whole thing.

"What am I telling whom?" Kiernan asked. His long legs were stretched out in front of him, and one arm dangled over the back of his chair. If you didn't look too hard, you might have mistaken him for a prosperous guildman's son out for a night in town.

I frowned at him. "Your parents. The court. Everyone. You've disappeared, as far as they're concerned, four nights in the past week and a half. You have to be telling them something."

"I told them I've met a fishmonger's daughter and that she's playing hard to catch," he said blandly. "That my courtship has so far been dismal—fish thrown at me, nets dropped on me from rooftops, horrible stuff—and that I'll have to devote much more time to sweeping her off her feet."

I clinked my fingernails against the side of my mug, my scowl deepening. "No, you haven't." It came out as more of a question than I had meant for it to. I didn't think he would really tell anyone that, but you never quite knew with Kiernan.

Kiernan took a slow draw from his mug of ale and then set it down. As he wiped a hand across his mouth, I saw that he was trying to hide a smile. "No, I haven't," he said finally. "I haven't told them anything. You forget, dear Sinda, that I'm only five months shy of eighteen. My parents seem to think that I need to, how did my father put it, 'get any ramblings out of my system' before I settle down as a proper adult. They're letting me run positively wild these days."

"As if you hadn't before," I snorted.

He shrugged. "The last few days, they're just happy that I've done something besides grimace and sulk in my rooms. I did a lot of that while you were away."

"I thought you kissed Lady Vivia while I was away."

Leaning forward across the table, he winked at me. "Yes, but only once, more's the pity." He shifted, as if he were going to sit back, but then he said, more seriously, "The truth is that I was miserable while you were gone. And particularly after our, um, visit in Treb. My parents threatened to take me to our Rithia holdings, to see if the fresh air would knock me out of my despondency. That was when I kissed Lady Vivia. I thought that a scandal would prove that I was still myself, and make sure they would leave me here. I had this idea that you might come looking for me, might need me, even after what happened, and I didn't want you to find me gone."

Warmth slid into the crevices between my bones, golden and sweet, like honey. I swallowed, not knowing what to say. "Your poor parents must have been mystified," I finally managed. "You've never been sick a day in your life."

"Oh, they knew the reason. They just thought . . ." He stopped, a falsely bright smile on his face. "Do you need another drink? I'm going to get more ale, so I can get you some if you want."

I nodded, watching him as he wove through the tables to the bar. He leaned on the counter, chatting with the serving girl as she produced two fresh mugs. He came back, bearing the drinks, with a jaunt in his step.

"That girl—Ani—she says that there's a troupe of jugglers staying at an inn in Flower Basket. They're going to perform tomorrow in the market just before dusk. If Philantha doesn't need you, maybe we go could see them."

"What did your parents think, Kiernan?"

"Pardon, my rosebud?" A confused look stole over his face, but I knew better.

"After I left. You said they knew why you were upset, but that they thought . . ." I trailed off, raising my eyebrows expectantly.

He sighed, then pushed my mug toward me. "They hoped that I'd make friends with her. That I'd forget about you."

The warmth was receding, replaced by the beginnings of crackly ice. "With Nalia."

"Yes."

I reached for my mug and managed to slop some of the liquid on the table as I raised it. I wasn't sure I wanted to know the answer, but I couldn't seem to help myself. "And did you? Make friends with her?"

Kiernan looked torn. He glared at his cup, then took a big enough swallow that he choked. Eyes watering, he said, "Sort of. She's . . . She's nice, Sinda. She was raised in that convent, but you wouldn't guess it—she's not stuffy or cold. She's nice. And my father wanted me to make sure that I didn't . . . snub her. He said that everyone knew how close I was to you, and that it would hurt our family if I seemed to dislike the princess. So I went whenever she invited a group of us to play games in the hall

EILIS O'NEAL

or go walking. And she had heard about you, and me. She asked me questions, sometimes."

My face felt puffy, like when I had been holding back tears. "Like what?"

He shook his head and shrugged. "Things you did. What you were like." He smiled at me, but weakly. "I left out the parts about your being pretty much unable to walk without hurting yourself."

Trying for levity, I stuck my tongue out at him, but it was halfhearted.

"At first, I felt like I was being disloyal to you. I didn't want to like her. But then I thought, well, that the two of you are really in the same boat. And I hoped that someone was being kind to you, so I thought I should probably be kind to her."

"Oh yes," I said sourly. "She's suddenly the princess and I'm suddenly nobody and we're in the same boat."

"Well, you are," he said more forcefully than I would have expected. "Neither of you asked for this. She was pretty lost herself at first. Everyone trying to curry favor; nobody really talking to her. She needed a friend."

I wanted to snap at him, or maybe crawl into bed with the covers up around my ears, but I just looked down. I was, I realized with a flush of mortification, jealous. Jealous of Kiernan liking Nalia, of finding her, even in the tiniest way, a replacement for me. Was this how Kiernan had felt when I had thrown Tyr in his face in Treb—all hot and cold at the same time? But I had been trying to be spiteful, and he wasn't. Even through the hurt, I had to admit it was different. Still, it didn't stop me from saying, somewhat sulkily, "Would you rather be with her now? You can go, if you want. I'm sure there's something going on at the palace that would be more interesting than being here."

"A play, actually," he said. "There's a Farvaseean troupe of actors staying at the palace. They're performing some new comedy tonight. It's supposed to be quite good."

I could feel my forehead pinching as I stared resolutely at my lap.

"Nameless God, you can be a stupid cow."

I jerked my head up. "How dare—" I sputtered, but Kiernan was shaking his head and smiling.

"Don't you see? I'd rather be here than watching ten Farvaseean plays."

The sincerity in his voice made me aware of how petulant I must look. "Sorry," I muttered.

"It's all right," he said easily. "I expected you to ask me about her before now." We sipped our drinks in silence for a time, before he added, "I think she's guessed that you're here, though. She said something to me the other day that made me think it."

I swallowed, not wanting to show how much that scared me. "Will she tell?" I asked. "I don't—I just don't want anyone to know. Where I am, that I'm here. I don't know why."

"I don't think so. Still, I wouldn't be surprised if she came looking for you. I think she has questions."

Which was a problem I had not even considered. I didn't know how I felt about talking to Nalia, and I wasn't sure I was ready to find out. But I had ruined enough of one evening, so I only said, "Well, we'll see about it when it happens. Now, tell me about the jugglers."

EILIS O'NEAL

CHAPTER EIGHT

It wasn't as simple as that, though. The next time I saw Kiernan, we quarreled about it.

"She has figured it out," he told me.

We were sitting in the garden behind Philantha's house, watching the water in the little fountain splash into the basin at the bottom. It was a small space—no one but nobles had room for sprawling gardens inside the city. Surrounded by a tall stone wall, it contained the fountain and circling walkway, with various herbs and flowers growing near the walls. The balcony above teemed with more life, but it was still a pleasant place. I had been lounging with my back against the warm stone lip of the basin, and I jerked so hard that I banged my right shoulder painfully. Eyes watering, I said, "What makes you think that?"

"She said, 'I know you're seeing her. I want to meet her.' It doesn't get much clearer than that."

I rubbed my shoulder. I thought about asking Kiernan if I was bleeding from scraping it against the stone, but only gritted my teeth instead. "What? Does she expect you to bring her to me?"

From the bench he was sitting on, Kiernan shuffled his feet against the ground, then said, "I think she does."

I felt my cheeks go hot just as my spine seemed to turn into an icicle. I didn't *want* to meet Nalia, didn't want to get any closer to her than I was right now. I didn't care that she was the princess, that it was her right to ask me to dance with a goat in front of all Goldhorn district if she wanted to. I knew only that I had no desire to lay eyes on the girl whose life I had been living until that spring. I would rather have crawled back to Treb on my hands and knees in the pouring rain without a cloak.

And yet.

I had been her. Some rebellious part of me wanted to look at her, to see the real thing, the thing I was supposed to have been. To see what she was doing with the life that had been mine. And it scared me, because I knew what I would find. I had seen it in that brief moment when she had disembarked from the carriage to greet the king and queen.

She was a princess. The real princess, all grace and silky movements and warm laughter. Something I, in my clumsy, shy, small body, had never been. To see her would force me to acknowledge it, more than I did now. And I was scared.

"Well," I said, getting up, my hands on my hips, "you'll have to tell her that you won't. That it's just not possible."

He folded his arms, a stubborn expression on his face. "You know I can't do that, Sinda. She's the princess. She'll be queen someday. If she asks, I have to do it."

"You didn't do what I told you to often enough!" I retorted.

"We're not talking about taking the last spice cake on the plate! You know that I'll have to bring her if she asks."

I did know it, but I didn't want to hear it. "Fine! Just do whatever Nalia wants. Bring her here. But don't be surprised if I don't answer the door!"

With that, I stormed out of the garden, slamming the door into the house behind me. Through the window, I saw Kiernan start toward the door, then stop. Slowly, he turned around and left through the garden door, the one that led into an alley that connected to the main street.

"What did he do?"

I whipped around, startled. I had been so immersed in my own thoughts that I hadn't even noticed Philantha standing into the doorway to one of the sitting rooms.

"Pardon?"

"Well, in my experience, it's usually the man who bumbles about causing most of the problems in relationships of romance," she said. "So, naturally, I assumed that your young man has done or said or thought something that caused you to come bursting in like a hurricane. Am I correct?"

I shook my head so violently the braid coiled around my head threatened to come loose. "We're not in a . . . relationship of romance. He's just my friend."

Philantha made a sound suspiciously like a snicker. "Truly?" she asked. "I suppose that's why he's been with you most evenings."

"Like I said, we're *friends*. And we haven't seen each other in a long time."

She raised an eyebrow. "I may not care about it—or at least I didn't, until recently—but I do hear some of the court gossip when I visit the college. The noble students, they bring it with them, you know. And one of the stories is how the Earl of Rithia and his wife are scrambling to find eligible matches for their son."

I felt suddenly dizzy for no reason, and a hot flush—disturbingly like the jealous feeling I had experienced at the inn—rushed through me. "Matches?" I repeated.

"Girls, young women, marriageable prospects. Strange, how suddenly they started. Right after the princess came back, it's been noted. As if they had had hope for another match before, and it was ruined."

"Me?" I asked. "People think Kiernan's parents wanted him to marry me? That's . . . ridiculous. Princesses don't marry earls—a duke, maybe, but not an earl, not unless he's foreign and brings some grand alliance. And besides, we're just—"

"Friends," Philantha finished. "I know. That's what you keep saying." She eyed me, before saying, "They haven't had much luck, though, from the gossip. He's polite to everyone they trot out, but nothing more. But that's neither here nor there, since you don't love him."

I glared at her, my face and chest still filled with that rush of heat.

"In fact, he's made you angry, hasn't he?"

"He did. Well, I said . . . Yes, we fought. He says that Na—the princess—wants to see me. And I told him that he couldn't bring her to me, that I didn't want to see her. He said that if she asked, he would have to. But he's wormed his way out of stickier situations than that. He could find a way to avoid it, if he wanted to."

"Then perhaps he doesn't want to," Philantha answered before gliding away up the stairs and out of sight.

I had plenty of time to mull over Philantha's words, because

EILIS O'NEAL

I didn't see Kiernan for the next three days. It was the longest we had been parted since I returned to the city, and even through my anger at him it drove me to distraction. I mangled my spells even worse than usual, spilled ink, and tripped so frequently that Philantha threatened to call Kiernan to the house herself and turn him into a sparrow if we didn't make up. Her eyes glinted dangerously when she said it, and only that was enough to force away a bit of my muddleheadedness. But I made up for it by spending my free time mooning about on windowsills, staring in the direction of the palace. I thought about sending one of my message spells to him at least five times a day. But each time I raised my hand to conjure the tiny ball of glowing light, I dropped it. I wanted to see Kiernan, but I wasn't ready to forgive him yet. As for Philantha's other charge, it was obviously silly. We were friends, as we always had been.

Still, why did it seem like every time I turned around I was fighting with Kiernan? We had rarely fought before, and then only over unimportant things. *Maybe,* whispered a seditious part of me, *you didn't have enough of a spine before. You were too shy to fight with anyone, even him.* Or maybe I was just turning into a prickly, irritable person, a sort of walking thornbush. Or maybe, despite my protests to Philantha, something was shifting between Kiernan and me, taking a path the end of which I couldn't see.

On the third day, I managed to botch the locating spell Philantha was teaching me badly enough that, instead of finding the needle she had placed in her desk, I flung all the drawers out of their slots and against the wall.

"You aren't concentrating," she snapped, pointing at the

drawers so that they flew back into their places. "You have to envision just the needle, nothing else."

"I know, I know," I mumbled as I slumped down on a stool. "I just . . ." I had been wondering about Kiernan, if he was talking to Nalia right then. It was afternoon, the time when the palace nobles sought the cool of the indoors before dinner. I felt wrung out, as tired and cranky as a wet cat, and also something else. Something that reminded me, though I wanted to deny it, of jealousy. "I'll do better," I offered.

"No, I think enough of my study has been upended for one day, or perhaps even five," Philantha said with a shake of her head. "There's an apothecary—strange man, very tall—in Wizard's district who promised to order me some Farvaseean blood fig seeds. They should be in by now. I want this whole jar filled, or as much as he can manage." Pushing a rabbit skull and paint palette aside, she found a squat, empty jar and shoved it toward me, along with a handful of coins.

I nodded and started toward the door. "I'm sorry," I said over my shoulder as I reached it.

"Remember what I said about the sparrow," Philantha huffed.

It was a gray day, with low clouds pressing on the tops of the buildings. The palace, I saw when I glanced involuntarily toward its hill, was obscured by the fog. I stared at the shifting mist for a moment, then shook myself and walked away from the house. I had taken only ten steps, however, when the tie on my shoe came undone, forcing me to stoop to relace it.

Only then did I notice the man.

He was thin, with unremarkable brown hair and a long,

slightly mushy-looking face, dressed in common brown leggings and a tunic. No one you would ever think to look at even once. He had been rubbing at the metal railings that led up the steps to the house across from Philantha's, his cloth dark with polish. I would never have noticed him, except that the abruptness of his movement caught my eye as I bent to tie my lace. He stopped, just when I did, and did not move until I had straightened and walked on.

Don't be foolish, I told myself. *It's just a coincidence.* But I couldn't stop the prickly feeling on the back of my scalp, and I managed to sneak a look behind myself after turning two corners.

The man was following me. He walked half a block behind, his eyes not focused on me. He looked like any other common man hired for a day at one of the merchant houses, on his way home or to his next job. But he took every turn I did, and never fell back farther than a half block.

My heart was racing now, but I didn't know what to do. Should I simply make my way back to Philantha's? But she might not believe me, what with my strange behavior over the past few days. Should I call a city guard? No, a guard would certainly not believe me, for I felt sure that the man would melt away before I finished drawing breath. A treacherous part of me longed to flick my fingers, summon a message ball, and send it straight to Kiernan, but even in my fear I couldn't make myself do it.

In the end, I decided to keep going to the apothecary. There were people on the streets; there was no way for the man to abduct me, if that was his plan. *And why should it be?* I argued with myself. Who would want to have me abducted or even followed? I was no one important, not now.

The apothecary's shop sat on a street near the college that housed several other shops which wizards patronized. The owner, who was indeed tall enough that I had to stretch my neck to look at him properly, filled my jar and took the money without saying much. I thanked him, then paused to glance out the window before leaving. I didn't see the man, which made me think that I really might have been imagining things.

You've been silly, I thought. *Get hold of yourself and go home.*

As I stepped out of the shop, however, I forgot to check down the street for the man, because I was immediately distracted by the strangest sensation. It was as though I was a doll on a string, and someone was tugging on that string, drawing my head in the direction they wanted. I couldn't help turning to the left. For a moment, I saw nothing but the quiet street, and then a figure moved out of the shadow of a nearby building. Not the man who had, or had not been, following me. This person wore a long brown cloak, and something about its lines reminded me of the clothing worn at a convent or monastery. A memory itched in my mind, but before I could put it together, the person drew the hood back, and I almost dropped the jar of seeds.

We didn't look the same, not really. Close enough to be cousins, perhaps, but never twins or even sisters. Nalia was taller than I was, and longer of limb. Her hair looked like polished wood, whereas mine tended to be more the color of dark tea. The features of her face were more cleanly cut, her nose sharper and brows more arched, all except her lips, which were full and rosy pink. The similarity was there, but it was like looking at a view of myself through water, with every feature altered by the waves.

EILIS O'NEAL

We gazed at each other for a long time, and then I said, "We'll attract attention if we keep standing here. And I'm guessing only Kiernan knows where you've gone, so you won't want that."

A little flush of color painted itself prettily across her face. "Will you walk with me then?" she asked.

I bit my lip, all other concerns vanishing from my mind, and nodded.

We walked in silence, each of us sneaking glimpses of the other out of the corners of our eyes, before I said, "There's a statue, I think, of Queen Conavin around that corner. She's the one who—"

"Granted the land for the wizards' college," Nalia finished. At my startled look, she shrugged delicately. "I was tutored well in the convent, and even more so since I've been here. They seem to want me to know everything you . . . everything a princess should know, and they think I should know it as quickly as possible."

Another silence, this one a little heavier than the last. "There are benches," I said. "We could sit there."

"Lead the way," she said.

The statue of Queen Conavin was set a short way off from the street in a small round cul-de-sac. It was life-size, or nearly, with the queen gazing toward the wizards' college, her two hands held out in a gesture of giving. Nalia paused as we made our way toward the benches placed around the statue, her head tilted back to regard the stone face. It was hard to tell, for the statue was more than two hundred years old, but I thought you could see the resemblance, mostly in the slant of their cheekbones. I sighed.

The sound seemed to recall to Nalia that I was waiting, because she smiled apologetically and came to sit beside me on the bench the farthest from the road. But instead of speaking, we avoided each other's eyes and stared at our laps. She wore a dusky blue gown, the sleeves cut to fall just below the crook of her elbow. If she had shifted, I might have been able to see her birthmark, my old birthmark, the three tiny reddish dots set on her inner arm. She remained still, though, and the silence between us grew more and more uncomfortable. But just as I was about to open my mouth, Nalia said, "I've been thinking about this for weeks, and now I hardly know where to begin."

Her voice trembled, so slightly I wasn't sure if I had actually heard it, and when I looked, I saw that there was just a sliver too much white around her eyes, a fraction of tension gripping her mouth. Vulnerable, I realized. The Princess of Thorvaldor felt as naked and strange as I did, as unsure of what to say. It made me want to simultaneously hug her and slap her across those elegant cheeks.

"Start at the beginning," I said, though it came out a bit ragged. "Why did you seek me out, Your Highness?"

She did flinch then; the last words had been more acrid than I had meant. "Don't call me that, please. I didn't come here for that."

"Then what did you come for?" I asked, resisting the urge to rub my hands up and down my arms.

"To see you. You were all I thought about, on the way from the convent. I thought that maybe I would get to meet you, that you would still be here, but you weren't. And when I was lonely, when I missed my home, I kept wondering where you were and if you were missing your home."

"Well, if that's all you wanted to know, I can tell you about it." The words rolled out of me in a torrent, sharp and biting. "If you want to hear how I cried myself to sleep missing my friends and my room and my . . . everything, I can tell you. If you want to hear about how I couldn't even make a life for myself with the one real family member I have left, I can tell you. I can tell you about how the one friend I thought I'd made turned out to be no friend at all, about how the wizards' college wouldn't take me because I'm too poor. Will it make you feel better to hear those things?"

For an instant, Nalia looked as startled as if I *had* slapped her. But then she straightened her spine, her shoulders going hard, and her chin rose. "I didn't ask for this, you know. I didn't ask for them to come and tell me that I was the princess. I was happy with my life the way it was—I didn't want to take yours! And now I'm just . . . trying to understand, and I thought—" She let out her breath in a whoosh, staring up toward the gray sky. "I thought I might, a little better, if I met you."

Another barrage of attacks came into my mind, and I almost let them loose. Just then, though, I noticed how one of Nalia's hands gripped the coarse fabric of her cloak, rubbing it back and forth between her fingers as if it were something comforting. The cloak smelled sweet, I realized. It had none of the slightly herby, musty smell of clothes that the palace servants had packed into trunks because they wouldn't be much used.

"That's not just for disguise, is it?" I asked.

She narrowed her eyes, waiting for another caustic remark, but when none came, she nodded once. "I wouldn't let them take it. They gave me new clothes at the convent, for the carriage trip, but they hadn't sent a cloak. I said I was cold, and they let me bring this. After I got here, I hid it before they could take it away."

I leaned forward, elbows on my knees and face buried in my hands. It would be easy to hate her. To be filled with righteous indignation at having been snuck up on. To rail at her for what her family had done to me, how they had used me and then cast me aside. I wanted to hate her for taking the life that I had thought was mine.

I couldn't.

Kiernan was right, I thought with a miserable, smothered laugh. Neither of us had asked for this. It had all been decided by others—the king and queen, the wizards they had asked for help, the Nameless God, even, when he sent a prophecy of death upon the princess's birth. The two of us hadn't had any control over it. And I was tired of being a thornbush, of yelling at everyone around me. Maybe, by not hating Nalia, by forgiving her for the life she now possessed, I could really begin to be Sinda, and not just the false princess.

"I'm sorry," I said, taking my head out of my hands. "All I seem to be doing lately is arguing with people. Let's start again, shall we? I'm Sinda, and you're Nalia."

Nalia had still looked frosty when I started talking, but by the end, her face had softened. "I'm sorry, too. I knew you wouldn't want to see me, and I came anyway."

"Sometimes you have to," I agreed. It had started to mist, and tiny droplets of water clung to her hair. I could feel the wet seeping through my dress, but neither of us moved.

"I don't have long," she said. "I've been coming here for the past few days, for a little while, thinking you might come."

"Why?" I asked.

"You told Kiernan that Philantha sends you on errands. So I've been going to each of the shops he said she frequents, while he lies to anyone who asks where I am." She blushed again. "I wanted to wait outside your house, but I didn't have the courage. I think this way took more time, though."

I twisted my fingers together, then let them relax. "Did he tell you I was here, in the city? Is that how you knew?"

I saw consideration flash through her eyes as she tried to decide whether or not to tell me. I waited while she let out a small breath and then said, "Yes and no. I mean, he did tell me where he thought Philantha sends you, but I figured out you were in the city by myself."

"How?" I imagined a ring of spies, all ready and willing to do the new princess's bidding, even as I knew how silly that was. *I* had never had spies, after all, nor heard of any sixteen-year-old prince or princess who did.

Her cheeks reddened a bit. "Kiernan. We were introduced soon after I arrived. And everyone seemed to like him, and he seemed to like everyone else. Everyone but me." I must have looked startled, because she smiled wryly. "Oh, I doubt many other people knew it. That's one thing I've noticed—the people who live in the palace rarely look beyond themselves. They're so concerned about, oh, their positions, and who's in favor with whom, things like that."

I grinned at her. "That's true. But it always seemed like everyone noticed my tripping and falling over things every time I came into a room."

"No one's mentioned it. All I've heard is how you were very

quiet, very studious." She paused, and I knew that she was leaving something out. Maybe that I had been so quiet and studious that they should have known I could never be the princess. I didn't say it, though, and she went on. "So, Kiernan. He always came, if I made an invitation, but I could tell that he didn't want to like me. I knew he had been your friend, and I told myself I understood how he might hate me for taking your place. But really, I wanted him to like me so much it hurt. I thought, since he liked you, that, if he liked me, too, I might feel more like I was really the princess. It took a long time, but he finally seemed to warm to me. It was overnight, almost, like he had made some decision while lying in bed."

I didn't say anything, remembering Kiernan's words. *I hoped that someone was being kind to you, so I thought I should probably be kind to her.*

"After that, I could tell that his . . . moods stemmed from missing you, and not disliking me. Then, one day, he said he was going to visit a friend outside the city. He gave a different name, but I guessed that it was a lie, that he was really going to see you." She swallowed, and there was the slightest hint of nerves in her voice when she said, "It didn't go well, did it?"

I recalled shouting at Kiernan, turning my back on him, the hot wetness of tears on my face. "No," I said. "It didn't go well."

"I didn't think so. He was worse when he got back. He didn't come out of his rooms for days. But then, all of a sudden, it was like a light came back on inside him. And I thought there was only one thing that would cause that to happen. You."

There was something sad in her eyes, in the line of her mouth.

EILIS O'NEAL

"We've been friends since we were children," I said. It sounded like an apology, and maybe it was. I wondered if she had left a friend like that behind at the convent, if she couldn't see that person now because she was the princess. I wondered what else she had left behind.

She shook herself, so slightly that I wouldn't have noticed, except that it made the raindrops in her hair tremble. "I made him tell me," she said. "He didn't want to. Don't be angry with him."

I didn't answer. The ache of anger at him had diminished a bit while I talked to Nalia. Part of it, I realized, had been born of the fear I'd had about meeting her, and I had just pushed it off onto Kiernan so I wouldn't have to face it. But that was something I'd have to work out with him, not her.

Nalia reached down and plucked a blade from the clump of grass that was stubbornly trying to grow between the flagstones surrounding the statue. I was gazing toward the palace, lost in my thoughts, and she must have misinterpreted the look. "Did you love it very much?" she asked softly, braiding the grass through her fingers.

"What? Living there?"

"Being the princess."

Part of me wanted to laugh, and another part, a little part, wanted to cry. As it was, I sort of hiccupped, then rolled my shoulders into a weak shrug. "Yes. No. I don't know. I mean, it was my life, and I was happy most of the time. I knew who I was, I knew what I was for. I tried to learn enough to be a good queen. But I never really . . . fit in, I suppose. I didn't like the grand dinners, with everyone watching me, because I was sure to spill something down my dress. I didn't like having to make conversation with every duke's son and foreign noble's daughter, and never getting to be let off dancing at a ball. I could do it all, but it made me nervous. So, yes, I miss it. It was all I knew." I looked into her face, so like and unlike my own. "But sometimes, it's a relief, too. It's easier, just being Philantha's scribe."

"Yes," she whispered, "I know."

A bell sounded somewhere in the district, marking the hour. It was later than I had thought. Nalia turned in the direction of the bell, her fingers rubbing her cloak again. She would have to go soon, or risk having every guard in the palace searching the streets of Vivaskari for her. She would have a hard enough time explaining as it was, for the mist had turned into real rain, and she would be soaked through by the time she reached the palace.

There was a question I had wanted to ask, but it kept getting stuck somewhere in my mouth before I could speak. Finally, though, with the ring of the bell still in my ears, I forced it out. "How is my . . . the queen. How is the queen?"

Nalia looked down at her lap. "She misses you, I think. She doesn't talk about you—neither of them do. But I caught her crying once, when she thought she was alone. I was standing just outside the doorway, where she couldn't see me. I was about to go in to her, but then my . . . then the king came. He held her shoulders and I heard him say that she had to bear it. That she had known, that there was nothing else they could have done. She stopped crying for him, but she still looked sad."

My throat burned and I had to shut my eyes to keep tears from spilling out. I had thought that I wanted to know that she missed me, but knowing it didn't make me feel better.

"I'm sorry," Nalia said. "I'm sorry, but I have to go. They'll miss me soon."

I nodded, eyes still closed. When I heard the sigh of her skirt brushing against the ground, I opened them and stood. We stared at each other without saying anything until Nalia finally gave a tight little smile. "Thank you. I'm sorry I sneaked up on you, but I had to. I had to know."

"I understand." I did, now. It had hurt to talk to her, but it had been healing, too, as if a painful boil inside me had been lanced. "If you go in through the corridor that leads past Lord Trenbalm's rooms, you probably won't be seen by anyone. There's hardly anyone around there this time of day."

She grinned. "Thank you."

She turned then and had almost reached the street when I thought of something. "Wait!" I shouted. She glanced back at me, quick and smooth as a deer. "What was your name, before?"

It hurt. I could see it in her face: an ache at recalling it, but also relief, a release like water breaking through a dam.

"Orianne," she said. "It was Orianne."

I inclined my head. Orianne. She watched me for a moment longer, and then I was alone beside the statue, rain dripping down my face.

I had made it back to Philantha's house before I realized that I had not asked her if she had sent the man in brown, nor had I thought to watch for him all the way home.

CHAPTER NINE

I told Philantha about it after I returned to the house. Not all of it, or even most of it, the largest omission being that of my possible follower. I said only that I had met Nalia in the street and that we had spoken. But I did ask her about that tugging I had felt just before I saw Nalia—the sensation of being drawn toward her.

"I was standing there, outside of the shop, and then I felt like I *had* to look in her direction. I didn't even know anyone was standing there, but I glanced that way all the same. It was like . . ." I shook my head, searching for a comparison. "Like there was a string between us, pulling us together."

Philantha paused, her pestle resting on the edge of the small bowl in front of her. "Did the princess seem to feel it, too? Did she say anything about it or, for that matter, did you ask her if she had felt it?"

"No," I admitted. "I was shocked to see her, and I forgot."

Philantha clinked the pestle against the side of the bowl in irritation, the sound sharp enough that I winced. "A wizard must always be aware of magical phenomena. You remember the story of Engahar Yarren?" I nodded, wincing again with the memory of the grisly story. "Good. Keep it in mind next time you feel a spell that you didn't cast affecting you."

Little cat's paws of trepidation frolicked up my spine. "A spell?" I asked. "You think it was a spell?"

She peered into the bowl, then shoved it toward me. "Do you suppose that these seeds can be ground much more finely than this? I don't—they looked absolutely pulverized to me—but it never hurts to check, after all." When I agreed, she snatched the bowl back and set the pestle aside. "Yes, I think it was a spell, or rather, the effects of a spell. The spell that made you appear to be the princess was, from what I can tell, a sort of transferring of a tiny bit of the princess's essence. They pulled out a little bit of her soul, for lack of a better word, and transferred it to you. They used it to mask your own essence so that, to any probing wizards, you would appear to be the princess. Things were made easier for them, of course, because who would ever think to try to look for another person hiding, as it were, under the princess's own skin?" She wrinkled her brow and crossed her arms. "Now, for all that they took only a tiny piece of her soul, it was a powerful spell. It made you appear to be the princess in every way, even pushing the magic inside you so low that it reasserted itself only a long time after the spell was broken. I think—though I may, of course, be wrong—that you will always feel that . . . current if you are near Nalia."

"There was part of her in me?" I asked.

Philantha gave a quick shake of her head, neither a yes nor a no. "As I said, it's only a theory. I tried to ask Neomar about it—I told him I was professionally curious—but he wouldn't tell me anything. In any case, it *is* only a theory, so it may not be the truth, but I think it is. In fact, it sounds as if they weren't able to get every last bit of her soul, since you're feeling drawn to the original. As if they accidentally left a little of Nalia in you." Gazing off into the distance, she narrowed her eyes in thought. "Such an odd spell, really. They would have had a time of it if the princess had died as a child, while she was living in that convent. The spell would have fallen apart then, and your magic would have come back to you, just as it has now. They wouldn't have been able to say you were the princess then. But I suppose there was no other way to do it. But now I really have to start to work on this"—she shook the bowl of powder around a little so that it swirled up the sides and then fell into the bottom again—"or it will lose its potency. Blood fig seeds are notorious for it."

After that, I wandered, restless, through the house. I wanted something to occupy my mind, something other than thoughts of my conversation with Nalia or the unsettling idea that parts of us had been exchanged during the spell laid on us. Or the idea that some unknown person was having me followed. I knew that I should use the message spell to send word to Kiernan, to tell him that he had been right about Nalia, but every time I began the spell, I stopped. I wasn't ready yet; it was all too fresh, too tender, like a newly unbandaged hurt. Some of the wounds within me might have been lanced by talking to Nalia, but that didn't mean I wanted anyone else prodding them. So I made a general nuisance of myself, bothering everyone from Gemalind, who sent me scurrying from the kitchen in a cloud of flour, to Tarion, who tolerated my presence in the stable until I accidentally levitated several curry combs, spooking Philantha's mare. After being evicted from the stable, I returned to the house, shuffling along the hallways and occasionally entering a room only to leave again after a few moments. Even the library held no appeal for me, and I eventually found myself at my own door. Sighing and unable to think of anything else to do, I opened the door, went inside, and flopped down on the bed to stare up at the ceiling.

What was Nalia doing? Had she made it back to the palace? I wondered if she had felt the . . . remnants of the spell they had worked on us. I rubbed my eyes, irritated with myself. I hadn't thought to mention it at the time, and now I couldn't ask her. Maybe I could have Kiernan ask her, if I ever managed to let him know that I wanted to make up.

With a growl I pushed myself up and scanned the room, desperate for something that would let me stop *thinking* so much. I was tired to death of pondering my situation, of worrying about who I was and who I wasn't. *Please,* I thought, sending a petition to the Nameless God, even though I knew it was, in most respects, an unworthy request. After all, the God had better things to worry about than one dissatisfied scribe girl. Still, I closed my eyes and prayed, *Please let me stop. I just want to be me—I just want to be useful and . . . content. I want to stop wondering if I'll ever feel whole and just be whole. I want to have a purpose, one that I can look at without feeling like I'm less than I was.*

If I was expecting some sort of sign—a clash of thunder in the rainy sky or a tremor of acceptance in my breast—I was waiting in vain. Nothing happened, not even a breeze against the window. Feeling silly, I kicked my feet against the side of the bed a few times until my eyes fell on my desk, which was littered with papers and books I had borrowed from the library. Well, I thought, if the Nameless God wasn't going to drop everything to attend to my needs, I might as well clean up.

My room, to tell the truth, wasn't really messy; it took only a short time before the desk was straightened. In the process of cleaning, however, I found a pair of gloves that had fallen behind the desk. Not one of the well-used pairs that I had purchased to help Philantha gather plants, but a set of leather riding gloves that I had taken with me when I left the palace. I picked them up, finally recalling that I had gotten them out several weeks ago for an excursion out of the city with Philantha. She had decided against it at the last minute, however, and I must have dropped the gloves onto the desk and then swept them off without realizing it. Shrugging to myself, I opened the chest that still contained the things I had brought from the palace and started to put them away. As I did, my eyes fell on a roll of fabric lying gently atop a folded dress.

The map to King Kelman's Door. I hadn't thought about it since I had returned to the city. Now I felt a pang of guilt as I carefully picked it up and spread it out on the clean desk. It wasn't mine, had never been mine. I should return it to the palace, where it could be put somewhere safe, somewhere other than an unused nook in the library where two children could find it. The pang increased, throbbing in my chest as regret joined the guilt. *It would have been something,* I thought, *if we had been able to find the door.* I let my fingers glide across the surface of the map, intending to roll it up, but just then, something happened.

I read a word, one of the untranslatable runes written across the bottom of the map.

I didn't breathe for so long that, when I realized it, I had to gasp for air and ended up coughing violently. Only once I had control of myself did I dare to glance at the runes again.

They were the wizard's language. Something I had never studied as a princess, something that even wizards hardly used anymore. And these were not even the most recent incarnation of the language that Philantha had insisted I study, but a more archaic version, with little curls on the ends of some symbols and what looked like abbreviated forms of some others. Still, I could read at least every third word, bending over the desk in my room.

Take . . . who . . . Door . . . Let . . . known . . . one . . . blood . . . Door . . .

What had Kiernan guessed that last day in the garden? That the runes might be a code, or a magic language? It looked as if, against all odds, he had been right.

I was gripping the desk with my hands so forcefully that my knuckles had gone white. There were too many words I didn't know, or words that were so different from their later forms that I couldn't recognize them. And there were several words at the very end that I had never seen in any form.

But, I realized as a grin broke across my face, I had a wizard's library downstairs, full to bursting with books on spells and magical theory and even treatises on the various incarnations of the wizard's language.

Words, I thought blearily. *It might be words. Or fish.* I squinted once again at the rune on the map, then shifted my gaze to the open book that sat propped against a stack in similarly thick volumes.

Why would anyone ever make the runes for words and fish look so similar? I wondered. *Were they trying to make a joke?*

Outside the library, the clock in the hall tolled twice and then fell silent. Leaning forward on my elbows, I massaged my temples and thought about laying my head down on the table. But no, I was close, so close to reading the runes that I could almost imagine myself standing at King Kelman's Door, watching it open up before me. I had to keep going, even if I was tired enough to go to sleep on the uncomfortable wooden chairs of the library.

I had been researching for hours, pausing only to wolf down some supper and go back in the library before my stomach had finished growling. It had been slow going, trying to decipher the archaic runes running across the bottom of the map. At times, I had considered taking it to Philantha, who I thought might be able to read them without resorting to half a dozen cracked and moldy books. But each time I despaired of finding the answers myself and picked up the map to go to her, I imagined Kiernan's face when I told him that I had shared our secret with someone else. Each time, I sighed and vowed to search just a little longer for whatever rune was currently giving me fits. And finally, in the late hours of the night, it had come down to only four untranslated runes standing between me and the answer.

Words, I decided. *It must be words. Fish just can't be right. Royal blood*—for that was the phrase before it—*and royal fish? No. Definitely not.* I wrote *words* down on my sheet of paper. Only three runes left to translate, I realized with a shiver.

But I couldn't. The clock in the hall rang three times, and then four, and those last three runes remained stubbornly

EILIS O'NEAL

untranslated. I couldn't seem to find any runes that truly resembled the ones on the map in any of Philantha's books. Every time I thought I had it, I saw that the slant of one line was wrong, or the curlicue on the top faced the wrong way.

Maybe they were older than the others. Maybe they were so old that Philantha didn't have any books that referred to them. Or maybe they weren't wizard's runes at all; maybe they were something else entirely. I shook my head to clear it. I had everything but those last three runes. Perhaps I wouldn't really need them. I could go ahead and assemble a translation from my notes and see.

Clearing a space for a blank sheet of parchment, I dipped my pen into an inkpot and slowly transcribed my notes. Then, taking a shallow breath of excitement, I read the words that had eluded Kiernan and me for so long:

Take heed, all who would attempt the Door of the King. Let it be known that only for one of royal blood and royal words will the Door appear.

The words, so stark and formal, stared at me from the parchment, my own handwriting looking somehow foreign and strange. *That's why it was never there for us,* I thought dimly. *We were looking in the right place, but I didn't really have any royal blood in me, and so it never appeared.* Disappointment warred with the thrill of discovery; I had imagined myself being able to open the door, and now, unless Nalia was standing beside me, I never would. A clever spell, Philantha would have said. It truly was a secret created just for the royal family, one that would be no good without them.

I was rubbing the place where my birthmark had been, I

realized, and I hastily pulled my hand away. I wondered vaguely what the last three runes were, for the message was clear enough without them. Maybe they were just the name of the wizard who had created the door, a signature of sorts. Wizards, even Philantha, were a vain lot, I had come to realize, and it wouldn't be odd for one to want to preserve his own name on such a document.

My hand had strayed to my arm again. This time I pinched the spot so hard that it turned white and then pink, and tears sprang up in my eyes. *Stop it. You're just disappointed that you won't be able to see it. But you were never going to see it anyway. It's no different now.* Which raised the question I had wrestled in my room that afternoon: What was I going to do with the map?

I should give it back. That was the right course, the proper thing to do. I could give it to Kiernan and he could easily sneak it back into the library. He could even pretend to find it so that it could be preserved as it should have been all those years ago. No one would know that he had given it to me. I let my fingers graze the edge of the map. Yes, it belonged in the palace, with the family for whom it had been created. Even if Kiernan had given it to me as a gift, as something to bridge the gap between my two selves. Still, there was no way I was giving it back without first bragging a little to Kiernan of how I had solved the mystery.

I pushed back my chair, decided. Reading my translation had burned away the exhaustion of the night, so that I felt oddly clearheaded and my limbs buzzed with pent-up energy. I put away the books I had pulled from the shelves, swept up my scraps of paper and notes, and rolled the map upon itself, tying it loosely with a ribbon. And then, without knowing why I did it, I left Philantha's house and headed for the palace.

EILIS O'NEAL

Morning had not yet broken the dark sky, though I felt a hint of coming warmth as I followed the streets out of Goldhorn, King Kelman's map cradled in my arms. I walked quickly, not knowing why I hurried any more than I knew why I felt so compelled to visit the palace now. I could seek out Kiernan after the sun had come up, after all, and right now it seemed likely that the palace guards would turn me away for coming so early. Still, I kept going, as if the Nameless God himself had laid his hand on me and pushed me forward.

As the palace walls reared into sight I slowed. I had no story to tell the guards, and I knew I must look a sight, with my hair half escaped from its braid and my dress wrinkled from sitting so long. I didn't stop, though, and as I neared the guards I heard myself saying, "I have a message for Kiernan Dulchessy from the wizard Philantha."

It was dark, and the guards were tired from the long night. Neither recognized me, either as the false princess or as the scribe who had occasionally sought out Kiernan. "Can't wait until a proper hour, can it?" the one on the right asked.

"If it could, do you think I would be here now?" I asked.

"S'pose not. Wizards," he grumbled to his companion. "Glad I don't work for one."

I was glad that I did, though, for he moved aside and, after giving me directions to Kiernan's chamber, turned his back to me.

Now that I was there, I felt the beginnings of embarrassment as I made my way toward the wing of the palace that housed minor nobility, taking the garden path rather than going through the palace itself. Why had I thought it was a good idea to come now?

I was going to look silly, banging on Kiernan's door to tell him . . .
what? That we wouldn't ever have been able to find the door? As
interesting as my translation might be, I suddenly wasn't sure it
was worth being woken up for before dawn. Especially when I
hadn't spoken to him in days.

I halted, taking a step back and then a step forward and
dithering with myself. No, I was already here, I told myself, I
would keep going. But, even after thinking it, I felt strange, like
something was pulling me back, slowly but inexorably. I was so
caught up in my own thoughts that it took a moment before I
realized that it wasn't my imagination, that I really did feel a
tugging deep in my chest.

It took a moment longer to realize that I had felt this sensation before.

Nalia, I thought, startled. She was somewhere nearby. Odd
that she should be out so late, or so early, depending on which
way you looked at it. Without meaning to, I turned toward the
palace. A stand of tall bushes edged the building, softening the
line of the gray stone, and I stood in their shadow. It was lucky,
because when a soft light flared up in the window nearest me,
its brightness didn't reach me. I remained in darkness, watching
curiously.

It was some noble's room, though no one occupied the bed,
despite the hour. Instead, two figures stood facing each other in
the center of the room. One was cloaked, so I couldn't make out
the face, and the other was Nalia.

She was wearing a robe, long enough that most people
probably wouldn't have noticed the hint of lace peeking out
from beneath it, and her hair fell unbound in long ripples down

EILIS O'NEAL

her back. I furrowed my brow as I realized that the lace was her nightgown. What was she doing out at this hour, wearing nothing but that?

I didn't have much time to ponder it, though, for as I watched, Nalia raised her arms, palms extended upward. She did it slowly, like someone moving through a dream, and it was that oddness that made me take two steps forward, so that my toes reached the edge of the bushes' shadow, to peer at her face. Under the creases of sleep and the dark smudges below her eyes, Nalia's face was blank, as smooth and uncomprehending as a sleepwalker's. The hand not holding the map rose toward my throat, and I pursed my lips in confusion as the other person in the room put out his or her hands and placed them atop Nalia's. It made me look toward the figure, and when I did so, I had to rub my eyes and try again.

I had thought the other person was cloaked. But when I tried to look more closely, my eyes slid away without grasping even the color of the person's hair or the shape of the body. A sight shield, I realized with puzzlement. Philantha had shielded herself only a few days before so that I might see how the spell rendered an object blurry, undistinguishable, preventing an onlooker from recalling what it looked like.

What? I thought, or began to think, because at that moment, something happened that made my heart contract painfully and my ears buzz like a nest of hornets.

A golden haze, faint at first, then bright, sprang up around Nalia, enveloping her. In my mouth, I tasted the iron flavor of blood.

A golden haze. The Hall of Thorvaldor. The king and queen

watching. My birthmark vanishing and something I hadn't known was there inside me disappearing as well.

The golden haze was falling away. Even with only one lamp lit, I could see Nalia's arms quite clearly, outstretched as they were. The birthmark on her arm was glowing, the three red dots hot and bright looking. Then, as I watched, they faded back to their normal appearance, and I could barely make them out.

The shielded figure was saying something; I could almost hear the words through the glass windows, but not quite. "Let me hear," I whispered, sending out a tendril of a spell toward the window. It was hardly anything, the weakest of attempts, because I was frightened that the shielded person would feel the spell and detect my presence. It wouldn't work, I knew it wouldn't. I had made the spell work only twice before, and I was hardly feeding it any power now. And yet faintly, so faintly I could barely hear it over the rushing in my ears, I heard, "Go back to your room. If you encounter anyone on your way, tell them that you felt ill and went in search of one of the palace physicians. Remember none of this."

The person's voice was spelled, too, so that it sounded neither male nor female, young nor old. Beside the figure, Nalia dropped her hands and walked toward the door. Now that I knew to look for it, I could see the languor of control in her movements, the force of the spell guiding her. She opened the door and left, shutting it quietly behind her. Inside the room, the other person swayed suddenly from the exertion of the spell, grasping the back of a nearby chair. The person stayed there, gripping the chair, for long moments, and I waited, my heart in my throat, hoping the sight shield would drop.

EILIS O'NEAL

It didn't. The person seemed to regain a measure of strength, for he or she straightened and, after glancing around, headed for the door.

Outside, I shuddered, convulsing over and over as the gray light of morning filtered into the palace gardens.

Nalia, or at least this Nalia, the girl once called Orianne, was not the princess. She was as false as I had been.

CHAPTER TEN

I stood, pressed against the scratchy bushes, and tried to think.

Had that really been what I thought it was? Was there no other explanation for what I had seen? Another spell, maybe, one that needed to be done at a certain time, to explain the strange hour. Or perhaps some remnant of the spell that had been performed on us as infants, some unforeseen mistake that needed fixing. Except that I knew the spell had to be renewed every so often, because the king had told me that was what had been done to me. Except that the shielded person had told her to remember none of this, had erased any memory of what had happened. Except that she had been under a spell of control, one that made her unable to resist.

I wrapped my free arm around myself and shook my head. No. I knew it in my bones, knew it in the same way I knew the blood running through my veins. I had lived under that spell my whole life, had seen it pulled off me in the Hall of Thorvaldor. And I knew, I *knew* that it was the same spell, only being renewed this time, instead of removed.

And she had no idea. I would have known it even if I hadn't seen the glazed look on her face, hadn't heard the command to forget this night's work. I had sat and talked with her just that afternoon, though it seemed a lifetime ago. She had no idea. She truly thought she was Nalia, just as I had thought I was.

There was a snap in the bushes, and I whirled around, getting a face full of twigs and leaves, only to see a bird poke its head out of the foliage. It cocked its head at me, as if surprised to see a human standing there so early in the morning, and then flew off. I took a breath, trying to calm my racing heart.

Someone had lied to the king and queen, had brought them a second false princess, using the very spell that had fooled everyone about me for all those years. A sound, something between a laugh and a sob, croaked out of me. Philantha had been right; it was a clever spell indeed. So clever that someone was using it against the king and queen, knowing that they would never think to check closely to make sure the girl brought to them was the real princess. Who else would she be, after all, when so few people had known?

Only five people, I realized as bile rose in my throat, five people in all Thorvaldor. The king and queen had confided in three wizards: Flavian, who was dead, Melaina, and Neomar.

They might have told someone, I supposed dully. It might be someone other than them. But if Nalia—no, Orianne—was not the true princess, it spoke of a plot conceived long ago, when the infant princess was first switched for not one, but two other babies. If they were not guilty, they would not have told someone else, not then. Not early enough for that imaginary someone else to do anything about it. No, it must be one of them—Neomar or Melaina.

Melaina, with all her beauty and magic, ready to step into a place of power at the college as soon as Neomar retired. A baroness, one of the king and queen's closest advisors. I felt sick thinking of it.

And Neomar, I realized, the sick feeling strengthening, another close advisor. A man who had refused to tell Philantha about the details of the spell, even after the princess had supposedly been restored, when it would do no harm for other wizards to learn the mechanics of what they had done.

I was shaking, and had been for a long time, if the fatigue that gripped my muscles was any clue. It was light now, the thin yellow light of true morning. What should I do? A vision of myself storming the palace in search of the king and queen, shouting news of my discovery to the rafters, filled my head and was squashed just as quickly. I could see the people of court whispering, murmuring to one another that I was making up stories out of vengeance or that my fall from grace had left me a little mad. I could see the king and queen shaking their heads, then ordering me sent from the city—or worse, locking me up for maligning the name of their lost daughter. I didn't *know* that they would do such a thing, but the thought was enough to make me skittish. I imagined telling Philantha, but she was too odd, too ostracized for her strange ways to be believed with such a wild tale. I cast about for someone else, but my world was small now, too small for something like this.

Kiernan, I thought finally. He might not be a wizard or a member of the royal family, but he was my friend. And he was someone who, I hoped, would believe me. For now, that would have to be enough.

Feeling as weak as a newborn foal, I stepped from my hiding

EILIS O'NEAL

place among the bushes, back onto one of the many paths that wound through the palace gardens. But the gardens, usually so beautiful to my eyes, seemed full of dark places where anyone or anything could lurk unseen. I felt exposed as I started off toward the Dulchessy family's chambers. Whoever the shielded figure had been was playing a dangerous game, and I had no reason to believe that person wouldn't hurt anyone who found out about it. My neck prickled as I passed several gardeners about their business, and I hunched down, trying to avoid being noticed. I wished I had the power—and control—to place a sight shield on myself, but I didn't.

Finally, after what felt like hours, I ducked inside the proper wing and turned the two corners to Kiernan's rooms. He had his own quarters now, not within his family's but connected to them. I glanced around and, seeing no one, rapped hard on the door four times. I also sent a small thanks to the Nameless God for Kiernan's reluctance to allow his family's serving people to stay with him at night—pranks were much too hard to pull with servants hovering around. At least I didn't have to worry about talking my way past anyone to reach him.

It took a while for him to answer, so long that I was anxiously shifting from one foot to the other by the time he opened the door.

"Sinda?" he asked groggily, blinking at me.

"Let me in," I gasped, then pushed past him without waiting for him to move aside. "Close the door!" I insisted after turning around and seeing him still standing there, the door half open.

Annoyance flashed across his face, but he shut the door. He was still wearing a long night shirt, and his bare toes curled against the cold stone floor. "I thought we weren't speaking," he said. "Have you come to apologize for acting like such a"—he shrugged, obviously looking for a word—"a princess?"

My jaw dropped, just a little. In my fervor, I had completely forgotten that Kiernan might not be happy to see me. "I—yes, no—I," I stuttered, my tongue feeling thick and useless. "What I mean is—"

"What's that?" Kiernan interrupted, pointing at the map still in my hands.

I had forgotten that, too. "King Kelman's map. I translated it, the part we couldn't read before, but that's not—"

"You translated it?" The annoyance lessened slightly as a familiar, mischievous light brightened Kiernan's eyes.

"Yes, I did, but—"

"I can't believe it! What does it say?"

"Kiernan, please, listen—"

"Does this mean we'll be able to find it?"

"Maybe, but—"

"We could go now! I'll get dressed—"

"She's not the princess!" I shouted.

He had been reaching for a pair of breeches hung over the back of the chair, but he stopped in midreach, confusion tightening his face. "What?"

I was breathing hard, raggedly, and darkness pricked the edges of my vision. Dropping the map on Kiernan's bed, I grasped my elbows to try to stop the trembling of my arms. "I saw her, just now, with someone. The person did a spell, the same spell that they did on me, only in reverse. To keep it there instead of to take it off. She's not the real princess, Kiernan. She's not Nalia."

Kiernan's arm dropped heavily to his side. "Start over," he said, his own voice abruptly raspy. "Start at the beginning."

So I did. I told him about meeting Nalia and the feeling that had drawn me to her, about realizing that I could translate the runes on King Kelman's map and what they said, about the way that only someone really royal could have ever opened the door, about coming to the palace and seeing the shielded person place a spell on Nalia. He didn't speak, not in the whole time that I told the story. When I finished, he stood silently, then went over to a small table by his bedside, where a pitcher of water and a cup sat. Pouring the water into the cup, he handed it to me, and I gulped it down gratefully. It was only when I had drained the glass that he spoke.

"Sinda," he said. It was too gentle, his voice, not at all like his normal one, and I flinched as if he had struck me.

"You don't believe me," I mumbled.

"I—" He ran a hand through his sleep-tangled hair and let out a whooshing breath. "I don't *want* to believe you. I'm good with . . . games, pranks, little things that don't matter. And if you're right, this is definitely not little. I don't want to believe in some sixteen-year-old conspiracy to place the wrong girl on the throne. I want to think that this is just some delusion you've made up, because you're unhappy."

"But I'm not, or I'm trying not to be." Crumpling a handful of bedclothes, for I had had to sit down halfway through my story, I stared at my lap. "I know that I'm not the princess, that I never was. I'm not doing this out of . . . revenge or something. I'm not making this up, Kiernan."

"But the spell—that spell that drew you toward her—Philantha said it was because part of your . . . essences being exchanged. Doesn't that mean she has to be the princess?"

He sounded hopeful, as if I were a history master who had

posed a particularly difficult question to which he had finally figured out the answer. "I don't know. Maybe it just means that they had to put part of the real princess in both of us, and that's what I'm feeling instead."

He frowned again, briefly stymied, before saying, another blush of hope in his voice, "No, wait! Here's a plan. We could ask her to come with us, to that place in the wall where Kelman's door is. If she is the princess, it'll open for her, and if she isn't—"

"Then she'll know she isn't," I cut in. "And then she'll probably run straight to the king and queen and tell them."

"Well, what's wrong with that?" Kiernan shook his head at me. "If she isn't the princess, they'll have to know, won't they?"

I jerked to my feet, my hands balled into fists, and starting pacing. "Don't you see?" I demanded. "Whoever did this, whoever I saw under that sight shield, is powerful, so powerful that they're about to pull off a coup under the noses of the king and queen with absolutely no one the wiser. And this isn't some sort of . . . game. They've been planning this for years, probably since before we were switched. And that makes them dangerous. If they see their plans being uprooted, they'll do something to stop it. They might kill the king or queen. They'll certainly try to hurt whoever exposed them, whoever found out about what they did."

Kiernan blanched. "You. They'll hurt you."

"Us," I corrected him. "You know, too, now. They'll hurt us, or your family, or who knows how many other people. The stakes are too high, and they'll be too afraid of losing."

I turned on my heel, at the end of my line of pacing, then

stopped. Squaring my shoulders, I stared at Kiernan. I wanted him with me, so badly that it was like a fire in my chest. I didn't want to walk into this tangle of intrigue and power alone; I would, if I had to, but I didn't want to. I wanted him, my friend, who had always managed to get us out of scrapes before, laughing all the while.

"I'm not making this up, Kiernan. I wish—Nameless God—I wish I were. But I'm not. And I'm scared. Please, you have to believe me."

Kiernan bowed his head and closed his eyes, like someone shuttering a house against a coming storm. "I believe you," he said softly. Then, raising his head and meeting my gaze, he said it again, more forcefully. "I do."

I hadn't realized how much tension I had been storing between my shoulders, but it fell away in a deluge, leaving me feeling weak and loose-limbed. For a moment, I couldn't speak, but then I cleared my throat and said, "Well, good. Now we just have to figure out what we're going to do about it."

"Tell me again where the room was," Kiernan said, glancing up at me from the floor of my room in Philantha's house. We had left the palace as quickly as possible. I couldn't help but imagine spells planted throughout its rooms, all designed to let whoever I had seen know of anyone talking as we had been. It was probably silly, but I couldn't help it. Luckily, Philantha had left me a note saying that she was going to visit a friend in Flower Basket and wouldn't be back until the evening, so no one would care if I spent the day with Kiernan.

"I was on my way to your room and I was walking by those

tall bushes. You know, the ones you hid Laureli Montage's doll under when you were eight." Kiernan nodded, a smile twitching his lips at the memory.

"It was the . . . third window from the corner," I said, squinting my eyes as I tried to remember.

Kiernan ruffled a hand through his hair. "I think that's Berend Yari's room."

"The scholar?"

He nodded. "But he isn't here now. He left weeks ago. Some trip to research the properties of Farvaseean lichen." He snorted. "I overheard one of the librarians saying that she had received a letter from him just a few days ago, and he expected to be there until autumn. And besides, the man is . . . colorless. You can barely see him even when you're talking to him. I don't think he has the stomach for rebellion."

I scowled. I had known it wouldn't be that easy. No matter who had worked the spell on Orianne, it hadn't been done in that person's own room. "Do you think he would have let someone else use his room, if they threatened him, maybe?"

"I think he would wet himself and then faint if someone even mentioned a coup in front of him," Kiernan said flatly. "More likely the person just used the room, so no one would see Nalia—Orianne—coming to their own. Which leaves us with—"

"Melaina and Neomar," I finished. "I know."

"Wizards. Really powerful wizards. The head of the college and his very likely replacement." Kiernan groaned, then laid his head against the side of my bed. "Well, you know both of them better than I do. Which one do you think it is?"

It was a question I had been pondering myself. Unfortunately, though, Kiernan's words were a bit optimistic. I didn't really know either of them. Melaina was a baroness—her husband, the Baron of Saremarch, had died years before—so she attended court functions and sat in on council meetings. She had never been anything but polite to me, though I had mostly seen her at a distance. And yet she had always made me feel . . . strange when she looked at me, as if she could see into my thoughts. She was beautiful, as cool as dark water, so lovely that she made me feel even more awkward and shy whenever I saw her. I had never sought her out and, aside from those probing looks, she had never shown much interest in me. And Neomar, though he advised the king and queen in matters of magic, had spent most of his time at the college. He had always been much too busy to do more than nod at me in greeting, rarely even taking the time to meet my eyes. Neither had seemed, until now, a likely candidate to stage a coup.

But, I thought with a shiver, *Neomar refused to tell Philantha about the spell.* Why? Because he feared that, if she truly understood it, she would see through his plans? Maybe. And he had wanted her to tell him how I was progressing with my magic, wanted to keep an eye on me. Did that have something do to with this? Still, nothing explained why he wanted to place Orianne on the throne instead of the real Nalia.

I sighed and rubbed my temples. I was tired from my night of translation, and my thoughts felt like they were coming through thick sludge. "I don't know," I said. "But we have to do something. I can't get to Melaina—she doesn't keep regular rooms at the college. But you could . . . watch her, follow her maybe. And maybe we should go to the college, follow Neomar or break into his rooms or something."

"Breaking and entering," Kiernan said wryly. He had been watching me rub my head with a worried expression on his face.

"I'm not sure those are the kind of wild oats my parents want me to get rid of, but they'll do in a pinch."

I laughed, which I think was what he wanted, but as the laughter subsided, he said, "But you're sure we can't go to the king and queen? They'll be able to . . . do it properly. Haul people in and question them, search Neomar's and Melaina's rooms openly."

"We can't. They'll think that I'm mad, or bent on revenge, and that I've—I don't know—used my wiles on you to make you believe me."

Kiernan raised an eyebrow. "Your wiles?"

I flushed, but pushed on. "The point is, they won't believe us. It sounds crazy. And we might end up tipping off the traitor, letting them know that we know."

Kiernan looked stubborn. "What about Philantha? She really likes you—I can tell. Maybe she could help us."

I had thought Philantha too outcast from the wizard community to be much help, but Kiernan made me mull it over again. Maybe he was right. It would be a relief to have someone else on our side, and even Philantha would be better believed than me. I had started to nod when he continued, "After all, she's a wizard. She knows both of them, knows things about—"

But I didn't hear anything else. I felt cold and hot at once, as I remembered Philantha in her study, Neomar's head bent close to hers as they looked at an ancient scroll. What had she said? *We did start at the college in the same year, and even his prestige hasn't stopped us being friends.*

Could Philantha be part of it?

No. I shoved the thought away from me as soon as it surfaced. Silly, absentminded Philantha, who didn't even want the prestige that wearing her wizards robes would bring, try to take over a kingdom? It was like trying to believe that a butterfly had designs on the throne. No, I was overtired and muddleheaded to have even thought it.

But she was Neomar's friend, however improbable that friendship might seem. When she went to the college, I knew, she almost always saw him, if only to say hello. She was much more likely to believe him than me, especially when I had no evidence other than what I had seen. Would she tell him? Warn him that I might make accusations against him, because they had been friends?

Could I tell her only part of it? Make it seem that I thought it could only be Melaina, and have help at least with that investigation? No, I decided. Because it took only a small leap to go from Melaina to Neomar, and Philantha would surely make it. Which led me back to where I had been to start: with her possibly giving our hunt away.

Kiernan had seen that I had gone into my own head and sat waiting for me to come back, I realized. So I explained my thoughts to him. He didn't like it, but finally he nodded reluctantly.

"So we can't tell anyone until we're sure we know who it is, until we have proof," I finished. "Whoever did this is clever. If we don't have proof, real proof, they'll probably find a way to slip out of it. And speaking of proof, we should start by going to the college—"

"No." Kiernan was standing in a flash, his hands on my shoulders, keeping me from getting up out of my chair. "You're exhausted. You can barely keep your eyes open."

"I'm fine," I insisted, even as a rush of exhaustion rolled over me like an ocean wave.

"You're not. Look, it's not going to be as simple as getting into Neomar's public study. He's not going to keep evidence of regicide lying around where anyone can find it. You need to rest, and then we'll go."

But something Kiernan said stopped me from really hearing the last part of the sentence. "Regicide?" I asked.

Kiernan nodded. "You know. Killing of a monarch? I know she wasn't a monarch yet, but she would have been, so . . ."

Slowly, through my fogged brain, it made sense. "You think the real Nalia is dead."

He let his hands drop from my shoulders. "Isn't she? If they switched Orianne for you, instead of the real Nalia, it stands to reason that they killed the princess then. So no one would notice a third infant in the switch. And if they're going to put Orianne on the throne, they won't want the real princess still alive somewhere."

I shook my head. "She's not dead, Kiernan. They need her, to keep the spell going. Without the real princess alive somewhere, the spell won't work. Philantha told me she was almost sure about that. Whoever did this, they'll know where she is. They'll have kept her alive because without her their plan won't work."

I rose from the chair and took two steps to collapse on my bed. It was all catching up with me now, the whole long day; I wouldn't be able to stay awake much longer. I managed to lift my heavy eyes to Kiernan, who stood watching me.

"This isn't just a matter of finding out who planned this and exposing them," I managed to say as fatigue washed over me. "Nalia is alive. The real princess is out there, Kiernan, and we're going to have to find her."

CHAPTER ELEVEN

I slept the rest of the day and woke the next morning only when one of the maids knocked on my door and told me that Philantha was waiting for me downstairs.

"A lecture, she says, on, oh, something magical," Briath said as she headed back for the door. "Can't remember the words she used. But she says you're to go with her, and now."

I scrambled out of bed, trying to smooth my wrinkled clothes as I went. As I reached for the comb on my desk—my hair looked like several birds had been at it with their beaks—I saw a small square of paper, folded over on itself and sealed with a blob of wax from the candle by my bed. Cracking it open, I recognized Kiernan's hand.

Don't you dare get up until you're rested! When you are, send one of those message lights and I'll come. In the meantime, I'll talk to O., see if she remembers anything about last night. And I'll find out if anyone saw M. or N. wandering the palace last night. Don't frown like that! I'll be sly.

I was frowning, I realized, which made me let out an irritated huff of breath. He knew me too well. Still, even his promise didn't make my fears go away. Kiernan might think he was subtle enough to question Orianne, but I worried that his natural exuberance might give him away. And if the traitor thought that Kiernan knew about the second false princess . . . I shuddered, laying the note back down. "Be careful," I whispered, then lifted my comb to my hair.

Finally decent, I hurried down the stairs to find Philantha wearing her black wizard's robes over a dress that I knew had a rather large ink stain on the front. "There's a lecture—Hemmel's giving it, the old bore—on transference of energies from, well, you'll see. It's doubtful Hemmel will have anything really useful to say—I remember when he was a student and he was always so . . . rule bound, and that's very limiting, always remember that—but you never know. It might be useful to you, though, so I thought we'd go." With that, she flung the door open and marched out into the street, me at her heels.

It was a fine, clear day, without a cloud to be seen, and I found my head clearing as well while we walked. It seemed I had recovered from my sleepless night, and the edge of shock at what I had seen was being ground down a bit by time and distance. It was still sharp, but I was gradually getting used to the idea that Orianne was not the true princess. Now if I only knew what to do about it. Well, I would start by trying to get away from the lecture and at least look at Neomar's rooms. That way, when Kiernan and I came back, we would know what sort of fortifications we were up against.

We made good time to the college, stopping only so that Philantha could examine a bird's nest blown from a garden tree into the street. She pronounced it too mangled to be of use, though, and left it there. Once at the college, we hurried to one of the great lecture halls. I had been in several for various ceremonies throughout my years as the princess, and this one was no different. A bowl-shaped room with stair-stepped stone benches, all leading down to a small stage where the wizard would speak. Wizards sat scattered around the room, mostly green-robed Novices, but I noticed a smattering of blue and purple robes as well. We chose spots in the middle of the room, near a balding man I recognized as one of the few wizards who deigned to visit Philantha.

"Neomar's not here?" she asked the man as we settled ourselves. Unprepared to hear his name, I nearly fell off the bench with my jerk of surprise. "I thought he was in agreement with Hemmel, more's the pity. One of his only failings, poor man. Still, thought he'd come to support him."

"Haven't you heard?" the man replied, and I recalled that his name was Sarcen Belveer. "Neomar's gone. He left town this morning, gone to the country for the air. He claims he'll stay there until at least autumn." Sarcen shook his head. "I told him, just the other day, that he looked peaked. And now I hear this rumor about redvein fever. . . ."

I stopped listening, my mind whirring. Neomar gone, and only this morning?

Philantha was shaking her head, a shocked look on her face. "I can hardly believe it," she said. "He didn't say anything to me, stubborn man, and I saw him just a few days ago. I have several concoctions that I've been working on, and they might have been helpful."

Sarcen nodded, but just then a man sat down on the other side of him and he turned to greet the newcomer. With his attention diverted, I asked, trying to keep the perturbed note out of my voice, "But what about his experiments?"

Philantha looked confused, so I barreled on, "I mean, doesn't Neomar have experiments, like you do, in his rooms? Will someone else be watching them now, or did he have to abandon them?"

Philantha snorted. "Experiments? Neomar? He hasn't done a practical experiment on his own in years. Administrative duties keep him from it, I expect, and he was always more of a thinker anyway. His breakthroughs have always been . . . less tangible, more theory. He hasn't left any pots boiling or feathers charring."

"That's good, really," I managed. "I mean, someone might get into his room, while he's gone, and mess them up. By accident, I mean."

She waved a quick hand in the air. "Oh, his rooms will be guarded with powerful spells. Any wizard worth his salt wouldn't leave his rooms open in a college full of nosy young things. No one will get into Neomar's rooms. Even if he was sicker than a wet cat, he'd have set up spells a Master would have trouble breaking. Still, I wish he had told me. Maybe I should make a trip to see him, take some of my new potions, if we can get the . . . mishaps in them worked out. . . ."

Hemmel, the wizard giving the lecture, was mounting the stage below us. As the crowd quieted, I felt my heart sink. We would never get into Neomar's rooms now. If he were here, coming and going, we might have had a chance. He might have forgotten to place his usual protection spells one afternoon, or simply left the door unlocked in haste one day. But now the rooms were sealed and would be until he returned in autumn.

I let my chin drop into my hand, elbow propped on my knee. We would have to look for clues to the identity of the sight-shielded person elsewhere.

"He's gone, you're sure? And there's no way to get into the rooms?"

Running a finger through the sweat left on the table by my glass, I nodded. "I walked off after the lecture, told Philantha I needed to get some air while she talked to her friend. I ran all the way across the college to his rooms. Told his secretary I was supposed to deliver a message to Neomar, but he turned me away. The same story, just like Sarcen had said." I rounded my back, pulling my shoulders apart to ease the tension in them. It had been two days since the lecture, and I hadn't slept well. I kept having dreams in which a faceless girl called out to me, and though I went stumbling across fields and streets and mountains to reach her, I never did.

Kiernan let his mug thud down onto the table in disgust. "Are you sure he was telling the truth? He might have been lying to you."

"I doubt that the whole college is in on it. If it is Neomar, he wouldn't have told anyone else."

"Well, it is suspicious, don't you think?" Kiernan asked. "His leaving right after what you saw. Maybe he used up too much of his magic renewing the spell and wants to hide it from everyone. Or maybe he's scared someone saw him and wants to lie low for a while."

"It could be." I had no idea how much energy it would take to renew that spell, especially for one person alone. Kiernan was right; it looked suspicious.

Kiernan tipped the front feet of his chair off the ground as he leaned back, head tilted up to the ceiling. "Autumn. Anything could happen by then." The chair legs slammed back down as he leaned forward. "And I didn't find anything out from Orianne. She didn't even remember any strange dreams from last night."

"Had anyone else seen anything?"

"Not a mouse. You're right. Whether it was Neomar or Melaina, they were being too careful." He laced his fingers together and cracked them. "Well, if we can't search Neomar's rooms, what about Melaina's?"

I bit my lip, thinking, but ended up shaking my head. "At least at the college, I could have brought something from Philantha's, claimed to have been leaving it for him if I'd been caught. You know, just played the fool, as if I didn't know I wasn't supposed to go into his rooms. He might have accepted that, particularly if I waited until Philantha really wanted to send him something. But what could we say if we were caught in Melaina's rooms? You've never said three words to her outside of court functions. And besides, Melaina has all of House Sare to leave evidence of any plotting in. She wouldn't bring it to the palace, where servants she doesn't really know clean her rooms every day."

Kiernan grimaced. "So what do we do now?"

I let myself slump. The inn around us was loud and bright, the yellow light from the lanterns flickering on the walls, the people tired and happy, their day finished. It made me want to climb under the table. I had no idea what to tell Kiernan. It was too much; I should go to Philantha, or the king and queen, or any adult who might listen. Except that I didn't think the king and queen would really listen, and Philantha was already thinking about trying to visit Neomar in the country. I wanted to trust her unconditionally, but a tiny voice inside kept prodding me with doubts whenever I truly considered going to her. Which left us alone. And I didn't know how to save a country. Substitute princess, failed dyer, scribe—none of those roles had prepared me for this. I was out of ideas, and after only three days.

I closed my eyes, shuttering myself against the despair that grappled me. If only the oracle at Isidros had never made that prophecy. It hadn't come to pass, had it? No one had tried to assassinate me before my sixteenth birthday, so there hadn't been any need for a false princess in the first place. And if they hadn't felt the need to switch me with the princess, whoever it was wouldn't have had the chance to make a second switch. The throne wouldn't be in danger, and I wouldn't be trying to protect it. Why, why that vision? Shouldn't the oracle have seen that it wouldn't come true?

Something rippled down my spine, fanning out at the base like tingling waves. Isidros. That was where all this had started.

"Sinda?" Kiernan had seen that I wasn't paying attention to him, and I felt him reach out to touch my arm.

My eyes flicked open, meeting his gaze. "Isidros," I said. "We're going to Isidros."

CHAPTER TWELVE

It took six days to reach our destination. I would have thought that would be enough time for my nerves to settle, but as we sat there, staring up the road to the temple at Isidros, I had to grip my horse's mane to stay upright. My heart pounded in my ears, and my vision felt swimmy.

"What if they won't help us?" I asked faintly.

"Don't think that way," Kiernan answered. "After all, who could resist such fine and feckless-looking nobles? They're monks and sisters, and one oracle. They won't have seen anything like us in the God knows how long. They'll be dazzled."

"Or irritated that we're disturbing their contemplations," I muttered.

Kiernan pulled on the reins of his horse, which was trying to graze on some thistle growing on the roadside, then flashed me a look. "You're forgetting yourself, *Lady Valri*. As my sister you are a charming, slightly twitter-headed girl with scholarly aspirations and a bizarre interest in the prophecies of the latest oracles. If you weren't, I probably would have stayed in court rather than accompany you on such a journey."

I sighed. "Of course, *brother*."

Kiernan pursed his lips at the slight edge in my voice, but only kneed his horse forward and said, "Come on, then. There's no use waiting."

He was right, of course. So I tapped my horse's sides, following Kiernan and the road toward the temple gates.

The journey to Isidros might have been shorter if we had had better mounts. But I had balked at the idea of taking any of Kiernan's family's horses—too much evidence to point back to his involvement—and so he had rented our mounts from a livery stable in Flower Basket, one unlikely to recognize the face of a young noble. Not nags by any means, but also not quite used to extended journeys, the horses tended to flag toward midafternoon.

I didn't mind, really. The road had cut away south from Vivaskari, meandering briefly through the farmland and then forest that surrounded the city. Most of the forest spread north of the city, however, so the road had soon entered more open country again, covered in farms that gave way to gently rolling hills by the third day. The hill country of Thorvaldor was home to shepherds, goats, and sheep, drawn by the grass and room for herds to wander. I had never been there; when the royal family left the city, we had gone north, to the cool lakes and deep forests. This was different, more sparse and rugged, but not without its own beauty. The openness, the scarcity of people suited me just fine in my present mood, I discovered. I was a jangle of nerves, but the thought that we could see anyone coming for miles comforted me.

I had another comfort: Kiernan. He had taken control of the practical side of our journey, choosing where and when we would stop, making sure we had enough water and food to reach the next town, checking our horses' hooves for stones at every rest. He begged a salve from the innkeeper on the first night after I slid off my horse and could barely walk into the inn because of the sores forming on my legs, now so unused to long days of riding. Not that he had let such responsibilities diminish his natural enthusiasm. He sang as we rode, flirted with innkeepers' daughters to get us cheaper rooms, and generally made a spectacle of himself. He told me, when I felt guilty, that lying to Philantha had been necessary for the good of the country. (I had told her that Aunt Varil had come down with a sudden, potentially dangerous illness, and that I felt it was my duty to go to her, as her only living relative. Since Philantha had been in the middle of an experiment when I told her, she had only waved her hand and told me to be back when Aunt Varil was well or dead.) Kiernan also came up with the story that we would tell at Isidros. A pair of siblings, we were the slightly impoverished Lord Aldarich and Lady Valri. I would claim to be writing a book about the history of the oracles of Isidros, and he would claim to have accompanied me to keep me safe on the road.

Now, as we approached the walls of Isidros, I wondered if anyone would believe our story. I felt grimy, even though I had taken a bath at the inn the night before, and I knew the wind off the plains had blown my hair into a tangled puffball around my face. I didn't feel much like a lady scholar, but I set my shoulders and pushed on.

The road led directly past the temple before winding away over the hills. A wall surrounded Isidros, broken at the front by two large, plain doors. Both stood open to reveal a courtyard made of flagstone, and we directed our horses inside. Isidros, I quickly grasped, was not one structure but a community made up of many buildings, like a tiny village. At the far end of the courtyard stood what I took to be the temple itself. Long, shallow steps led up to a columned pavilion, which in turn connected to a domed building, similar to the temples in the city. To our right lay several shorter buildings with many windows, probably the rooms of the sisters and monks who lived here, and another building almost as grand as the temple. On the left and back were the practical buildings of any community—the kitchen, surrounded by vegetable gardens, the washroom, the stable, and such. They would not stand on ceremony here, I knew, and all the inhabitants, except the oracle, would be expected to cook and wash and sew. Beyond this lay a few more gardens, and then—I could see because the ground sloped down toward the south—a graveyard, surrounded by its own small iron fence. A mausoleum built with graceful, simple lines stood in the back of the cemetery, nearest the wall.

As I was taking all of this in, a young man dressed in a long brown robe approached, a solemn look on his face. "Be welcome in the presence of the Nameless God," he said, placing his hands together and bowing. When he straightened, however, an easy smile graced his lips. "I am Brother Paxson. How may we help you?"

Swinging down out of the saddle, Kiernan handed his reins off to a Novice dressed in pale robes instead of the brown ones. Kiernan reached out a hand to help me dismount, then turned to Brother Paxson, saying, "I am Lord Aldarich, and this is my sister, Lady Valri." He paused, flicking a glance at me; we had agreed that I should explain our "quest."

I smiled, hoping that Brother Paxson couldn't see the way my hands were shaking. "I'm writing a book," I began. I hoped my voice sounded light and unconcerned. "A scholarly treatise on the history of the oracles of Isidros. I was hoping to speak with the oracle, and perhaps look at the records left by her most recent predecessors. The library in the palace has very good records up until the twenty-fifth oracle, but not very much on the last five. I think the librarians have been reluctant to leave the comforts of the city to obtain the records." I tried to wink conspiratorially, even though I probably just looked like I had something in my eye.

The monk inclined his head. "Of course. I do not know if the oracle will be able to meet with you in person—there are many pilgrims who come seeking her guidance, you see, and she does not have time to meet with them all. But I will see, and you can surely meet with Brother Seldin, our abbot. He will be very helpful for your research."

With that, Brother Paxson led us to a building broken into several small rooms, each with a narrow cot, and one currently empty communal room. I gathered that pilgrims and visitors stayed here as they awaited an audience with the oracle. He left us there, and after a while a sister came bearing a jug of water, two apples, and a half loaf of brown bread. She placed the food on a small table and then left.

"Do you think they'll let us see her?" I asked after checking to make sure no pilgrims sat in the tiny bedrooms.

Kiernan shrugged through his bite of apple. "If they do, what are you going to do? Just ask her about the prophecy?"

I twisted my hands in my lap. Truly I had not quite figured

out my plan, even with the long hours on horseback with nothing else to do besides stare at the roadside. "I don't know," I admitted. "Maybe. It depends."

"On what?"

"I don't know. I'm just going on a . . . feeling. It all started here. There has to be something, some sign. But I don't even know if she's the same oracle who made the prophecy about Nalia."

I didn't get any further, because just then Brother Paxson opened the door and beckoned us forward. "You're lucky to have come on such a quiet day," he said. "Brother Seldin can see you now."

Brother Paxson led us toward the large building I hadn't recognized, murmuring greetings to the robed men and women whom we passed. They all had a serene quality about their faces, so at odds with the tautness I felt in my own.

Kiernan was talking to Brother Paxson, though I hadn't been paying attention to the conversation. When Kiernan jostled me surreptitiously with his elbow, however, I heard him say, "Now, you'll have to remind me. I know my sister's told me before— probably five times—but I just can't recall how long the current oracle has served."

"Fifteen years," Brother Paxson said amiably.

"Of course, of course," Kiernan answered as I dropped back a step. Fifteen years. So she would not have been the one to make the prophecy. Which meant that any information I found would have to come from somewhere else. But where?

"Relax," Kiernan whispered as we entered the building and Brother Paxson stepped ahead to lead the way. When I glanced at him, I saw a smile quirking the corners of his mouth. "How can you be nervous? Don't you see? We're in a library."

To my chagrin, the knot in my stomach eased the tiniest bit as I breathed in the scent of paper and dust. It was so familiar, the smell of so many books together, and it comforted me. As Brother Paxson led us past several large rooms with books on shelves going up to the ceiling, I couldn't help slowing just a little to glance inside. Most of the rooms also contained tables, at which sat brothers and sisters with books and scrolls in front of them. All of the doors stood open, save the one at the end of the long hall we had walked. It had a symbol painted on it: an open eye, the sign of the oracle. Another man stood there, waiting for us, and Brother Paxson nodded genially to him before leaving us.

The abbot, Brother Seldin, was an older man, his graying hair curling about his ears and deep lines etching his face. Even so, he stood straight, and I could see that the muscles in his forearms had not gone soft with age. "Be welcome," he said, smiling at us. "So, Brother Paxson says that you are writing a book about the oracles, and that you wish to see the records of their lives." I nodded, and he seemed pleased. "It is a good thing, I think, for someone so young to have an interest in the oracles. Though you are welcome to search the other collections, I expect that what would be most helpful to you lies in here."

One hand had disappeared inside his robes, and from them he produced a ring of keys, thick and jangly. Sliding a long key into the lock of the door, he twisted it, then led us inside.

This room had none of the airy openness of the other rooms of the library. It was small and somewhat dark, with lamps set at intervals that Brother Seldin hurried to light. Only one wall held any books, I noticed, and they were all small volumes, each with the same red spine. Set into the middle of that wall was a cabinet of black wood with a silver lock.

"Here you will find the journals of the oracles," Brother Seldin told me. "All the oracles kept journals of the visions sent by the Nameless God, as well as some details of their own lives. You may read them, though we ask that you use the greatest caution and not take them from this room. Some are very fragile."

"There are no names on them," I said, as I gently took one of the last on the shelves and opened it to its first page. This was exactly what I needed. Surely the prophecy would be mentioned, or more than mentioned; maybe the oracle would have written about it in detail.

Brother Seldin shook his head. "The oracles give up their names. It brings them closer to the God, who also has no name."

I had known that once, when I studied such things as the princess, and as a "scholar" I should certainly have known it. I found myself flushing. It didn't help my disguise to make such silly mistakes. "Of course," I said hurriedly. "I just thought that they might be listed here, in their journals." Sliding the book back into place, I glanced to the end of the shelf, which stood empty. "Shouldn't there be a few more?" I heard myself asking.

"There are, but, unfortunately, I cannot offer them to you for your research." Brother Seldin gestured to the black cabinet. "The journals for the last three oracles are in here. We keep them separate, as no one but the oracle herself is allowed to read them."

Kiernan made a strangled noise that he belatedly managed to turn into a cough. "We can't read them?" he asked.

"No one can." The monk's voice was gentle, but firm. "Some of the prophecies contained within them may not yet have come to pass, and it is for no one but the oracle who made the prophecy and the pilgrim who asked the question to know the answer until they do. The only exception is the current oracle. I'm sorry, but these are our ways."

I turned my head away, hoping that he took it for mere disappointment. The word didn't cover the way my heart had sunk. The glow of my excitement vanished like a candle being blown out. I didn't give a fig what the other journals said; those oracles hadn't made the prophecy for Nalia. If we couldn't read the journals of the most recent oracle, we had come for nothing.

"We understand, of course," I managed. "Thank you. The rest will be most helpful."

He left the door open, so I slowly pulled another journal from the wall, took it over to a table, and sat down, setting the book in front of me as if I were going to read it. After a moment, the chair beside me scraped the floor as Kiernan pulled it back.

"Don't worry," he said in my ear. "We'll find another way. We can sneak in at night or something, break open the cabinet, and read the journals then."

I shook my head, trying to ignore the burning behind my eyes. "There's a spell on it. I can feel it. Philantha showed that kind of spell to me. Only the key can open that cabinet. You couldn't even burn it up, or chop it apart with an ax."

"Then we'll get the key."

"We don't know where it is."

"We'll find it. Or maybe we can skip all this and just ask the oracle where Nalia—the real Nalia—is, since you're sure she's alive."

It was a thought I had been toying with myself, though I hadn't mentioned it to Kiernan. Could I just ask the oracle to point me toward Nalia, give me the name of the town, of the street where she lived? Somehow, I didn't think it would be that easy. Prophecies tended not to be that specific; there was generally room for interpretation.

"Maybe," I said, not believing it.

We stayed in the room until late afternoon, pretending to read the journals and taking fake notes. Even the allure of the books didn't tempt me now, however. I could feel myself slipping into a dark place, despite Kiernan's efforts to cheer me. I had no idea what I was doing. I had to admit that now. I had come running off to Isidros because I had no real ideas about how to find Nalia or decipher the identity of the spell-shielded person. What was I playing at? I couldn't do this. I was just a scribe with magic I could hardly control, not a savior of Thorvaldor.

My thoughts seemed stuck on the same path, wheeling around and around themselves without going anywhere new. I felt heavy, my dashed hopes weighing me down. Was this what my aunt had meant when she said I gave up too easily? Maybe there was something else I could do, but in my misery, I couldn't see it. Finally, though, my dark thoughts were interrupted by the sound of someone entering the room. It was, I realized after a moment, Brother Paxson.

"The oracle will see you, if you wish," he said simply.

Since I didn't have any other ideas, I nodded, trying to look excited. Again we walked through the library and out onto the grounds. The wall cast long shadows in the afternoon light, and several sisters and brothers sat on benches in the shade, paring vegetables for the evening meal.

As we mounted the shallow steps leading into the temple, I wondered what I would say to the oracle, mostly to distract myself from my suddenly weak legs. Would she tell, if I revealed that I was not a lady scholar but a girl on a more desperate quest? And if I did, would she have any information that could help me? Despite the malaise that had gripped me, I felt a tingle of real excitement as we entered.

The inside of the temple was cool and dim, the domed ceiling arching high overhead. Our feet echoed on the stone floor, for the entire space was empty, save for a small circular dais set in the exact center of the room. A hole had been cut in the top of the dome so that a shaft of sunlight fell into the room, the only light other than a few lanterns hanging on the walls. At noon, the light must pour directly downward, but now it had moved with the sun and only vaguely illuminated the still figure sitting on a thin mat on the dais.

Brother Paxson stopped only a few feet from the door. "I will leave you now. Do you wish to go together, or alone?"

"K— Aldarich can stay," I murmured.

"You will approach and kneel," he said. "Do not speak until she speaks to you."

I nodded, and a moment later, he was gone, the door shutting softly behind him.

Kiernan and I looked at each other, both unmoving, and I had a sudden urge to reach out and take his hand. I blushed at the thought, surely brought on by the strangeness of the place, the eerie quiet, and the unmoving figure on the dais. I hadn't held hands with Kiernan since I was eight. Still, the thought jarred me enough to break the spell that had settled over me, and I took the first step toward the oracle.

She was not old, I realized as I came closer. I had expected a woman with gnarled hands and gray hair, but this woman looked no older than thirty, the skin on her face and hands smooth and pale. She sat with her legs folded beneath her, a long dress of blankest white pooling around her. Her hair was pale as well, a soft, thin honey color, and it fell unbound to the floor. Her eyes were light blue, nearly colorless.

Licking my lips, I knelt, letting myself rest back on my calves, my neck prickling. I heard Kiernan do the same, but I couldn't look away from the oracle's face. It was still, as motionless as the rest of her, and I knew she didn't see me.

She blinked slowly and I felt her suddenly focus on me, coming back from wherever she had been.

"Greetings, Princess-who-was," she said.

CHAPTER THIRTEEN

"*What?*" *The word* came out a squawk. Beside me, Kiernan tensed. "You know who I am?"

She nodded. "I saw you, three days ago. You were riding over hills, with a broken crown on your head. Do not worry. I will not tell." She smiled, but strangely, like a slightly mind-touched child.

"Do you know why we've come?" I asked.

She shook her head. "The God sends what he sends, and no more. I can ask, sometimes, for certain visions, but they are not always sent. I saw you coming, but he has not told me why." She cocked her head at me. "I see the crown, still. You have not put it aside. But you no longer wear it. It sits in your hands, as if you are keeping it for someone else."

It should have been unnerving, for her to see me, my motivations, so clearly. It wasn't, though; it was like looking into a very clear mirror for the first time. "That's why I've come. I wanted . . ." I swallowed. "I wanted to know about the prophecy, the one made about the princess when she was born. But you didn't make it, and Brother Seldin won't let us see the records of the oracle who did. The royal family . . ." My voice, already low, dropped to a whisper. My earlier fears had fallen away; somehow, I knew it was safe to tell her. "They've been betrayed. I feel like the prophecy has something to do with it, but I need to read it, learn whatever I can about it."

The oracle tilted her head, then shook it sorrowfully. "I cannot ask the abbot to change the rules that have governed this place for centuries."

"But please, you don't understand—"

She raised a finger, then let her hand go to her neck. From beneath her dress, she pulled a long silver chain, a silver key hanging from its end. At my incredulous look, she smiled. "I cannot ask them to change. I am only one oracle—there were others before me and there will be others after me. But I saw myself giving you this key, before you even arrived." She smiled again, and something a little more human sparked in her eyes. "If you wait until night, the library will be empty. They do not lock the outer doors. You can leave the key in the room, and I will say I left it by mistake."

With trembling fingers, I reached forward and let her lay the key in my hand. "If you're helping me, then you must know—" I breathed—"what happened. You can tell us who did this, who betrayed the king and queen."

Again she shook her head. "I am not given to see the past."

I frowned, confused. "Then why are you doing this, giving me the key?"

That serene smile. "Because I saw myself giving it to you."

"Then," I asked breathlessly, "then the Nameless God . . . wants me to succeed?"

A crease formed between her pale eyes, and she blinked

sorrowfully. "No. Or rather, the God cares naught for such earthly things as thrones, and who sits upon them. The visions he sends me are not visions of his will. They are merely glimpses of what may come, but even they are rarely certain. I give you the key because I saw myself doing so, but I cannot say it is the God's will."

I swallowed my disappointment. "Can you see what will happen? What I should do?"

The oracle gazed at me for a long time before saying, softly, "When I look at you, the path of the future is crooked. There are too many branchings, too many chances. Too many choices. Even the God cannot see it."

It made me feel small and scared, more alone than I have ever been before. Even the Nameless God, in all his infinite knowledge, could not see my path. Which meant that I had no chance of seeing it.

Something warm touched my hand, curling under my fingers and then clasping them firmly. With a start, I looked down and saw Kiernan's hand holding mine. He grinned at me, as clearly as if he had heard my thoughts. No. I would not be alone.

It seemed there was nothing else to ask. "Thank you," I said, and the oracle inclined her head.

"May you be guided by your knowledge," she said, and I sensed that it was the phrase of closing.

It had all happened so quickly. I stood, feeling foolish as my skirt caught on my foot and I stumbled, brushing the oracle's knee with my hand as I caught myself. My face flushed, but when I glanced at the oracle in embarrassment, I saw her staring at me. Her body, so languid before, had gone oddly rigid, and

EILIS O'NEAL

her pupils had expanded so far that I could barely make out the ring of blue around them.

"Are you— Is everything all right?" I asked.

As if my words had actually struck her, she startled, then slumped fractionally, her head hanging. Then she raised her head to look at me. "It seems a key is not all I am to give you," she said, then paused, eyes flicking down.

"What did you see?" I asked.

"I saw a triangle," she said finally, "set in a storm. One of its sides crumbled and fell away, leaving only two."

A triangle. I frowned and then gasped as I realized what she must mean.

"Is that all you saw?" Kiernan demanded.

The oracle nodded. "I do not command the visions," she said sadly. "They command me. I cannot tell you what it means."

A triangle. Three girls, all bound together. One side falling away, crumbling.

Dying?

"Don't worry," I mumbled. "I think I know."

The oracle bowed her head, the light from the hole in the dome above brushing her long limbs, and did not answer.

"You aren't going to die," Kiernan whispered through the darkness.

We sat in one of the bedchambers for pilgrims, me on the cot and Kiernan on the floor. He was sitting with his knees bent, elbows resting on them. If I looked at him, I knew I would see his eyes flash even in the dark. So I leaned my head back against the stone wall and said nothing.

"She might not have meant you," he continued. "It could be Orianne, or even the real Nalia."

That did make me look at him. "Great," I said sarcastically. "So we find the real Nalia and then somehow get her killed. That would certainly be doing the kingdom a favor."

Kiernan huffed in irritation, then took a breath. "I didn't mean it that way. And besides, not all of those visions come true. The one that started this whole mess didn't."

I didn't answer. I felt numb, had felt that way since stumbling out of the temple. Even the key hidden inside my fist hadn't been enough to bring me back to myself. I had allowed Kiernan to lead me to the pilgrims' quarters, overheard him tell Brother Paxson that I was too weary with study to leave that night. I had eaten the food brought to us, nodding mechanically in thanks, then sat down on the cot and let my mind wander.

A triangle. One side crumbled away, leaving only two. Try as I might, I could think of nothing else it could mean. Only that if I found the real princess, one of us—Nalia, Orianne, or me—would die.

"And even if it was a true prophecy, we can fight it. We know about it now, so we can be . . . alert, careful. We can keep them safe. We'll keep you safe—*I'll* keep you safe." Kiernan pushed himself up off the bed and came to sit next to me. "Come on," he said, reaching out a tentative arm and putting it around my shoulders. "I just got you back. I'm not going to let you die."

Closing my eyes, I let myself lean against him. He smelled nice, even after days of travel on horseback. And he was warm and solid, and my friend.

We stayed like that long enough that I felt a little of the

EILIS O'NEAL

numbness leave, melted away by Kiernan's warmth. "Sorry," I said finally. My voice sounded a little choked, which made me pull away from him in embarrassment. "It's a strange thing to hear, that's all."

Kiernan had let his arm drop from my shoulders, but his fingers now brushed my arm nearest to him. "I'm sure it is," he said. He was gazing into my eyes as he said it, though more deeply than seemed necessary.

My heart was suddenly hammering in my ears, and I was overly aware of how close we were. "It must be near midnight," I stuttered. "We should . . . We should probably try the, uh, library."

Kiernan blinked, then pushed himself up, one corner of his mouth pulled in. "Of course," he said. Then a mischievous grin broke across his face. "Now, *this* should be fun."

It only took sneaking across the moon-shadowed courtyard for me to decide that my definition of fun differed drastically from Kiernan's. I nearly jumped out of my skin when some sort of animal—a night bird or a bat—landed in a nearby tree with a loud rustling of leaves. At least, though, the heart-thumping terror that came with the idea of being caught pushed all thoughts of the oracle's latest prophecy from my head. Luckily, we made it to the library without seeing anyone. Kiernan gave the door a gentle push, and, true to the oracle's word, it swung slowly open.

The library was quiet, so our footfalls seemed like thunder in my ears. No lamps remained lit in the hallway, and we had to feel our way one step at a time. There was one tense moment when I managed to trip over my own skirt and collide with a closed door, but no one came to investigate. Finally, we made it to the door painted with the oracle's sign, went through, and hurriedly closed it behind us.

"We're going to have to light at least one lamp," Kiernan whispered. I nodded, hoping he could see me. Luckily, with no windows in the room, only the bit of light escaping under the door could give us away. Feeling slightly blasphemous, I whispered a prayer for forgiveness to the Nameless God and approached the black cabinet. The oracle's silver key slid silently into the lock, and the door popped open as I twisted.

Six journals stood in the cabinet—at least one of the oracles must have been a heavy writer. I reached for the last, then brought it over to the single light Kiernan had lit. Carefully, trying not crack the spine or bend a page, I opened it.

Twenty-third day of autumn, year 1145, reign of King Antaine II. Today the rites were finished. It seems strange somehow, to think that I am now the oracle. I only wish that my family had been able to attend, though I know that it is a sacred rite, and can be viewed only by my religious brothers and sisters, and not my kin . . .

"This is it," I said, forgetting to keep my voice down in my excitement. Kiernan clapped a hand on my shoulder, his eyebrows raised meaningfully. "Sorry," I said in a lower voice. "But this is the right one. It starts in 1145. . . ." I flipped through the pages, finally stopping over halfway through. "She wasn't oracle for very long," I murmured as I scanned the pages for the date I wanted. "Just seven years. Here!"

I slowed as the dates neared my birthday, finally stopping as my eyes found the words I wanted.

EILIS O'NEAL

The king and queen came today, seeking the prophecy for their coming child. The queen seemed to have made the journey well enough, given her condition. They came to the temple, but when I asked the God to send the prophecy, I was struck down by visions of horror. A high room with thrones at the end, and lying before them in a pool of blood, a girl, pale with death. A golden crown lay near her, the blood spreading out toward it. Behind her, fifteen lamps winked out. They asked for more, but the God would not answer. I can only think that it was the unborn princess, and that she may die in the palace before her sixteenth birthday, a victim of murder.

I turned the page, but there was no more about the princess. Instead, it went on to an account of a merchant's wife and her petition. I sat back, letting the book fall closed, my hand between the pages.

"But we knew all that," Kiernan said angrily from over my shoulder. "Couldn't she have written a little more? Something helpful? Nameless God, it was about the princess!"

"The God doesn't care who sits on the throne. That's what the oracle said, remember? I guess it wasn't any more important to her than any other prophecy." I realized that I was fighting back tears. I had been right. Coming here hadn't helped at all.

"Let me see that," Kiernan demanded, and I handed the book over to him without a word. I could see his eyes moving as he read, but then he sighed, laying it facedown on the table with a shrug. "Someone needs to teach them to be a bit more thorough."

I picked at the back cover, letting it fall open and then closed again, not caring in my disappointment if I caused any damage. I had to work to keep a sob out of my voice, so I ended up sounding like I had a bad cold. "I just thought that surely there would be something here, that it would help . . ." Just then, however, something caught my eye. I stared at the last page of the book. The writing, unlike the clear hand from the beginning, had gone choppy and hard to read, as if the oracle had been weak and shaking when she wrote it.

The illness has progressed quickly. I am unlikely to live much longer, not with this fever clutching at me so tightly. The prophecies have gone anyway, for days now, and I cannot see my own end. It is fitting, perhaps, the God's justice.

Of that which I have not written, I will write now—I fear the God's wrath if I do not, though I fear it already for what I have done. I have commanded the record to be buried with me, sealed in a container. The monks will not question it, for it is my will. And perhaps, if I acknowledge it somewhere, the God will take pity on his servant when I meet him.

I frowned, then read the lines again. They didn't make any sense. "There was something she hadn't done, or said," I murmured, trying to work it out. "Whatever it was, it scared her. I think she wrote it down when she was dying and had it buried with her."

"You think it has something to do with the princess?" Kiernan asked.

I shrugged. "I don't know. But whatever it was, she felt guilty about it. She was frightened. We should try to find out what it was—we don't have anything else to try."

He shook his head in disgust, then slid the journal back

into the cabinet. "If she had it buried with her, it's no use to us, unless you plan to go digging up some moldering body, and even then . . ." He grimaced in disgust.

I frowned and licked my lips, an image forming in my mind. "I don't think we'll have to," I said slowly.

"I'd feel a lot better about this if that spell had worked," Kiernan hissed.

"Don't tell me that *I'm* going to have to drag *you* along," I whispered back. "This is a real adventure, Kiernan. Just think, if we manage to get out of all this without being killed or imprisoned, you'll have such stories to tell the ladies at court."

"Are you sure that this isn't blasphemy? We're going to desecrate the grave of the Nameless God's chosen ones."

"We aren't going to desecrate it," I insisted. "We're just going to look around it. And besides, since when have you worried about blasphemy?"

He snorted, but softly. "Let's go, then."

I nodded, hoping he could see me in the darkness. The barest sliver of moon hung in the sky, casting little light, and while I was grateful for the cover, it also made it hard to see. And I, too, wished that I had managed to cast a weak version of a sight shield on us—a sort of "don't see me" spell. But I hadn't, so we would have to make our way across the grounds of Isidros the old-fashioned way.

We went slowly, creeping from shadow to shadow, praying that no one would decide to sneak to the kitchens for a late-night snack or to fight sleeplessness by taking a midnight stroll. My heart hammered in my chest so that I felt a little faint. This was more than sneaking into the library. We would have been in trouble for that, I felt sure, but I also knew it would be nothing compared to what would happen if we were caught disturbing the remains of the oracles themselves.

The gate on the iron fence surrounding the temple's grave-yard creaked as we inched it open, just wide enough to let us slip inside. I peeked hastily behind us, sure someone would have heard it, but no one came. It didn't make me feel better, though, but worse, as if fate were only waiting until we were completely committed to this course before clamping down on us. Sweat trickled down my back by the time we reached the mausoleum I had seen that morning, its pale stone walls rearing up above us. We crouched on the far side of it, around the corner from the door, and then Kiernan darted around to test it.

"It's locked," he breathed when he returned. "Really locked. We'd make enough noise to wake Vivaskari if we tried to force it. Are you sure she'll be in there?"

"It said something about all the oracles being entombed there in one of the journals I read today." I sat back on my heels and bit my lip. "I'll have to try a spell then."

Which, I thought as I hunched my shoulders in front of the door to the mausoleum a moment later, *could be as loud as trying to knock the door open with a battering ram.* Kiernan shifted from one foot to the other, keeping a watch for any approaching monks or sisters. I closed my eyes, trying to ignore the shivery feeling brought on by standing in a graveyard in the dead of night, forcing myself to think about what Philantha would do. Except that Philantha would know a real spell to open the door, and she would be able to make it work. When

I looked inward, all I felt was power roiling inside me without control.

Well, fine, I thought. *If that's how it's going to be . . .*

Raising my hands, I placed them on top of the huge lock set into the thick wooden door. Then I let go, releasing the inner walls that held my magic at bay. Energy pulsed through my hands and threw me backward to collide with Kiernan. We tumbled to the ground in a tangle as a terrific pop and sizzle sounded from inside the lock.

Kiernan had landed on top of me, his elbow digging into my ribs. But neither of us rose; instead we listened to see if anyone else had heard us. When no one came, I shifted to make his elbow move.

"Sorry," Kiernan said, smiling. "Are you all right?"

"Yes," I said, but it came out smaller than I had meant it to. I could feel heat flushing my neck, and I scooted out from under him before he could see my face. Scrambling over to the door, I wondered what was the matter with me.

Kiernan was right behind me, and he pushed the door open with a grunt. "The lock's . . . Well, they'll know someone's been here. It's well and truly broken. We'll have to leave before they notice it."

He glanced at me with that small smile on his face, and my stomach flipped for no reason. "Ladies first," he added with a grimace.

I took up a torch from one of the two brackets beside the door while Kiernan took the other one. Then, swallowing, I managed the spell to light them and stepped into the tomb.

CHAPTER FOURTEEN

The mausoleum had been built with the centuries in mind. It was a large building, made to hold the remains of oracles throughout the years, and it had not yet been filled. At least whoever had designed it had not thought to house each oracle's body in its own stone coffin. Instead, open niches lined the walls, each with intricate designs carved around the dates of the oracle's life. The light from the torches flickered around us as we peered into the niches, searching for the most recent. Little remained in the nearest ones, nothing but scraps of the fabric wrapped around bones. The sights, combined with the coldness and stale air of the tomb, made me shiver. Not finding the oracle we needed, we plunged farther into the gloomy tomb.

"What will they do when they run out of space?" Kiernan asked as he squinted at the numbers above one niche. "Not this one."

"Build another mausoleum?" I suggested. The oracles had not been placed sequentially, I found, which meant we had to examine each niche individually. My skin crawled as I tried to push away the thought that real bodies lay inside the shrouds.

We were near the back of the occupied niches when Kiernan called my name. "Sinda! I think I've found her."

Hurrying over, I raised the torch to view the year of death, then shivered with excitement and fear. A pure white shroud wrapped around the oracle's body from head to foot. Some dust and cobwebs marred its blankness, but it was fully intact.

"This is it. She said it was in a container, so let's look for it." A moment of searching around the niche, however, yielded nothing. "I think we'll have to take her shroud off," I said reluctantly.

Kiernan's shoulders twitched, but he laid his hands on the fabric and pulled. The fifteen-year-old shroud fell open to reveal the last oracle.

She had not decayed as much as I would have thought, and I realized belatedly that the monks must embalm the bodies, or ask a wizard to cast spells over them, before bringing them to the tomb. Dark hair clung to the skull, I saw before I forced my gaze away from the face. It seemed rude, somehow, to stare at her. Instead, I concentrated on the rest of her, a task made more difficult by the guttering light from the torch. Her hands had been folded serenely across her stomach, but nothing lay in them. Finally, however, I noticed a small metal container lying on the crook of her right arm. Holding my breath, I reached in, trying to avoid touching the oracle, and pulled it out.

Copper, with a tight lid fitted over the top, so that I had to bang it against the wall to loosen it. Finally, however, I pulled the lid off and reached inside, coming out with a rolled piece of paper. My voice trembling slightly with nerves, I read the words aloud.

"'I find, in these last, clouded hours, that I cannot go to the

God with this unsaid. I have hidden it, all these years, but the God knows all, and I must acknowledge it before I meet him. All the prophecies I made, I made for the God. I made them truly. Save one. Of that, I will write now, and hope the God will forgive me.

"'In the year of the crown princess's birth, the God sent his prophecy for her. I did not relay it to the king and queen. Instead, I gave them a false prophecy, one that would make them think the princess would die unless they hid her away. I was not alone in this, but even now, with the God's judgment coming, I cannot find it inside myself to name that other.

"'The true prophecy, unacknowledged until now, I will give. I saw a girl, alone, who did not know herself. She stood at the walls of a palace, looking up at it from the outside, her hand inside her shadow's.'"

That was all. I turned the paper over, hoping for more, but found nothing. Slowly, I raised my eyes to Kiernan's face, just as a voice cut through the dark tomb.

"Who's there?"

We both froze, our eyes locked on each other. Kiernan made a "what now?" face, but I could give only the smallest shake of my head. We had no reason for being down here, no excuse that could get us out of this.

"Who's there?" the voice insisted again. Steps echoed in the dry air of the mausoleum, but they sounded tentative, as if the person didn't know whether or not he wanted to investigate on his own.

A mixed wave of horror and relief crashed through me as

EILIS O'NEAL

Kiernan handed his torch off to me and silently freed the sword that hung at his waist. I knew from watching him in the training yards that he knew how to use it. Still, I shook my head more vehemently, and he nodded. He wouldn't hurt the intruder, just scare him if needed.

We didn't have any more time to figure out our plan, for just then the figure, dressed in the long robes of the monks, reached the edge of the torchlight. He was a paunchy man with a squishy-looking face. And, for all that he may not have wanted to enter the tomb alone, he hefted a staff in his right hand, looking poised to use it.

"Who are you?" he demanded. "What are you doing in here?" He glared at us, but then he noticed the torn shroud lying in disarray over the body of the last oracle. His face went purple as rage seemed to seize him. "Grave robbing! Disturbing the oracle! Come with me, or I'll—"

With a cry, Kiernan leaped forward, his sword out. The monk jumped backward, raising his staff to block the blow. Except that Kiernan didn't try to strike the monk. Instead, he feinted suddenly to the side and shoved him with his free hand. The monk's staff slashed through the air as he stumbled sideways, but he missed Kiernan. The monk crashed into the wall, and Kiernan followed, knocking the staff aside with his sword. It clattered across the floor to land at my feet, and I kicked it away into the darkness.

The monk crouched against the wall but didn't move, his eyes on Kiernan's sword. "I'm sorry," Kiernan said, and brought the pommel of his sword down on the man's head. The monk's eyes rolled up, and he slumped to the side in a faint.

"Are you all right?" Kiernan asked as he sheathed the weapon.

"Yes," I croaked, my throat dry. My mind was racing. We had attacked a monk of the Nameless God. . . . The oracle had given a false prophecy to the king and queen. . . . If one monk had heard something strange, enough that he had come down to the cemetery to search the mausoleum, more might have heard us as well. . . . The oracle had been in league with Neomar or Melaina, but there was no telling which one. . . . We needed to leave, before the monk woke up.

"Sinda." Kiernan had taken hold of one arm. "Can you do something, a spell, to make him forget that it was us down here?"

I was shaking, I realized, trembling like a sapling in a strong wind. But I took a deep breath and tried to focus on Kiernan. "Maybe," I said finally. "Philantha, she was trying to teach me a confusion spell. But I never got it to work—I kept making her forget everything we were doing instead of just getting confused."

"Can you try it anyway?"

Nodding and handing the paper and container to Kiernan, I squatted down in front of the monk to place my hands on either side of his head. I could feel the magic in me just as I had outside; it wanted to burst out of me, to run rampant through me. But I couldn't just unleash it as I had out there, or I would risk hurting the monk beyond repair. So I concentrated, focusing on letting just a tiny stream of magic slip out of me. *You don't know why you came down here,* I thought to him. *You looked around and saw that the shroud had fallen open, but nothing else was wrong. You were tired, so you sat down for a moment and fell asleep.*

EILIS O'NEAL

I had no way of knowing if the spell had worked, but I finally had to drop my hands when the pressure of a building headache made black spots swim in my vision. No matter what the monk said, it wouldn't fool the temple forever; eventually someone would notice that the lock had been blown apart. The monk himself might notice when he left. But it might give us enough time to leave, and hopefully our false names would confuse anyone searching for the culprits.

I took the oracle's confession from Kiernan and rolled it back into the metal container. Then, slipping it into a pocket of my dress, I said, "Let's get out of here."

A day later, we sat in the mostly empty common room of the Brown Cat's Tail, a rather dingier inn than those we had stayed in on our way to Isidros. Still, we had decided to avoid the places that a nobleman and his sister might choose, just in case my spell had failed and Isidros decided to send riders looking for their grave robbers.

"So," Kiernan said after taking a bite of his dubious meat pie, "what did we learn on our grand adventure?"

His naturally buoyant spirits hadn't taken long to reassert themselves once we were on the road with no sign of pursuit. He felt sure that the note we had left, claiming my sudden desire to research the cave where the original oracle had had her first vision as our reason for a night departure, wouldn't attract any undue attention. "Scholars are like that," he had said. "They won't think anything of it."

I, on the other hand, felt fretful on the road, glancing behind us often enough that Kiernan asked if I had a crick in my neck.

I worried about the effects of my spell on the monk and about being caught by pursuing religious folk. I worried about the meaning of what we had discovered, and about the prophecy given to me by the current oracle.

Now, however, I spread my fingers on the table to tick off points. "We learned that the oracle gave a false prophecy to the king and queen, one that would make them want to hide the real Nalia away and put someone else in her place. There never was any chance of the princess being killed in the Hall of Thorvaldor. Which means that the oracle was either in league with or coerced by Neomar or Melaina. I think she was in on it, though, because of the guilt she felt. She knew what she was doing was wrong, and it haunted her until she died. We learned that one of the three of us—Nalia, Orianne, or me—will probably die if we attempt to find the real princess."

"That's still debatable," Kiernan interrupted. "Not all prophecies come true."

I shrugged. I had managed to keep from dwelling on that part of our discoveries, if only because I was so preoccupied with trying to figure out which of the two wizards was more likely to have persuaded the oracle to help them. But it hung at the edge of my thoughts, ready to pounce if I let my mind drift.

"Still," I continued, "we don't have to worry about that until we *find* the princess. And to do that, I think we need to know if it's Neomar or Melaina we're dealing with. She said that she wished her family had been able to attend her investiture. So maybe she's related to one of them."

"But how can we find that out, without walking up to them and asking, 'So, your sister wasn't the oracle who betrayed

EILIS O'NEAL

Thorvaldor, was she?' I think, maybe, that might make them suspicious."

I took a drink of my ale and smiled grimly. "The palace library keeps the records of every noble family in Thorvaldor— all the deaths and all the births, even of the minor lines. So that certainly includes the Harandrons of Saramarch."

"But what about Neomar?"

"He's an Ostralus. They were titled when he became the head of the college. He'll be in there, too."

CHAPTER FIFTEEN

Six days later, in the early afternoon, we rode back into Vivaskari. I hunched in the saddle as we approached South Gate, but the guards at the city walls gave us only the briefest of looks before allowing us to ride in. I had been half expecting to be met with guards bent on taking us into custody for our escapades in Isidros, so I breathed a sigh of relief as we rode away from the gate.

"I have to go back to Philantha's," I told Kiernan after we had returned our horses to the stable in Flower Basket. "It might be a few days before I can come to the palace."

He nodded. "I'd go through the records myself, except that I don't even know where to start. When you want to come, send me a message."

"Look for it in a few days," I said, then paused. I wanted to hug him, to thank him for going to Isidros with me. A few months ago, I would have done it without hesitating. But something was changing between us, something I couldn't name. He was clearly ill at ease, too; a faint line had worked its way between his eyebrows, and he shuffled from one foot to the other.

"Thank you, Kiernan," I said finally, wrapping my arms around myself.

The frown deepened momentarily, and my stomach flipped. But then the frown had vanished, and Kiernan was saying brightly, "You could have done it on your own. I only lent a certain foolishness to the enterprise."

Once, I might have slapped him on the arm or tugged his hair for the lie. Now, I only scowled and said quietly, "That's not true, and you know it. I couldn't have managed without you. You're my best friend, Keirnan."

He swallowed, suddenly serious. "I know. Listen, Sinda, I—"

Whatever he was going to say, he didn't get the chance. A passing chicken cart suddenly lost a wheel, spilling its load into the street. Several of the coops burst open, filling the air with squawking chickens and white feathers. We both clapped our hands over our ears, and Kiernan finally shouted, "Should I walk you back?"

"No," I yelled over the commotion. "I told Philantha I was going to Treb. She'll know better if she sees you."

"Until I hear from you then," he called, and we each hurried away alone.

Philantha spared only a cursory question for the state of Aunt Varil's health before pulling me into her study to examine her latest experiment. I was tired from the road, but somehow, being among the bottles and bubbling potions of Philantha's work made me feel more relaxed instead of more exhausted. Philantha's house had become my house, I realized, something like a home.

For several hours we stirred pots, shredded herbs, and generally tried not to blow ourselves up. When Philantha finally felt that the mixtures were simmering in just the right state of thickness, she turned to me and asked, "So, did you have a chance to practice your magic at all?"

"I did," I acknowledged. Then I thought about the lock that I hadn't been able to open without blasting it apart, the failed spell that would have made us hard to notice. Maybe the monk wouldn't have come searching for intruders if I had been able to work them properly.

My shoulders drooped. If only I could rely on my magic. I was going to need it to find Nalia and restore her to the throne. I felt sure about that. But it worked only in fits and starts, nothing I could count on.

And if it failed me, if *I* failed, someone might die.

"It didn't always work, though," I admitted sadly. "It never does."

Philantha looked up from the pile of discarded stems that she had been sweeping into her hand. Letting them fall to the ground, she came to stand in front of me.

"Listen," she said, pushing her flyaway hair back behind her ears, "because I probably won't remember to tell you again for a good long time—Nameless God knows I can barely remember what lessons I've taught you, much less to give you praise. You have power, Sinda, and it's not your fault that it lay dormant for so many years. If you had been like any normal wizard and discovered your talent as a child, I have no doubt you would be working your way through the ranks right now."

I sat silently while she turned away and bustled about with pots for a moment. I had almost decided to ask if there was anything else she needed me for, when she gave one of her little

EILIS O'NEAL

bird shakes and fixed her eyes on me. "I don't know if I told you, but the last time I had an apprentice was fifteen years ago. He was a good lad, nice and solid, but then his family had some Farvaseean blood, and I've never met a truly reckless Farvaseean. Makes them boring, really. But he'd do any spell you asked—like a good dog, he was, very well trained."

"I'm not much like that, I guess," I mumbled.

"I let him go," Philantha said. "No less than four college wizards on my door the next day, begging me to change my mind. But I wouldn't. There was no real potential there, no room for imagination.

"I don't care how long it takes you to get control of your magic, Sinda." She grinned and cocked her head, looking off into the distance. "Because I want to be there when you do. I think—and I'm rarely wrong about these things, you know—that it will be something to see."

Four days passed before I felt caught up enough to send a message spell to Kiernan. In my absence, Philantha had purchased a boxful of crumbling books from a tinker who promised that they held rare and forgotten spells. So far, I had found only some recipes, a history of the founding of the Wenthi capital, and what looked like half of a very melodramatic play, which might have made me laugh, except that I was strung out with nerves. Part of me wanted to dash up to the palace that minute so that I would finally know the name of the person I was fighting against. The other part, however, wanted nothing more than to stay in Philantha's house forever, to keep everyone—Orianne, myself, and Nalia—alive.

But I had never been one to put off duty for too long; it

had been imprinted in my bones as the princess, and it seemed unwilling to go away as a scribe. So, when I had at least glanced into all of the new books and decided it unlikely that any of them held powerful spells, I begged an afternoon off from Philantha and sent my message to Kiernan.

He met me outside the gates, a long cloak in his hands. "I thought it would be better if fewer people saw you wandering around here," he said with a shrug. "If it's Melaina, she's likely to be at court, and if it's Neomar, he might have left a spy."

I took the cloak and settled it over my shoulders, pulling the hood up around my face. It was hot, too hot for the warm weather, and I thought I must look very peculiar. But the guards barely glanced at me as I trailed behind Kiernan—a perk of coming through the gates with the Earl of Rithia's son.

The library was located in the main part of the palace, rather than the wings reserved for minor nobility. I hadn't been back there since the day my true identity had been revealed. It felt strange to walk the halls toward the library, as if I were wandering through a dream or a ghostly palace. Or as if I were the ghost, the unreal one. I felt light, insubstantial, like a strong wind might pick me up and carry me away.

I must have looked it, too, because halfway to the library, Kiernan reached over and linked his arm through mine. We had often walked that way, before, though it had never made my heart thump against my ribs as it did now. But it was a comfort, too, and in this way we entered the library.

We glanced around and, seeing that no one had noticed us, went quickly to a table in a corner that I knew few people wandered past. "You'll have to ask one of the librarians for the

EILIS O'NEAL

genealogies," I whispered. "Here, I made of list of the years I want." I slid it toward him across table. I had gone back at least twenty years further than I thought really necessary, just to be safe. "If they ask why you want them, tell them that you're—I don't know—researching the bloodlines of a girl you like or something."

Kiernan flushed at my words, looking ready to argue, but I only flicked a hand at him. "Go!"

It didn't take long for him to return with the huge volumes. They were tall and wide, big enough for a scribe to have drawn family trees on each page. "Let's try Neomar first," I said. That book was bound in dark green, the writing in it not yet faint with age. Neomar's family, along with all the other families in the book, were new nobles, only recently titled. Still, I turned the pages carefully, until the name Ostralus caught my eye.

"Here he is." I jabbed his name with my finger, but then paused. "But there's nothing . . ." I shook my head. "Look, it says that he was an only child, and his parents are dead. And his father's only brother died without any heirs—all before Neomar was thirty. He hasn't had any close family for years and years, long before the oracle was instated. But I thought—I mean, I thought it really might be him. He wouldn't tell Philantha about the spell they put on me, and he didn't want her teaching me. He said he wanted her to report on my progress, like he knew I was a threat. And he left the city right after what I saw in the garden."

"The oracle might have worked with him without being related to him," Kiernan offered. "That was just a guess on our part. She could have been coerced, or was maybe just a friend."

"Maybe," I conceded, but without much feeling. What if we

were chasing moonbeams here? What if this wasn't the way to find out who the oracle had been working with? I didn't have any other ideas, at least not any safe ones.

Laying the green book aside, my stomach tight, I reached for the most recent of the other volumes. The older nobility's records took up much more space, and Kiernan had brought me three red-bound books.

The listing for the Harandrons took up four pages on its own. I scanned the names, finally coming to the one I wanted. "Look," I said, pointing, "she wasn't a noble herself. She married Theodrin Harandron, the Baron of Saremarch. He died before I was born."

"Just by a little," Kiernan said. "See? Only a few months."

I barely glanced at it, though. "There should still be a page about her family, since she married a noble. Ah, here." I flipped the page, though Kiernan caught it to hold it upright between us, to keep looking at the previous entry. "Kiernan," I said, my heart thumping, "she had a sister. Alethea. She died of . . . redvein fever. And she died—Kiernan, the date's the same as the one carved over the oracle."

Kiernan snapped his eyes up to me. "There something else," he said in a strangled voice. "You might not have noticed, but Melaina had a baby."

I shook my head. "No, she doesn't. She doesn't have an heir at all."

"She died. According to this, she had a girl who died the day she was born. And that was just five days before Nalia was born." He went white suddenly, even his lips turning pale. "But what if her baby didn't die? What if she only pretended that she had?

EILIS O'NEAL

And instead of sending the princess to that convent, she made sure her own daughter went instead."

"Orianne," I whispered. I felt cold, so cold that I pulled the heavy cloak around me more tightly. "Orianne is Melaina's daughter."

It all fit—the sister who had been the oracle, who might have helped her sister subvert the throne if she asked. The baby born just a few days before the real princess.

The king's words, suddenly remembered, echoed in my ears. *Nalia has been raised in a convent some distance from here— Melaina took her there a few days after her birth.* It would have been the perfect time to switch the babies. So easy, with no one the wiser.

I could imagine the scene in my head. Melaina, their trusted advisor, pale from childbirth and the apparent death of her baby, sitting before the king and queen. "No, please," she would have said. "I can still take the princess. It will give me some comfort, to know that I am ensuring the survival of the Thorvaldian throne. And I have performed healing spells on myself—I am well enough to travel, though my heart is aching."

Yes, I thought. Yes. That would have worked on a king and queen desperate to hide their child.

"But why?" Kiernan's question jolted me out of my thoughts. "Just to place her own daughter on the throne?"

"It's reason enough," I began, but then stopped. Kiernan had let his page fall over the tree showing Melaina's family, but I flipped it back with ice in my veins. The tree filled the page, with Melaina's and Alethea's entries at the very bottom. But it was the top that made me close my eyes with dread.

"Melaina is a Feidhelm," I said. "This isn't just about putting her own daughter on the throne. This is a vendetta."

"I don't understand," Kiernan hissed.

I pressed my lips together, then drew them back and shook my head. "You never paid enough attention to the history master. Four generations ago, a twin girl and boy were born to the throne—Aisling and Angar. Aisling was the elder, but only by a few minutes. When the old king died, she inherited the throne. But her brother, Angar, thought that he was the better choice, and he led a rebellion against his sister. They fought for almost a year, but he was finally taken and executed as a traitor. His wife was killed, too, when she refused to surrender to Aisling even after Angar had died."

I grimaced; it wasn't my favorite story of Thorvaldian history, particularly because I had worried about Angar's ghost for months after hearing it. "But there was a daughter," I continued. "She was just a little girl, and Aisling wouldn't hear of having her killed as well. But she did strike her from the royal family so she would have no claim on the throne. I think the daughter was just grateful to be alive by the time she grew up, and she married a wealthy merchant named Feidhelm. The Feidhelms have never caused any trouble—I doubt most people even remember who they are at all."

"But Melaina remembered," Kiernan said. "And she thinks that her family ought to be on the throne."

Just then one of the librarians shuffled past, reading while she walked. She didn't look our way, but it made me aware of how many people might overhear us. Standing abruptly, I ripped the

EILIS O'NEAL

pages out of the volumes, ignoring Kiernan's shocked expression at my defacement of library property. "We'll take these with us. Who knows? They're the official records, and she might come and destroy them if she thinks someone's found out about her. Let's go back to Philantha's. We can talk there."

I waited in our corner while Kiernan replaced the books, and then, after peering around the shelves to make sure no one was watching, we slunk from the library. I flipped the hood up to cover my face as we stepped into the hall. My head was spinning so hard that I barely registered my route, though it didn't matter; my feet knew the path anyway. Melaina was Orianne's mother. She had used her sister's position as the oracle to make a false prophecy, faked her baby's death, and switched her with the real princess and me with Orianne. Did I have enough evidence to go to the king and queen now? I wanted so badly to tell them, to let someone else worry about saving the kingdom. But all we had as proof were a few scraps of paper, and she was their friend, the person they thought of as their child's savior—

I collided with someone as I turned a corner, the genealogies falling from my hand as I fought to stay on my feet. "Pardon me," I said as I reached down to pick them up.

I froze, however, as the person I had hit said, in a voice as dark as a winter night, "Sinda Azaway. What a surprise to see you here."

I heard Kiernan inhale sharply and suddenly his hand was on my arm, pulling me back toward him a few inches. I straightened, my eyes locked on the face of Melaina Harandron.

CHAPTER SIXTEEN

"Melaina," I said dumbly. For a moment, I felt like I was wrapped in a thick blanket, and then my nerves exploded in a riot of sensation. *Run! Get the papers! Stay still! Don't let her see anything's wrong!* All contradictory, and none of it helpful. "I mean . . . Baroness. I apologize."

She laughed, a sound like low bells, and shook her head. She wore her long dark hair pulled away from her face and secured with a silver clip that still allowed half of it to spill down her back. Her green eyes were sharp as pine needles and rimmed with heavy lashes. Her skin was creamy and soft looking, her lips full. No wizard's robes today, but a long gown of crimson silk. Still, you would never mistake her for someone other than a wizard. Power emanated from her; you couldn't help but look at her and want her to smile at you.

Except that I didn't want her to smile at me. I wanted only to run away.

"Please, don't," she said. "We've known each other too long for such formality. Please, call me Melaina, and I will call you

Sinda. Though I have to say, I did not expect to see you roaming the palace again." Her gaze flicked to Kiernan behind me. "But I can see that even the maneuverings of kings and wizards were not enough to keep you from your friends."

"Yes," I said in what I hoped was a light voice, though it sounded more strangled to me. "There's very little that could keep me away from Kiernan." *Please*, I prayed, *don't let her notice the pages*. They were still lying on the floor at my feet. Was there some way for Kiernan to grab them without letting her see what was written on them?

Melaina raised one hand to her chin and tilted her head, a quizzical look her on face. "Ah, yes. I suppose that playing scribe to Philantha leaves you time for wandering. She is not, I suppose, the most demanding of mistresses."

That threw me off balance. I had not expected her to know where I lived or what I did there. But I only smiled tightly and said, "I do have some time to myself."

Melaina didn't nod. Instead, her eyes flicked downward to the floor, and, before either of us could stop her, she had stooped and then straightened up, the pages in her hand. Her eyes sped back and forth across the names, and then she was staring at me. Her face, so smooth and cool a moment ago, had hardened like ice on a pond.

"A lot of time, I see. Digging into the past, Sinda?" she asked. Her voice was still calm and light, but with an underlying sharpness now, like a knife wrapped in velvet. "Again, I am surprised."

"A project," I squeaked. "For Philantha."

"Really? It looks quite revolutionary." She held the page showing her daughter's birth out in front of her, her thumb resting just below the day of birth and death. "Perhaps you can ask her to tell me about it, next time I see her."

"I—" I started, but then took a step back. Power was building in the hall, roiling out of Melaina. I glanced down and saw her free hand flashing through signs, stoking her magic, and I swallowed hard as I recognized one of them. A spell of forgetting, one so powerful it might make a person forget their own name. "No," I breathed. "Kiernan—"

"Lord Cavish," Kiernan called, waving frantically down the hall. Melaina whipped around to see a minor lord exiting one of the rooms that led into the hall. He smiled and hurried toward us, oblivious to the magic permeating the air around us. Melaina's free hand dropped and the power evaporated, though her grip on the papers tightened so much that they crackled.

"Kiernan," Lord Cavish said jovially as he neared. "I hope you've called me over to pay that little gambling debt you still owe me?"

"Yes, yes, that's just it," Kiernan rambled. Producing several gold coins from his pocket, he said, "Sorry I can't stay and chat, Cavish, but I have an appointment. It was good to see you, Baroness."

He reached out a hand, and Melaina had no choice but to hand the pages to him. "Of course," she said, no trace of anything but pleasantness in her voice. "We'll talk again soon. Stay out of trouble now, Sinda."

It was all I could do to keep myself upright as we strode down the hall and out toward the gate. Once we reached the city streets, however, my bravery fled and I started to run, Kiernan at my heels.

❖ ✠ ❖

"She knows," I said when we finally reached Philantha's house. We had raced into the garden behind the house, and from there we had snuck into my room. "She knows, Kiernan."

He had started pacing the minute we closed the door, but now he stopped. "Then we need to tell the king and queen. We can't keep this a secret anymore, Sinda."

I wanted to agree with him. I wanted to nod and say, "Of course. We'll go right now." But I looked at my bed, where the two ripped-out pages from the library lay beside the tiny scrap of paper that held the oracle's final confession, and I remembered Melaina's beautiful face. A face you wanted to believe. The face of a woman whom the king and queen trusted above all others.

"It's not enough," I said. "It's not proof. They won't believe us, and even if they did, we still don't know where the princess is. Do you think she'll tell them, just for the asking, after all this time, after all her plans?"

"There are ways to make people tell secrets," Kiernan answered grimly, but I shook my head.

"Nothing they do to her will make her tell. She's worked too long for this. She's strong, Kiernan. And clever. She might even have some plan in place to have the princess killed if it looks like the king and queen know what happened."

"I thought you said she needed the princess alive," Kiernan shot back.

"She does, as long as no one knows that Orianne isn't the real princess. But if they did, she might have Nalia killed, so there wouldn't be any heir left but Orianne. She *is* royal, Kiernan, or her four-times great-grandfather was. She's the best they've got, if Nalia dies."

"Then why not kill Nalia now?"

I rubbed my neck with my hand. An ache had started there and was spreading throughout my body. "It's better if she doesn't have to. Then there's no one calling for deposing Orianne, no one saying she's not worthy to be the heir. She's just the princess, no questions asked. But if she thinks it's all coming down around her . . ."

Kiernan dropped to his knees in front of me where I sat on the bed, taking my hands in his. "Please, Sinda. I know it's dangerous, but we have to tell someone. I'm—" He pursed his lips. "I'm worried that she'll try to hurt you. She almost blasted us in the middle of a public hall. She won't quibble about sending someone after you."

Like lightning flashing in a dark room, his words suddenly illuminated something I had forgotten. Ice formed on my spine, and I breathed in sharply before I could stop myself.

"What?" Kiernan demanded.

Nausea grappled with my stomach. "I think she already sent someone."

Kiernan's grip on my hands grew so hard that I would have yanked them from him if I could have. "What do you mean? When?"

"The day I met Orianne. There was a man who followed me. He was waiting outside the house."

A vein pulsed in Kiernan's forehead. "And you didn't tell me?"

"I was going to tell you, but I forgot, what with meeting Orianne and the map and seeing Melaina renewing the spell and going to Isidros. I didn't remember until right now!"

"Is he out there now?" Kiernan asked.

I shook my head, unsure. We stood up together, creeping across the hallway to a window that looked out onto the street. I didn't see anyone at first, but then I noticed a drab-looking man trimming the hedge in front of the house two doors down. I squinted—the sky had darkened since we'd been inside, gray clouds building up above the city—but finally had to nod. "I think that's him," I said.

Kiernan scowled fiercely down at the man, his normally happy features locked in tension. Then he stomped back into my room and rounded on me when I had followed him and closed the door.

"Don't you see? We *have* to tell someone now. If she was having you followed before you'd even found out about any of this, if she was worried about you then—"

"This is more important than me!" I shouted at him. Lightning cracked outside, covering my yell. Rain dashed against the window in a sudden fit of storm. "Don't *you* see, Kiernan? This is about Thorvaldor, about making sure the right person is on the throne. If I can't do this, then none of it . . ." I faltered, shaking. "None of it—my whole life, all the lies—none of it will have been for anything. I have to find her."

Kiernan gazed at me, eyes narrowed. "You think you know where she is."

I nodded. That morning, I would have said I didn't have the faintest idea of where to start looking for Naila. But now, now I knew who had hidden her, and I knew where to look. "Where would you keep something, if you wanted to be able to lay your hand on it in a moment but didn't want anyone else to find it?"

He went still, his face suddenly even paler. "Oh no," he whispered. "You are *not* going to Saremarch. That would be like—like walking into a trap. Melaina could catch you there and no one would ever see you again."

"That's where she is," I argued. "Melaina must have her there somewhere. Right on her own land, where she could get to her if she needed to."

"You aren't going. It's too dangerous. I won't lose you again."

"It's not your choice!"

"I'll tell them myself," he threatened. "The king and queen. *I'll* tell them, Sinda, if you won't."

"Kiernan," I started, "please—"

I didn't get any further, though, because just then the world exploded.

"Sinda, get down!" Kiernan shouted, but I barely had time to turn away as my window, the one looking out over the garden, burst into a thousand flying pieces. The glass shattered inward, exploding over us in a rain of shards. I felt some of them slice my skin just before Kiernan collided with me to knock me down below the near side of the bed. A second later, limbs from the tree that shaded the garden flew into the room. They smashed against the walls, and I felt Kiernan wrapping his arms over my head. Wind howled outside and rain washed through the broken window like a tidal wave.

This isn't a real storm, I thought as something heavy crashed into my trunk. It had come on too quickly, too strongly. Rain and glass and limbs whirled overhead, falling where they would, but I could see none of it. All I could see was Kiernan's face over my own, the thought I had just had reflected in it.

The storm raged for what seemed like hours, but I knew that it really lasted for only a few minutes. Slowly, the wind abated, and the rain began to fall more softly. When no other debris had blown into the room for a long count of heartbeats, Kiernan finally pushed himself up off of me. At first it seemed quiet after the noise of the storm, and then I made out the sounds of feet running through the house, the maids' voices calling out, trying to find everyone.

"Are you hurt?" Kiernan asked.

I moved my head in a motion that might have been a yes or a no. Kiernan himself was covered in tiny cuts wherever his skin had been exposed, and I knew I couldn't look much better. "Scratched," I managed. "And my back hurts from falling. But nothing serious, I think."

Now Philantha's voice rose above the others. "We have to go out to her," I said.

Kiernan nodded before lurching to his feet and holding out a hand to help me up. Glass crunched under our feet as we turned to survey the room.

My window had been completely demolished, so I now had a great gaping hole to the outdoors on one wall. Limbs, leaves, and what looked like a piece of shuttering from a nearby house lay helter-skelter across the room. Something had knocked my trunk onto its side; its contents were spilled in a pool before it. Rain had drenched everything on the window's half of the room, including the bed. My own hair, I realized, was dripping, and Kiernan wiped a hand across his face to rid it of water, leaving a bloody trail.

I licked my lips and tasted coppery blood. "We were lucky, I think."

"Lucky," Kiernan repeated, but his eyes were dark.

We stumbled out of the room and down the stairs into the main entrance to the house. There gathered Philantha's household, shivering together in a tiny knot. Philantha knelt on the floor, her hands working quickly to tie a bandage on Tarion's arm. She muttered a few words and light sprang up around her hands to coat the bandage.

"There," she said briskly. "That will hold you until I can take another look." She straightened as she saw us coming down the stairs, and her eyes widened. "Sinda!" she barked. "Come here! Are you injured?"

I waved a hand toward my face and arms. "What you see. The window exploded. I think a limb might have come through it." I wasn't going to mention that the window had exploded *before* the first limb flew into the room. "But we're all right."

She shook her head, lips tight. "Never in my life. Such a storm. Luckily only one pane of glass in my study broke, or there might be a crater where the house used to stand."

I swayed against Kiernan, then glanced up at him as he put his hands on my shoulders to steady me. I hadn't considered what would have happened if the storm had hit Philantha's study like it had my bedroom. A crater, I thought, would have been getting off easy.

"Philantha," Kiernan began, "do you think that the storm—"

I elbowed him sharply enough that he let out a *whoof*. "Was the worst you've ever seen?" I finished for him.

"Certainly was one of the worst, though I was once on the

coast during a hurricane, and that tops this by a wizard's leap," she said.

Kiernan glared at me, but he didn't ask any more questions. I knew what he had been going to say, however. But if Philantha thought the storm was natural, I wasn't going to let him persuade her otherwise.

"Well, we're all here." Philantha surveyed us, hands on her hips. "We should go out and see if anyone else on the street is hurt. Gemalind, come with me. We'll get supplies. Kiernan, Sinda, you stay here and clean yourselves off before you come help. No use scaring the neighborhood any more than it's already frightened, and you two look like you were rolling in glass."

Several hours later, Kiernan and I sat in one of the empty bedrooms, one that had been untouched by the storm. Both of us sported a multitude of bandages; Kiernan kept picking at his. My things lay in piles on the floor or spread out to dry; I had been too tired to organize them in the new room. The two pages from the library, which had been blown about and crumpled by the wind and rain, sat on a low table with four books covering their corners to try to flatten them back into shape.

"That was Melaina," Kiernan growled. "You know it, and I know it. This was the only house on the street to be hit like that, and your room was the worst of all. We should have told Philantha."

"No." I folded my arms, trying not to wince as the motion pulled at the cuts on my skin. "She didn't seem to think it was strange, and no one else on the street did."

"That was no normal storm!"

"I know. But we don't have any proof, and if we tell her we think it was Melaina, we'll have to tell her about everything else, too."

"Which I'm all for doing," Kiernan said. "There no reason not to now. We know it's not Neomar, so Philantha won't choose her friend over us. You've never said she's close to Melaina."

"I know, but . . ." I shook my head, feeling confused. He was right, we should tell Philantha, but something I couldn't quite identify was stopping me. "It could put her in danger," I said finally. "If Melaina finds out that she knows, too, she could try to . . . do something to her."

"Like she tried to 'do something' to you?" He leaned forward on his chair and let out a breath. "Nameless God, Sinda! She tried to kill you."

"She might not have been trying to kill me," I insisted stubbornly, even though I knew that was unlikely. "She might just have been trying to scare me. Make me leave it all alone."

Kiernan blew a derisive breath upward so that his hair flopped on his forehead. "It doesn't really matter. You scared her into acting rashly today. If she's scared, she'll be even more dangerous. Once she realizes that she hasn't stopped you, she'll try again. And she won't fail next time. The woman is at the end of a plan to steal the throne back for her family. She isn't going to let one girl get in the way of that."

Here we were. Back to where we had been before the storm turned my bedroom upside down. I gazed at Kiernan. His face was utterly earnest; I could see the worry and fear etched into it. He wasn't going to give this up.

"We can tell now," he insisted. "The king and queen. Philantha. *Someone* who can help us. Tell me why we can't."

I shook my head. "Please, Kiernan. We can't tell anyone. Philantha—she could be hurt. And as for the others, we still don't have enough proof. They won't believe it; they won't *want* to believe it. We should lie low, make her think that we've been scared into giving it up, and then, when she doesn't expect it, we'll slip away to Saremach and find—"

But Kiernan wouldn't budge; he glared at me in the dim evening light, his face set. "It's too risky. She'll be watching you even harder now, if she doesn't try to hurt you again. Either we tell, or we give it up for real, Sinda."

I felt like he had kicked me hard in the gut; I actually hunched over, my arms around my middle. "Give it up?" I gasped. "What are you talking about?"

"What does it matter if Orianne or Nalia sits on the throne? They're both royal, aren't they? And Orianne is . . . good. She doesn't know anything about this. She'd make a fine queen."

I shook my head, pushing myself up out of my chair. I couldn't believe this, couldn't believe what he was saying. "We can't— Melaina— They were renegades! Her family tried to depose the true queen."

"Over a hundred years ago!" Kiernan lashed out. "So long ago that hardly anyone even remembers it."

"No! It matters!" I was pacing now, my arms wrapped tight around myself. How could he say this? How could he think that I could just walk away from this? "It matters! If we don't find her, if then all of it—my life—" My voice broke. I could hardly breathe; my lungs felt too small to draw the air I needed.

But Kiernan had curled his lips up and closed his eyes.

"That's what it really comes down to, doesn't it? That's why we can't tell. This isn't about having enough proof, or even about Philantha getting hurt. You have to find her yourself. This isn't just about the country, or the throne. This is about you proving that you're not nobody. If you can't be the princess, you'll be the savior of the princess."

Another feeling of being kicked, but this one hit harder, right in a place I had been trying to shield. "No," I whispered, but it came out low.

"You can't be just a scribe, or a wizard. Nameless God," he cried, raking a hand through his hair. "I wish they had never found you, never made you think you were the princess. Nothing else will ever be good enough, not now. You'll never be happy. You'll throw yourself into danger, take it all on yourself, just to prove that they were all wrong about you. And I just— I just—"

And without warning, he stepped in front of me, grabbed my shoulders to stop my pacing, and kissed me.

If I thought being kissed by Tyr had been what kissing was all about, I had been wrong. This kiss trampled Tyr's kiss, threw it to the ground, and danced on its grave. It was like being kissed by sunlight, or joy. Kiernan's arms wrapped around me, holding me so tight that I thought his hands might leave impressions on my back. But his lips were gentle, moving with mine as if they had done it for years, warm and soft. Little tingles of pleasure licked through my body, from my lips to my toes. I felt my own arms snake up around Kiernan's neck, and I thought I might drown in sensation.

And then there was coldness as air swept between our bodies. Kiernan gave me one last graze of a kiss, and pulled away. I

EILIS O'NEAL

gasped, like a drowning woman who has just had the air snatched away from her by the waves.

"I love you, Sinda," he said, not shakily but with certainty. "I have for—oh, years—before I even knew that I did. I loved you when you were the princess, and I love you now. I just want you to be happy. And I want you to be safe. I don't care if you're the Queen of Thorvaldor or a pig keeper in Mossfeld." He brushed a hand down the side of my face, his thumb running over my lips. "But you do, don't you?"

Kiernan was staring at me, his laughing face for once as serious as my own. I wanted more than anything to put my arms around him again, to let him, my best and only friend, kiss me until the world ended.

I couldn't do it.

"I have to find her," I whispered. "I have to."

I took a step back, raising my shaking hands. The skin around his eyes crinkled as he frowned in confusion. Tears stood in my eyes as I called on my power, feeling it coil in me. This spell, I knew, my heart breaking, would work.

"I'm sorry," I breathed.

White light flared from my palm, shooting toward Kiernan and bathing him in its brightness. He flinched and shut his eyes, his hands raised in front of his face, and then it was over. I let my own hands drop as my shoulders sagged.

"What was that?" he asked raggedly.

"A spell." I could barely look at him. "To keep you from telling anyone about Nalia. You won't be able to talk about it, or write it down, or even tell anyone about the spell. It's a block, but just for this."

He swallowed, his eyes glassy. "You won't remove it?"

I shook my head. "Not until I find her. Once I do, the spell will end on its own."

He closed his eyes. He looked like a starving man turning down a feast, or someone who has betrayed his heart's desire. "I can't help you," he said finally. "With Melaina after you, and that prophecy . . . I can't— I can't watch you be hurt, Sinda."

Not have him with me? Not have him there to watch my back, to make me laugh when I felt defeated? It was bitter, like ashes and blood on my tongue.

He stepped toward me and wrapped me in his arms. I had the feeling he was trying to memorize me, to imprint the feel of me against him in his mind. His lips moved against my ear. "I love you. I'm sorry. Please, be safe."

And then he was gone, the door swinging shut behind him, and my heart—rebellious and cruel—went with him.

EILIS O'NEAL

CHAPTER SEVENTEEN

The next few days passed in a haze. I knew that I should be on my guard, should be watching out for another assassination attempt by Melaina or, at the very least, her spies. Perhaps, though, she felt it too dangerous or too soon for another large-scale attack, because no ill befell me. But even without that worry, I knew I should be thinking about Nalia. I was going to have to sneak out of Vivaskari without Melaina realizing it and go looking for her in the very seat of danger: Saremarch, Melaina's own holdings. I should be thinking about protecting my own skin and saving the kingdom.

I couldn't think about anything but Kiernan. Sometimes it was in anger, over his leaving me. He had betrayed me, I sometimes felt. But most other times, I understood. I was set on this course, one that had so little chance of succeeding. Even the oracle had given me only a one in three chance of surviving. I could see that he wouldn't want to watch me die. So I was torn between feeling betrayed and wanting to throw myself into his arms and demand that he love me forever.

It had been different when I was the princess. Then I had looked at his flirtations with other girls and at least told myself that his heart lay there. It had been easy to think that, even though he always returned to me after every infatuation, he wanted only my friendship. And he must have held it in, kept his true feelings to himself, knowing that I would never have been allowed to marry a minor lord of Rithia, no matter what his parents might hope. I would marry for political reasons; we had both known that. There had been no reason to acknowledge that we could ever be anything more than friends. But still, it had been a thin façade, one that I could have seen through, if I had wanted to.

And when I was no longer the princess? Had I known? If I really looked, had I known? Yes, I had to admit, I had. But it was like knowing that you need air to breathe or water when you're thirsty. Something I knew, but without ever thinking about it, without even really considering it. I had held Kiernan's heart for so long that I had forgotten I had it, tucked away beneath my own.

So, yes, I had known. Hadn't his face inserted itself between Tyr and me, no matter how I tried to forget it? Hadn't I felt somehow guilty when I'd kissed Tyr, as if I were betraying Kiernan? And hadn't he come looking for me in Treb, hadn't he been with me every day he could since I returned to the city? I had told Philantha otherwise, but hadn't I felt strange with him for weeks, awkward, knowing somewhere inside me that things between us were changing?

Or maybe they weren't changing. Maybe they were just now becoming what they had always wanted to be.

What I wanted them to be.

EILIS O'NEAL

Because I did. I had felt it in that one kiss, how things could be. And I wanted it. Oh, how I wanted it.

But I had thrown it all away, by putting that spell on Kiernan against his will, by keeping him from doing what he thought he must do to protect me. I had seen the look of shock on his face when I used my magic on him. I didn't know how he would be able to forgive me, after that.

I had destroyed my chance at happiness with the one person who had always understood me.

All to save the kingdom that had abandoned me, or maybe just to prove to myself that I was worth something.

But if I thought I could wallow in my own problems for long, I was mistaken. I learned that five days after the storm, as I stood in line at the apothecary's shop.

"It's the king," the woman in front of me was telling the apothecary. "He's ill. His physicians are all at the palace, and half the wizards from the college, too. They aren't letting much out, but I heard a rumor about redvein fever."

The apothecary leaned forward across the counter. "Redvein fever?" he exclaimed, shaking his head. "When it comes on so quickly, the patient is likely to die. I—" He broke off, staring at me over the other woman's shoulder. "Young lady, are you all right?"

For I had swayed without realizing it, reaching out blindly to steady myself against the wall. Redvein fever. I closed my eyes and shivered. Neomar. He had gone to the country because of redvein fever. And the oracle, she had died of it as well. One who could have threatened Melaina's plan and one who knew of it, and felt guilty. So strange, that they should catch the same disease. It was a rare disease, after all. Stranger, that the king should catch it as well.

Too strange.

I shook myself. "Fine, I'm fine," I said. "But the king—did they say if it was bad?"

The woman looked troubled. "Aye, child. They say he's slipped into fevered dreams already, and none can call him out of them. The queen and princess are by his side, day and night."

I bought the herbs Philantha wanted without even glancing at them. On the way home, it seemed that around every corner I found people talking about the king. They whispered that the physicians could do nothing, nor the wizards. They murmured that the princess looked so grave and beautiful, even in her grief, so much older than her years. And with every step, I became more sure.

Melaina was behind this. She had sent the illness by magic, killing her sister all those years ago, so she wouldn't have a change of heart and tell their secret. She had caused Neomar to become ill so that he would have to leave the city for the country, where he would never have the chance to notice the spell they had created still active on Orianne. Perhaps he, too, lay dying even now. And now she would kill the king, so that Orianne could become queen, making her that much more bound to the throne.

I had not moved quickly enough.

Kiernan, I thought suddenly, *I wish you were here.* Here, walking beside me, to tell me that it was not too late, that we would go and find Nalia and put everything to rights. To put his arm around me so that I could press my face against his shirt and shake with worry for the man I had thought my father. To smile his reckless smile and say that, together, we would find a way.

The yearning in me was so strong that I looked up, almost believing that he would be standing before me. But he wasn't there. I could only hunch my shoulders and press my way through the crowds of whispering people, feeling small and all alone.

So while the city held its breath, waiting for the king to live or die, I prepared to dethrone the girl it thought was the princess. I did so carefully, sneakily, always looking over my shoulder for Melaina or her spies. It slowed me down so that what should have taken little more than a day took four. I bought food supplies under the cover of running errands for Philantha's cook and convinced Philantha that the entire household should have new boots so that I might have some, too. I arranged to rent a horse from a stable while visiting one with Tarion, under the pretence of helping him carry home several bags of feed. During a trip with Philantha to the college library, I found a map of northern Thorvaldor, one that showed Saremarch in detail, and felt no qualms about tucking it under my cloak and leaving with it. I hid the pages I had ripped out of the genealogies under a loosened floorboard under the bed in my new room, along with the copper container that held the oracle's confession. After a second thought, I put King Kelman's map with them, just to keep it safe. I practiced spells that would make me appear older or younger, blonde or red-haired. Even then, though, with such high stakes in front of me, I could feel the magic clenched inside, stoppered up so that it was almost useless, and my letting it out only a dribble at a time.

Finally, though, I decided that I had done all I could, short of mounting a horse and riding out the gates of Vivaskari. The only thing I had not done was tell Philantha I was leaving.

If I could have, I would have dithered and put off telling her for as long as possible. I had no ready lie this time; I had deliberately not fabricated one because I felt, somehow, that it might taint my quest. But I couldn't tell her the truth either. Finally, though, when all my things were packed, I forced myself to walk down the hall to her study and knock on the door.

"Come in, come in! Look at this," she demanded as soon as I had shut the door. She held up a long snakeskin, thin and papery. "Now, I think that, if we apply Tabitha's law, we'll be able to— well, it's hard to explain, but I'll show you and then—"

"I'm leaving, Philantha," I interrupted softly.

She paused, blinking once, and then hurried on, "Well, I have to say it is an inconvenient time—I'd much rather you stayed to help me with this. In fact, I insist. You can go see Kiernan this evening. Now—"

I shook my head and laid a hand on her thin arm. "No. I mean, I'm leaving the city. I have— I have something I have to do. I wish I didn't, but I can't ignore it anymore. I have to go, and I don't know when I'll be back." I felt miserable—scared and alone and deserting Philantha in the process.

Laying the skin down on a table, Philantha turned her bird-bright eyes to me. They searched my face, and I wondered if she would be able to see the truth there. Melaina would have ripped the facts from my mind with magic, but Philantha only nodded.

EILIS O'NEAL

"I can see that," she said. "But never fear. All this"—she swung a hand out to indicate her study—"will be here when you get back."

No judgment, no questions, just simple acceptance. It made me want to tell her so badly that I nearly spilled the entire story there at her feet, just to have someone else behind me, to let someone else *know*.

I wavered, unsure, teetering on the brink of telling or not telling. But finally, when I should have opened my mouth, I didn't. Whether from fear for her safety, or what Kiernan had said—that I wanted to find the princess all alone—or both, I couldn't tell. Whether that was weakness or strength on my part, I couldn't tell. So I only smiled a shaky smile, nodding in agreement, and left the study as quietly as I had come. I picked up my bag from my room and walked out Philantha's door toward the stable where I had arranged to rent a horse. I didn't look back at the house, or behind it, toward the palace where the king lay dying and the second false princess sat worrying over him, and where Kiernan surely walked the halls, wondering if I had gone. I did not look back at all. I was scared that, if I did, I wouldn't have the courage to go on.

The holdings of Saremarch lay just two days' journey from Vivaskari. I wanted to fly down the road, but I feared that a lone girl in a hurry would attract the wrong sort of attention. I also had a healthy sense of my own vulnerability; the roads near Vivaskari were generally safe, but lone travelers could still tempt thieves and other desperate sorts. So I traveled moderately, trying to stay near farmers' wagons or merchant caravans, people who might help me if I started screaming. I knew that, if I were really attacked, my magic might decide to assert itself in my defense, but I didn't feel like I could count on it.

For most of the first day, I rode with my shoulders hunched, starting whenever I heard someone approaching from behind. It seemed almost ludicrous to think that I could have escaped the city without Melaina's spies warning her, but no pursuit came, and I began to think that, for once, my luck had held, that I had slipped by them. I stayed the first night in a roadside inn after telling its owner that I was going to visit my sick father in a town quite far from Saremarch's borders. The next night, dusk fell before I reached a true village, so I begged shelter from a farmer and his wife whose house sat along the road. They didn't have an extra room, but they piled blankets in front of the fire and I slept well enough, leaving them a coin at my departure.

On the third day, I reached the edge of Melaina's lands.

The holdings of Saremarch were not large. A little farmland, enough to bring some money to the Harandrons. Mostly, though, woods covered Saremarch. From the map I had pilfered from the wizard's college, I saw that three small hamlets dotted the farmland, forming a rough semicircle around the only true village, March Holdings, which lay on the edge of the farmland and the beginning of Thorvaldor's northern forest. The village had grown around House Sare, the seat of the Harandrons, and that was where I planned to go first.

It took only until midday to reach March Holdings. Smoke rose from chimneys, and the thin trails made my hands tremble so much that my horse tossed her head and sidestepped in confusion.

EILIS O'NEAL

What was I going to do? I had no real plan, I finally had to admit, other than to ride into town and start looking for a girl my own age with a triangle of red spots on her arm. I needed a story, but Kiernan was the one who could invent elaborate reasons for being where you weren't supposed to be.

My heart spasmed at the thought of him, clenching in on itself, and I had to force myself to breathe in and out slowly. *He isn't here,* I told myself. *You're going to have to do it on your own. If you don't find her, no one will.*

Which wasn't, I thought, the most heartening call to arms I had ever heard. But it was enough, somehow, to make me tap my heels against my horse's side and start toward March Holdings.

As I entered the village, I thought I must look like a ghost riding on horseback: pale and drawn, with shaking arms and legs. Surely strange enough to make people suspicious. Still, though I drew first glances, no one spared a second. There was a traveling tinker, his wagon stopped in the center of the village, who had attracted the attention of most of the villagers. Women stood examining pots and pans, while children ran underfoot, or waiting in line with items to be mended. Locating a tiny stable, I paid a copper to tie my horse there and breathed a sigh of relief when the stable boy provided a story for me.

"You from Hol's Landing? Come down to see the tinker?" he asked.

I nodded cautiously.

The boy grinned gap-toothedly. "Told my auntie there he said he'd be coming through this week. She tell you?"

I nodded again, but was luckily spared from having to actually produce details about his auntie when the stable manager whistled him up. I ducked outside into the sunlight, thinking. It looked like most of the village was nearby, either haggling with the tinker or gossiping together. And if word of his arrival had spread, there was a chance that Nalia might come to see him herself. Maybe all I would have to do to find her was wait.

So I waited. A bench stood alongside the one tavern, and I sat there, trying to make it look as if I were merely waiting my turn with the tinker. I glanced back and forth slowly, attempting to appear merely curious about each new person walking across the road, but I studied them all closely. Once my heart leapt into my throat, only to plummet when I realized that the girl I had seen was too old to be Nalia. The sun moved across the sky so that I had to shift on the bench to stay in the shade, but I didn't see anyone who looked like she could be the lost princess.

For a while, I tried to occupy myself thinking about what Nalia would be like. I imagined her looking like Orianne, with that same grace and surety of movement, stately even in the common girl's clothes she would surely be wearing. They were related, after all, so it figured that I ought be looking for someone similar.

Picturing what Nalia would look like took only so long, though, so my thoughts eventually turned to what I would do when—and if—Nalia ever appeared. I had spent so much time worrying about sneaking out of the city undetected and reaching Saremarch without mishap that I hadn't given a great deal of attention to how, exactly, I was going to get Nalia to come with me.

Should I just lay the entire truth out before her? But what if she didn't believe me? I had spent enough time worrying about being believed that it seemed entirely likely that she would listen to my story and think me mad or stupid. Or perhaps not. What girl wouldn't like to be told that she was really a princess? But still, thinking about telling Nalia the whole truth made my stomach flutter uncomfortably. Maybe a . . . modified version of the truth would be better. I could say that I was the representative of an unknown relative in Vivaskari, one who had recently died and left her an inheritance. There could be papers that needed to be signed, but that could only be dealt with in the capital. That should get her to come with me, at least. Then, on the trip back, as we began to know each other better, I could slowly tell her the truth.

That plan fixed in my mind, I settled back on the bench and resumed my vigil. But if I had thought coming up with a plan would somehow make Nalia appear, I was wrong.

This isn't working, I thought as the shadows cast by the buildings lengthened across the village. The tinker's crowd had dwindled as people began to make their way home for supper. One of my legs had fallen asleep, and my stomach was calling vigorously for food. *What should I do?* I wondered as I stood up and, for no other reason than curiosity, walked over to the tinker's wagon. *Go to each door and ask if anyone knows a girl about my age, who might or might not look a little like me?* I didn't like the idea of drawing any attention to myself; this was Melaina's village, after all, and who knew what sort of spies she might have in it? But I didn't have time to wait, merely hoping that Nalia would walk up to me.

The tinker's wagon held nothing of real interest, and I had turned away, wondering how much a meal at the tavern would cost, when something seemed to reach out and yank at me. I staggered to the side so that a man bartering with the tinker put out a hand to catch me.

"Miss? Miss, are you all right?"

I nodded without looking at him. I couldn't have looked at him if I had tried. Because there, staring at me from the middle of the road, her shocked expression surely mirroring my own, was the princess.

EILIS O'NEAL

CHAPTER EIGHTEEN

She stared at me, one hand going to her chest and a look of discomfort flashing across her face. A dented pot hung from her other hand; she had obviously been coming to see the tinker. But she could feel the same pulling sensation I did—that much was clear by the way she stared at me in confusion.

The sensation was much stronger now, as I gazed at the real Nalia, than it had been with Orianne; instead of a tiny bit of soul calling to the bit left in me, I was confronted with the entire thing. But it seemed to dwindle a little the longer I looked at her, as if the magic of the spell were satisfied that I had noticed it and settled back down. I shook off the man who had caught me and raised a hand toward the princess.

Instantly, a wary foxlike look gripped her face. She glared at me, her eyes narrowing to slits, and then she spun on one heel and hurried back the way she had come.

I stood dumbly for a moment. "Miss?" the man said again.

"Thank you," I mumbled. "I was just dizzy." Then I picked up my skirts and dashed after the fleeing princess, heedless of the murmuring that I left in my wake.

She had turned between two houses and started jogging once she was off the main road. A small dirt track led away from the village into the forest, and I could just make out her small figure in the deepening shadow. I followed, but more slowly now, until the track ended at a tiny house. At the door, she darted a look behind her and, seeing me, whirled around to face me, her hands on her hips.

"Well," she demanded, "what d'you want?"

She was small, even smaller than me; I could see that as I approached. Naturally fine-boned, she was not at all tall like Orianne. Still, even in the forest gloom, I could see that she was a shade too thin even for a naturally tiny person. There was a sharp, hungry look to her mouth and eyes, which made her seem only more like a fox.

Even so, she looked like the queen, if you knew what to look for. And I, having spent my entire childhood thinking the queen was my mother, did.

"I—I've been looking for you—" I fumbled. Suddenly words seemed to flee from me; I couldn't figure out where to start, what to say. I had found the princess, I was sure of it, and I couldn't string two words together with a needle.

"It's your doing this, isn't it?" She gestured to her chest, where she must still feel the spell pulling us together. "Some sort of trick? If Porter Handover put you up to this, Nameless God's teeth I'll, I'll—" Her face flamed and she tossed her head, throwing back her hair in anger. "You tell him, I know what he thinks of me, what he thought of my gran, but he's no right to send some hedge witch out to spell me just for coming into town."

"I'm not doing this," I said, shaking my head vehemently. "It's a spell, but I didn't cast it."

EILIS O'NEAL

"Right. And that's why I didn't feel it till I saw you staring at me in the street. That's why you chased me through the woods." Her fists were balled at her sides, the knuckles white. "I haven't forgotten what Porter did last time he saw me—my house still smells up and down of pond scum. And now if he's got some frog charmer working for him—"

"I *didn't* cast it," I insisted. "I swear I didn't. But maybe . . . maybe I can shield you from it."

She glared at me, chin high. She looked like she was a minute away from either slamming her door in my face or striking me with her bare hands. I felt shaky and unsure, completely unprepared to try a spell. The magic raged inside me, fanned to leaping by the feel of the spell that bound us together and my own nerves.

Be calm, I thought desperately. I could see the spell that might protect us from the pulling sensation—a simple, low-level shield. But if I botched it, put too much power it, the shield could send us both flying across the forest with its force. *Please, be calm.* I raised my trembling hands, but it was no good. I was too anxious, too scared of letting loose and hurting her. I lifted my face toward the sky, trying to hold back tears.

You can do it, someone seemed to whisper in my ear. That voice, as familiar as my own. I jerked, expecting almost to see Kiernan come stepping out of the woods. But it was my own head that had produced his voice. Still, that momentary calmness, the sense of rightness that had come with the memory, was enough. In my mind, I imagined a gentle blanket falling over Nalia and myself, one that blocked the feel of the spell pulling us together.

I heard her intake of breath as the spell settled. Her eyes were narrowed at me as I dropped my gaze to her, but more consideringly than suspiciously. "Did you do that?" she asked.

I nodded.

"You swear it?"

"I swear."

She pursed her lips, then said, "I'm Mika Varish."

"I'm Sinda Azaway. And like I said, I've been looking for you."

It was a tiny house, much smaller than Aunt Varil's—just one room with dirt floors, a small cot, and a few pieces of hard-used furniture. Inside, Mika heated some water on the hearth, crumbling a few leaves into it, and handed me the mug of weak tea. Then, her own cup in her hands, she sat down on one of the two chairs and waved a hand at the other. She regarded me over the lip of the mug as I sat down, then said bluntly, "You talk like a lady. And I've heard your name. They talked about you when they found the real princess. Everyone else forgot it, but it stuck with me. Why would you come looking for me?"

My tongue felt thick and dry, so I gulped down a swallow of tea, then almost spit it out when it burned me. "Can I see your left arm?" I asked when I could speak.

"Why?"

"Can I just see it?"

Another of those crafty looks came my way, but Mika finally held out her arm. Carefully, like I would approach an injured animal, I turned it over so that her palm faced upward. She wore a patched brown dress, the sleeves a little too short. Hardly breathing, I pushed up the sleeve covering her left arm.

Three small reddish dots, arranged to form a crude triangle, lay just below the crook of her elbow.

I let her arm drop, resisting the urge to rub the same spot on my own arm, and thought frantically.

My plan, conceived when I was sitting on the bench outside the tavern, waiting for a girl like Orianne to show up, now seemed ludicrous. Worse than that, I knew without a breath of doubt that if I lied to Mika, if I told her anything but the absolute truth, we would never have a chance. If I told my story about a relative and an inheritance back in Vivaskari, the moment she learned the real truth, she would cease to trust me forever. I had only been with Mika for mere moments, but I already knew that this girl had been treated more harshly than I had ever considered. Her eyes told it, the sharp little motions she made when startled told it, and the bluster she summoned when cornered told it. She had been deceived and harried too many times in her life, and if I lied to her, I would lose her.

I had trained myself, in the time since I had seen Orianne being spelled through that palace window, to silence. Only two other people alive knew anything resembling the truth of what had happened sixteen years ago—Kiernan, whom I trusted more than I trusted myself, and the oracle of the Nameless God, who had sworn herself to her own silence. Those long, long days of secrecy made me quake to think of telling anyone else, even the true princess, around whom it all circled.

But there was no other way. Not if I wanted to gain her trust, not if I wanted to save Thorvaldor.

"Mika," I said slowly, "what I'm going to tell you, it'll sound crazy. But you have to believe me." She waited without speaking, and I swallowed. There was no easy way to put this; I just had to say it. "Until I was sixteen, I had that same birthmark. Or it looked like I did. Really, it was part of the spell that made me seem to be the princess." Again, she waited. "Right now, the girl in the palace has those same marks, but hers aren't real either. Because she's not the real princess any more than I was. Someone tricked the king and queen, double-crossed them by switching the princess not once, but twice."

I set the mug of tea down on the rickety table beside me. "Mika, there's only one girl who has the real birthmark. You. You're the real princess. You're Nalia."

She sat still for so long that I thought she hadn't heard me. Just as I was about to repeat myself, though, she pushed herself out of her chair. "You're right," she said flatly. "I think you're crazy. Or better yet, I think that you're playing a trick on me, the crazy wood woman's granddaughter. So strange, so poor, out there in her hut. Funny, wouldn't it be, to make her think she was the princess?

"I'm not stupid!" she snapped, stepping toward me so quickly that I scrambled backward out of my chair. "And you can tell Porter Handover so! Get out!"

"I'm telling the truth," I insisted. I forced myself not to take another step back, though I wanted to cringe or flee from her anger. Even being so small, so wary, she radiated a kind of furious power in her indignation. "Please, you have to listen! I don't know Porter Handover—I don't know anyone in March Holdings. I *am* who I say I am."

She shook her head, her sharp face tight. "Don't believe you."

"Then how did I know about your birthmark, unless you go showing it off to everyone? I bet that hardly anyone knows about it. And that spell that you felt, I can explain it. When they switched us—all three of us—they had to put a little of your . . . essence, your soul, into Orianne and me so that the spells that make us appear to be you would stick. That's what draws us together, because there's a little of you in me." She had stopped coming toward me, but with a snarl still on her face. I cast around wildly for something that would persuade her to hear my story. "I bet your parents are dead, or you thought they were. And I bet that they weren't from around here, that someone brought you here when you were just a baby. You said you live with your grandmother—"

I had wanted her to listen, but I wasn't prepared for the look of pain my words caused. Her arms dropped to her sides as she lowered her head, her dark hair falling in front of her face. "Lived," she said softly. "I lived with my gran. She's dead now."

A picture of the king dying in the palace flashed through my mind, and I wrapped my arms around myself. "I'm sorry."

Mika shrugged, a small motion. "She was sick for a long time. A cough got into her chest. Wouldn't come out. We tried all the remedies she knew, but it was just forest lore, not proper medicine. Didn't have the money for that. See, Sinda," she said, plopping back down in her chair and waving a hand around the room, "that's what makes me doubt you. Look around. I'm no princess. I can barely get enough to eat—I'm hungry half the time. Half the people in town won't even talk to me, on account of us being so odd and poor. I think about leaving, but I can't even scrape together enough to move down to Hol's Landing. How can I possibly be the princess?"

"It's the person who did this," I insisted. "She must have had you sent here, where she'd know where you were. But she wouldn't have wanted you to have any power, not even a little, so she—I don't know—told the villagers not to help you and your gran, or put a spell on them to stop them from liking you. Something to keep you here, but so far down you'd never be able to leave."

Mika smirked as she shook her head. "And who'd have that sort of power?"

Something made me not want to say her name; it was as if I feared that, by naming her, I would call her down on us. But if I were going to make Mika believe me, I would have to. "Melaina Harandron," I whispered.

The name made Mika jerk in surprise. "The baroness? She's the one who did it?"

I nodded earnestly. "Please, just let me tell you the story."

For a moment, I thought she would refuse me. But then she stretched her legs out in front of herself. "Go ahead," she said wryly. "I could use a good story."

Night had descended fully by the time I finished, and I had gone through another mug of weak, forest-gathered tea. Mika sat picking at the small fire. Finally, she said without looking at me, "You're a good storyteller, but it's asking a lot for me to believe you. I mean, a sixteen-year-old plot that only you and your friend know about. Spells and baby switching and king killing. It sounds like the poems bards make up."

"It's true," I said tiredly. "I saw the oracle's confession myself. Melaina tried to kill me with a storm, or at least scare me into keeping silent. The king is sick and no one, not all the wizards and physicians in Vivaskari, can cure him. He'll die soon, and then Orianne will be crowned queen. On your throne. By the Nameless God, Mika, I swear I'm telling the truth."

EILIS O'NEAL

One corner of her mouth lifted. "I wish you were. It'd be something, to think that I wasn't really born to nothing. 'Cept that I don't know anything about being a princess. Even if you took me back to the palace and showed me to them—if we didn't get killed on the way—they wouldn't believe you."

"They would. You're the last piece of the puzzle," I insisted, though a little doubt had crept into my heart at her words. What if she was right? What if, even with the real princess beside me, no one believed me? After all, who was I? Just the false princess, a dead weaver's daughter, and an eccentric wizard's scribe.

"They'll believe us," I whispered. "They'll have to."

"I can't—" Mika started, then froze. "Did you hear something?"

"What?" I asked.

She rose, the fire poker in her hand. "I thought I heard something outside."

"I didn't hear anything," I began, but just then I did. The clink of metal and the snort of a horse. Then the low rumble of a man's voice, followed by the soft shuffling of a dozen feet moving forward.

"Mika," I whispered. "That sounds like men—lots of them."

"Maybe they aren't here to hurt us," she said, with her eyes on the door. But I could tell she didn't believe that. She had the look of an animal being backed into a corner, ready to fight or to try to dart away. From the set of her body, I could tell that this was not the first time she had felt that way, though the wideness of her eyes might have meant this was the worst time.

We couldn't just wait for them to come in and grab us. And there was no other way out, not even a small window in the back.

"They might not be ready yet. We could break out of the door, try to run. We might surprise them."

"Or they might skewer us like dinner," Mika hissed.

I shook my head. "If you die, the spell on Orianne could fail. She needs you alive."

"What about you?"

In my mind, the oracle said, *I saw a triangle set in a storm. One of its sides crumbled and fell away, leaving only two.*

"They'll catch us for sure if we stay in here," I insisted. "On three, we run. One, two, three!"

We burst through the door together and into a ring of armed men.

We had surprised them, and without that, we never would have had a chance. Perhaps ten men formed a semicircle near the door of Mika's house, half horsed and half on foot, two holding torches. Two of the horses shied, forcing the unhorsed men to skitter out of their way and opening a chink in their wall.

"Run," I screamed at Mika, who was still gripping the fire poker in her hand. She dashed toward the space the horses had created and had to swing the poker at the first man who approached her. Maybe they had been told not to harm her, because instead of reaching for his sword, he only ducked out of the way. That duck cost him as his foot slipped in the darkness and sent him to one knee.

I had tried to go the other way, to split their forces, but the men on my side of the circle regrouped more quickly than their comrades. Two advanced toward me, faces set. Magic flamed inside me, but too strongly, so I clenched down on it instinctively before letting out a thin, weak spell. The gust of power that

EILIS O'NEAL

should have frozen them in their tracks only slowed them, too tamped down to do any good.

I whirled, ready to follow Mika, and saw her grabbed by one of the men, her fire poker falling to the ground. He lifted her off her feet even as she twisted and fought like a wildcat; she drew blood on his face with her nails, and I saw her teeth clamp down on his hand. Still, he held on doggedly, only to suddenly cry out as a flash of silver spun through the air toward him from the forest. A second later he dropped her to the ground, a dagger protruding from his left shoulder. She rolled as she fell, then was on her feet and running toward the spot in the woods from which the dagger had flown. From the darkness, I heard a voice call, "This way!"

I might have made it, except that the sound of the voice made me stumble in surprise. *Kiernan?* I thought dumbly just as something *pushed* me and sent me sprawling on the ground. Then a second spell hit me, the real version of the one I had tried on the soldiers. My muscles locked in place so that I couldn't even turn my head.

"Go," I rasped, not knowing if Mika could hear me, just before my mouth froze shut.

"Find them," snapped another familiar voice, one that I had heard in my nightmares all too frequently these last few days. "She knows the woods, so hurry, before they get very far." A moment later, horse hooves thudded into my line of vision. I couldn't look up, but I didn't need to; even as my head swam and blackness edged my eyes, I knew who sat on that horse.

"Hello, Sinda," said Melaina Harandron.

CHAPTER NINETEEN

I woke on a pallet in a small dark room with every inch of my body aching. Raising my head, I had to clench my teeth to keep from moaning. Something had happened, something bad, and I couldn't remember—

In my head, a voice as dark as night said: *Hello, Sinda.*

I sat up so quickly that the blood rushed to my head, and it took a moment before I could see again. When I could, sweat broke out along my back as I gazed at my surroundings.

A room no more than five paces across. Stone walls. No windows to the outside, only a single door with a small, barred window set into it, through which a broken square of torchlight fell onto the floor of the room.

"Hello?" I said tentatively.

No one answered.

"Hello?" I called more loudly. "Please, anyone—I'm trapped! Someone, please, help me!"

Again, nothing. Standing up, I staggered over to the door, only to find that it had no latch on this side. I laid my hands against it, reaching for a spell similar to the one I had used to open the mausoleum's door in Isidros. But my magic caught inside me, blocked by something not of my making. I reached again, trembling, and still I couldn't bring it to the surface. So I banged on the door until my hands hurt from hitting it, without budging it in the slightest. The barred window offered no help. By standing on my tiptoes, I could press the side of my face to it and see a tiny sliver of hallway, but nothing else.

My heart, which had been beating faster than a humming-bird's wings, fell toward my feet. A line of sweat trickled down the side of my face, but I felt cold enough to shiver. There was no way out, no one to hear me.

"Please," I whispered as I slid weakly down the door and landed in a heap on the floor. "Please."

Not even a mouse answered.

I had no idea how long I waited in that tiny room. Six times men in gray uniforms, swords hanging from their belts, opened the door and entered. They left a tray of food each time, emptied the chamber pot in the corner. They didn't speak to me, not even when I barraged them with questions, and eventually I merely huddled on the pallet, watching them. I didn't even attempt any spells; my magic was well and truly blocked, as inaccessible to me as the other side of the door.

At first, my mind ran circles around itself. Had that really been Kiernan I had heard calling from the forest? It had sounded like him, and I would have known his voice anywhere. But he had said he wouldn't help me, had feared that something just like this would happen to me, and hadn't wanted to watch it. And surely he was angry with me because of the spell I had laid on him, too angry to forgive me so easily. I had seen the look in his eyes when he realized what I had done, and it had been one of betrayal. And yet, through it all, had he had a change of heart and come after me anyway?

Had Mika escaped, with or without Kiernan? She would know the woods, might know a place to hide from Melaina and her men. If Kiernan was with her, would he try to take her back to the city? The spell I had cast would have broken the moment I found Mika, so he would be able to tell the king and queen what had happened. Or were they both trapped like I was? Should I knock against the walls, as people did in stories, and hope that one of them knocked back?

Was the king alive or dead? Was Orianne still princess, or mere days away from becoming queen?

I explored the scant space in the room, looking for any way out. But it was as tight a cell as any dungeon. There would be no escape from here except by magic, and, try as I might, I couldn't reach mine. Perhaps the room itself was spelled, or maybe Melaina had cast one on me after I fainted outside Mika's house.

For the first two days—or what I took to be days—I lived in a state of constant fear. Fear for myself, for Kiernan and Mika. I vibrated with it, felt it hugging me from the moment I woke up until I fell asleep. Would she kill me, or torture me, or merely keep me in this cell until I was a tottering old woman? I didn't know, and the not knowing was worst of all.

But even fear has its limits. Gradually, though, when nothing changed, I felt myself settling down to wait. Melaina could have killed me as I lay on the ground outside Mika's house. She had sickened Neomar, had killed her own sister. She would not leave me alive if she could help it. She was a careful plotter, concerned about leaving no trace of her sedition. The only time in sixteen years that she had acted rashly had been when she sent the storm against me. She had plotted this coup to the last detail. But even her caution would not keep her from killing me now, because I knew too much.

That was, unless she wanted something. Since I was still alive, I decided, she must need something from me. And that gave me the slenderest strand of hope to cling to, the only thing keeping me from deepest despair.

So I waited.

And finally, after two days or four, Melaina Harandron came to see me.

"I apologize for the way I've kept you, Sinda," she said. "Even your aunt's house in Treb was, I expect, more luxurious than this."

I said nothing from my seat on the pallet. She had come alone, though I did not doubt a whole troop of guards stood in the hallway, ready to fling open the door if she so much as raised her voice.

She wore a simple gown of deep blue, her dark hair coiled around her head like a crown. Even the gown, though, did not seem as out of place in the cell as her voice. It was like velvet, so dark and melodious you wanted to fall into it and never come out. I held myself still, striving not to fall under its spell.

She shrugged, a delicate motion that belied the steel beneath her skin. "Still, it is the only room in House Sare that can keep you from using magic to escape, so what can we do?"

I breathed out sharply. "House Sare? Shouldn't you call it House Feidhelm?"

I saw her throat flash as she swallowed, but otherwise she seemed not to have heard me. She surveyed me and I, knowing that I must look a wreck from the God knew how many days and nights I'd spent in here, had to resist the urge to sit up straighter. "Sinda, it doesn't have to be like this."

"Like what?" I spat. I had imagined, while I waited, what I would say when she came to see me, but all my carefully prepared words seemed dim and far away. I felt a little giddy, reckless, with nothing to lose. "You betrayed Thorvaldor—you betrayed the king and queen!"

Again, that shrug, a tiny lowering of her head. "Betrayal is a harsh word. Rather, I like to think that I am righting old wrongs."

"No, you're just doing what your family's good at. Your ancestor betrayed his sister all those years ago. He tried to take her throne, just like you're doing now."

"But was he wrong?" she countered. "They were twins, after all. And by all accounts, Aisling was a weak queen, a bit stupid, really."

"It was *her* throne," I insisted. "If he thought she wouldn't rule well, he could have offered her counsel, helped her become a better queen. Not tried to depose her."

"As I should have done? Offered counsel to the king and let my daughter inherit a tiny barony when she has as much royal blood as your Nalia?"

"Yes," I growled, my hands in fists in my lap. "Yes, rather than what you did." I felt my face twist up as I stared at her.

EILIS O'NEAL

"You subverted the oracle at Isidros, then killed your own sister after she helped you. You sent redvein fever to Neomar and the king to kill them, too. You might have killed your husband, I don't know. You gave up your own daughter, switched her with me and the princess. You left Mika poor and alone. You made me think I was the princess. You ruined all those lives, and none of it has even touched you."

"Do you think so?" she asked, and, for the first time, I heard a raggedness on the edge of her voice. "As you say, I gave up my sister, my friend in the college. I gave up my daughter. I saw her only three times before she came to live at the palace, when I went to renew the spell on her. You will never know what those things cost me." He face had gone so white that it stood out in the dark room, and her hand shook as she raised it to her neck. "Do not say that none of it has touched me."

She stood in silence for a long time, her eyes on some distant point only she could see. Finally, she turned her gaze back to me. "But it has cost you, too. Has it not, Sinda?"

I watched her warily, nerves prickling along my back. She might have come to see me, but I didn't know what she wanted of me. Now, though, I thought we were getting closer to it.

"It cost you your place in the world, your very sense of who you were. Your entire life—a lie. The people you loved, so eager to get rid of you once they no longer needed you. And what did you have to look forward to when you left the palace? An aunt who didn't want you and let you go without a word of protest? A dotty old wizard when the college wouldn't accept you? Love from Kiernan, whose family will never allow you to have him now?"

I had stiffened with each sentence, the sliver of truth in each like a piece of glass rubbing against my heart.

"I've watched you, Sinda, especially after you came back to the city. I've kept track of you. But what I've seen, it has not been encouraging, has it?"

"Because of you," I managed, more weakly than I had meant. Her words were traps, briars meant to snare me, and I could feel them digging under my skin.

She shook her head, the light from the window catching the pins in her hair so they winked like stars. "Because of them. The crown used you and tossed you aside when it was finished with you. But they didn't have to. They could have helped you, rather than shipping you off to a backward village the same day they told you who you were. Is that why you want to restore Nalia to the throne? For all the goodness her family did you?"

The giddiness in me fell away as I scrabbled to keep up with her, to refute her. "No, they were right. I might have been a danger—"

"A danger?" Melaina laughed. "You? Poor, awkward Sinda, never anyone's idea of a true princess. Sinda, who left without so much as a fight, without asking for anything at all for the life they had stolen? So timid, so good at following rules." Her face hardened. "They wanted you out of the way, and they never thought about you again once you were gone."

I didn't answer. I tried to shake my head, but all I wanted was to wrap my arms around my knees and curl into a ball of misery. *True enough*, part of me whispered. *What she's saying is true enough.*

No, I told myself. *Not all of it.*

EILIS O'NEAL

But enough. Enough of it is true.

She regarded me as the thoughts swirled in my head, stared at me for a long time. Then, slowly, Melaina's face loosened, a smile curving her mouth.

"They were wrong, Sinda," she said.

"What?" I choked.

"They were wrong to send you away. You did have power, didn't you? It was just hidden by the spell that made you seem to be the princess. You have it now, all coiled inside you. I could teach you to use that power, much better than poor Philantha can. You could be powerful, Sinda, a force for good in Thorvaldor. That is what you wanted, isn't it, when you were the princess? To do what's right?"

She took a step closer to me, close enough that I could smell the sweet scent of her skin. "I want people like you around Orianne. People who can make her a strong queen, a good queen. And you, with all that magic inside you, with all the things a princess should know in your head, you could be her greatest ally. A wizard, a councillor." She smiled gently. "Someone even the Earl of Rithia would think good enough for his son."

She was painting a picture in my head, so vividly I could see it. Myself, no longer awkward and unwanted, but strong, striding through the palace in wizard's robes. Content, with a place in the world at last. With no more strife between Kiernan and me, because I would be safe from harm. It was what I wanted, wasn't it?

Yes, in my deepest heart, yes. I wanted to be respected, to be useful, to be loved. I closed my eyes, seeing it all.

And then I forced them open, the images in my mind scattering. "You can't find her, can you?" I asked.

Melaina's eyelids flickered in the dim light.

"You can't find her," I repeated. "She's out there with Kiernan, and you can't find them. That's what this is about, isn't it? You want me to tell you where they've gone. Well, I don't know. Kiernan's probably taking her back to the city right now. He's probably already there. They'll tell the king and queen and—"

"The king is dead," Melaina said, sharp as a blade. "He died the day after I left the city."

If I had been standing I would have staggered. Sitting, I clutched my stomach with my hands. "No." I shook my head. "You're lying."

"I'm not," she said easily. "The coronation will be in four days. I managed to convince the queen of that before I left. After all, her daughter might have survived the prophecy given at her birth, but who knows if whoever was foiled then might not try now, while she is vulnerable and uncrowned. No one can see her, not until she is crowned—not you, not Kiernan, no one but her mother and her most trusted councillors." She smiled again. "After that, she will have the entire army at her command, and every noble will have vowed loyalty to her. She will have been blessed and sanctioned by a priest of the Nameless God. She will be queen—the embodiment of Thorvaldor." Melaina tilted her head, eyes shining at me. "You know how much harder it is to topple a monarch than a mere princess—your precious Aisling proved that a hundred years ago. Once Orianne is queen, your words won't mean anything, even if you could find someone to listen to them. And then, then I can find your Mika at my leisure, and put her somewhere where no one will ever find her again."

"I found her," I said, "even with all your planning."

EILIS O'NEAL

She nodded gravely. "True. I've wondered how."

"Your own spell." But the taunt felt empty. I felt empty. Melaina had planned too well. Kiernan would not be able to get Mika to see the queen, and any story he told could be seen as a plot. Clever, Philantha would have said, very clever. "When I'm near her, I'm drawn to her. The same with Orianne. You didn't get all her soul out of me when you removed that spell."

"Ah." Melaina's mouth tightened. "I wondered if we had been able to get every last bit of Nalia that we put into you. I thought perhaps not. It worried me a little, but I had no idea that it would link you that way. A pity, then, that I didn't. Still, it didn't matter, did it? I was watching you before I saw you in the palace that day, and I've been watching you since then."

"You were a little slow in stopping me, though," I said. "I got here, didn't I? I found her."

Her cool eyes frosted a little more. "I had to make sure the king's illness was sufficiently progressed before I came after you. It was quite helpful, though, for me not to be in the city when he died. Fewer ties back to me, that way. I have you to thank for that."

"We'll stop you," I said roughly. "Somehow."

Melaina had turned toward the door, but she looked around at my words. Her voice lost its velvet, going tight as a bowstring. "You've already lost. Don't you see, Sinda? You're nothing, a nobody. A fake, meant only to be replaced by the real thing."

Breathing out sharply, she then smoothed her gown deliberately, brushed a bit of imaginary dust from it. "I won't see you again," she said more calmly. "I ride for the city today." She laughed, and it sounded like bells.

"There's a coronation, you see."

CHAPTER TWENTY

Two more meals came. Did that mean one day had passed, or two? I had no idea, not knowing how often Melaina chose to have me fed. Or even if she would have me fed at all much longer. I had little appetite, but I forced myself to eat anyway, unsure if more food would be coming.

What to do now? I couldn't help thinking of it, even though I knew that all my thoughts would make no difference. The king was dead, had been dead for days. Normally, it would be weeks before the coronation of a new monarch, after the country had had time to mourn the passing of the old one. But now, with Melaina stoking the queen's old fears for her daughter's safety, probably no one would look askance at a hasty coronation. They might not even wonder at how cut off the queen and princess were from everyone but a few councillors. The country was still in love with the idea of Nalia, the princess who had been hidden and then found again. No one would want to risk her.

Which meant that Melaina was right. Even if Kiernan had gotten Mika to Vivaskari, he would find no one to listen to our story.

We had failed, I realized miserably. Orianne would be crowned, and Melaina would then have the time to hunt down Mika and toss her away in a cell like this one. And I, well . . . what good would there be in keeping me alive at all? Probably she would keep me alive until she found Mika, on the slim hope that I would help her locate the real princess. But afterward . . . A triangle, one side falling away.

Perhaps, I thought dully, I should take Melaina up on her offer. I could pretend to have a change of heart and vow to protect Orianne instead of Mika. She would have me watched, of course, so closely that there would be little chance of my finding a way to subvert her. But there would be a chance. At least then I would be alive, and not trapped or dead. The thoughts swirled in my head until I had to shake myself out of them. Truly, I doubted that I could make Melaina believe I had given in to her. She had seen the vehemence in me already, and I had never been a good liar. I had always had Kiernan for that.

Kiernan.

I had been foolish, I supposed, in those few days after he had said that he loved me. Foolish even to let myself relive those words. Melaina was right; his family would never let him marry me. Philantha had told me how they were searching for a bride for him, now that there was not even the slim chance that the princess of the realm would choose her best friend. I had never asked him about it; something in me, unknown at the time, had always balked, hadn't wanted to know. No, I would never be allowed to marry Kiernan. Not even in a few years, once I felt old enough to marry, even if I had managed to learn enough by then to gain the rank of Novice wizard. I would still be poor and common and not good enough.

If he still loved me at all, that was. Hadn't I pushed him away, laid a spell on him that might have wrung all the love out of him? Even if he had come after me, it might have been out of pity, or the old debt of friendship between us. Probably he had stopped loving me, had seen how dangerous it would be to love someone like me.

I tried to push the thoughts away, but they sucked at me like a swamp. I had to be strong, I told myself. I had to think of a way out of this.

But there in Melaina's cell, try as I might, I could not see one.

I had been dozing when they came for me. Heavy footsteps on the stone floor of the hall and the sound of chain mail clinking woke me.

I pushed myself up from the pallet, lips and throat dry. Maybe I had been wrong about Melaina keeping me alive until she found Mika.

The footsteps paused, and I heard a voice say stubbornly, "The baroness said she wasn't to be moved."

"She also said she was to be kept alive. If that fire gets down here . . ."

"They'll have it out before that," the first voice argued.

"I'm not taking the chance. You might be willing to face her with that chit charred to a cinder, but I'm not. She's just a girl, Kev. A thief or somewhat. What can she do?"

A fire? House Sare was on fire? I sniffed the air but smelled nothing. Still, House Sare was large, and the smoke might not have reached . . . wherever I was.

The voices stopped, and then the door to the cell flew open,

EILIS O'NEAL

banging against the wall. One of the men shouldered his way inside, then gestured to me. "Show me your hands," he ordered. I raised my hands slowly. "We're moving you. Don't try anything. Just come with us, and you won't be hurt."

I nodded back at him and didn't flinch when he grabbed my upper arm and hauled me forward. The other man, Kev, glared at me as we stepped into the hall, then took hold of my other arm. Together, they hustled me down a narrow hallway toward a set of stairs. Through one open door, I saw wine bottles stacked to the ceiling, and I shook my head. I had been in some converted room of Melaina's wine cellar.

Up the stairs and down several more hallways. The men didn't speak; their bruising grips on my arms said enough. I had to take two steps to every one of theirs to keep up, so I didn't have a chance to find my bearings. Finally, they pushed on a set of doors that opened into a stable yard, and into chaos.

There was a fire. It blazed on the rooftops of the buildings across the stable yard, lighting the night so that I could see everything inside it. A line of people with water buckets had already formed, but it looked almost too late for their plan. Several servant women were trying to organize a group of scullery girls and stable boys, herding them toward the gate that led to the lawn and woods beyond the house. Men from the stables, where the fire seemed to burn most wildly, hauled frightened animals toward the gates. The entire household looked to be in the stable yard or fleeing it.

"Where should we take her?" Kev asked.

"Out the gate," the other man said. "We'll tie her to a tree, keep a watch." With that, they yanked me into the fray.

The stable yard was a large square, made up on three sides by the house and stable and on the last by the open gate toward which I was dragged. The fire roared furiously into the night sky, moving faster than the people trying to stop it, and the heat from its flames felt like desert wind. Glowing cinders rained down, and we had to dodge the people racing around with blankets to smother them. One landed on my arm, burning me, and I cried out, but my captors didn't even slow their steps.

Suddenly, shouts filled the air, followed by the sound of some part of the stable crashing down. Sparks flew higher, showering the stable yard, and then a pile of hay only a few feet in front of us exploded into flames. I tripped as the two men jerked me backward and landed in a heap at their feet. The blaze that had been the pile of hay shot upward in a column of fire, spewing flames and smoke. I felt dazed by the noise, smoke, and heat, by the crackling menace of the fire, but the men holding me showed no mercy. They pulled me up and, tugging on me, took a few more steps toward the outer wall and gate.

But I let my feet drag, as if the fall had stunned me even more than it had. Because there, at the edge of the stable yard, where no one noticed them in the confusion, stood two cloaked figures who were not fleeing or attempting to fight the fire. One had the hood of the cloak up, face hidden, but the other had pushed his hood back and was scanning the crowd so intently he looked like he was trying to memorize it. The wind that whipped the fire into more and more frenzy blew a piece of blond hair into his eyes, and I thought my heart might stop as he hastily brushed it away.

At just that moment, Kiernan's eyes locked on mine.

I didn't think, or worry, or hesitate. For once, the magic was there when I reached for it; maybe it rejoiced at being unfettered by the blocking spells in Melaina's cell, or maybe I was so desperate my own fears didn't get in the way. Whatever it was, the guards holding my arms flew suddenly forward, propelled by the wind Philantha had taught me to call up to float feathers across her study. They slammed into the wall before us and, before anyone else noticed, I picked up my skirts and ran.

Kiernan didn't speak as I reached him. He simply reached out and grabbed my hand so tightly that I thought the bones might snap. Then we were running, Mika's tiny, cloaked form on his other side. We dashed past a contingent of servants hurrying the same way, but they hardly seemed to notice three more people fleeing from the fire.

Behind us, the fire enveloping House Sare burned higher and higher as we disappeared into the night.

We ran for perhaps a quarter hour, Mika now leading the way. She slipped between trees and over rocks so easily it seemed like she had been born in the forest. She might have been able to run forever like some night creature, but I had been living in a cell five paces across for who knew how many days, with who knew how many meals a day. Finally, I had to yank my hand from Kiernan. Then, doubled over and gasping, I stumbled to a stop and braced myself against a tree.

The two stopped without a word, though Mika immediately set herself looking back toward House Sare, shoulders tense. It took long minutes, but finally I managed to breathe normally. Raising my head, I found Kiernan staring at me, a fierce grin splitting his face.

"You did it," he whispered fiercely. "You made the magic work. You tossed those guards away like they were pillows!"

I felt like I might laugh until I couldn't stand, or cry until I couldn't see. "You rescue me, and the first thing you say is about my magic?" I managed.

Kiernan hardly seemed to hear me. "I was wondering if I should charge them, and probably die doing it, and then they just flew away from you. You did it: you called it up just when you wanted it." He laughed delightedly, and I found myself laughing, too. "So we didn't rescue you," he added. "We just set the fire, made the diversion. You rescued yourself, Sinda."

Almost, I took the step across the space that separated us and threw my arms around him. But then, just before I raised my foot, Melaina's taunts in the cell seemed to echo in my mind.

You're nothing, a nobody. A fake, meant only to be replaced by the real thing.

Even flushed from running, his tunic dirtied from the dash through the woods, he looked so beautiful, so . . . noble. Melaina had offered me the chance to stand on equal footing with him, to be powerful enough that it would be possible to have him. Not just for kisses stolen here or there, but forever. And I had refused her.

I pushed the thoughts away, but that hint of doubt made me hesitate, and I saw Kiernan's face grow still when I didn't say anything.

"I thought you weren't going to help me," I blurted out. Kiernan's shoulders hunched slightly, but I pressed on. "I thought you said I was on my own."

I could see Kiernan flush even in the darkness. "I know what

EILIS O'NEAL

I said. But it was all a bluff. I wanted to . . . slow you down. I hoped that, if you thought you'd be alone, you would hesitate. And that if you hesitated, I could come back in a few days and talk you out of it. Stupid, really, because I knew how important it was to you. But honestly, I didn't think you'd go alone. I just wanted to stop you, keep you safe. I didn't ever really intend to abandon you. I would have gone with you, if I'd realized you were really leaving.

"But then, before I knew it, the king was sick, and you were gone. And just after I found out, the day before the king died, I overheard someone saying that Melaina was planning a trip back to Saremarch. Some sort of emergency with her estate, something so bad she had to go, even with the king so ill. I figured that she knew you were gone, that she was coming for you, and I realized how just stupid I'd been. I thought I was protecting you, but I just put you in more danger. So I slipped out before her—left a note for my parents saying I had urgent business outside the city and had to go. I expect they're combing the countryside in a panic for me right now. Anyway, I took a horse and rode faster than the Nameless God's breath to find you. I figured you'd come here first. I stopped in the tavern in March Holdings, and some of the locals were talking about a girl they'd never seen who scared another girl into running out of town. So I took a chance that it was you. But I was too late again." He gripped me by the shoulders, his hands hot. "I'm sorry, Sinda. I truly am. I should never have left you."

He hadn't really abandoned me. Maybe he had under-estimated my strength of will in this, but he hadn't abandoned me. Sweet, the words should have been sweet. But all I could hear was Melaina's voice in my ear, telling me that it didn't matter, that I would never be good enough for him, never good enough for his family.

I shook my head, pulling back out of his hands. "You were right, at least about what happened. She did catch me—she could have killed me. You were probably right to want to threaten to leave me, even if it was a bluff."

"No, I—"

I shifted away from him, my head down, but I could see the hurt in every line of his body. "Let's not talk about it now, Kiernan. Please, I'm glad that you came. You have no idea how glad. But we have other things to worry about."

I turned to Mika, who had been staring off toward House Sare during our exchange, as if she couldn't hear it at all. "What made you believe me?"

Mika snorted. "The soldiers. Why else'd they have come for us, unless you were telling the truth? And the baroness with them. I saw her, just before we ran off. I've seen her before, from a distance, but she's never come to my house. So I figured you weren't as crazy as you sounded." She grinned and jerked her head at Kiernan. "Your friend's a good convincer, too."

Kiernan snorted himself, shaking his head, but I felt a wash of relief knowing that the spell I had laid on him had broken just when I'd set it to—after I found the true princess. My relief was quickly replaced by another revelation, though. *They're friends*, I realized with surprise. But maybe it shouldn't have been so surprising. After all, he had been friends with Orianne, too.

"Then we all understand," I said. "Melaina told me that the king's dead, and that there'll be a coronation for Orianne in four days."

"Three days now," Kiernan interrupted. I could still see the hurt I had dealt him with my coldness, but, true to his nature, he had squashed it down until only I could have noticed it.

Then it had been just two meals a day, I counted ruefully before continuing. "She said that they're keeping Orianne away from almost everyone. Something about how whoever failed to hurt her before—the prophecy and all—might try now, before she's crowned. Which means we only have one time that we'll be able to see her and the old queen."

"The coronation itself," Kiernan said. "They'll have to let people in for that."

I nodded. "But even then Melaina will have set precautions. Her people will reach the city before we do. She'll be watching for us."

"So how'll we get into the coronation?" Mika asked. "Won't there be guards and soldiers?"

"A lot of them," I said grimly. I bit my lip. "I don't know how we'll get in. I'll figure it out on the way there. Maybe Philantha will have an idea; we can go there first."

"We have horses tethered just a little farther on," Kiernan said.

"Not that I can ride mine worth the Nameless God's toenails," Mika put in.

He waved a hand to shush her. "Can you make it?" he asked me.

I smiled. I was tired and hungry, scared almost out of my wits at what we had to do. But for now, I was with him again, with my best friend, and that was enough to give me strength.

"Lead on," I said.

CHAPTER TWENTY-ONE

We had to hurry to reach the city before the coronation, but we also had to stay off the road. We kept to the woods as long as we could, then cut across farmers' lands, following the tracks they used to see to their fields. There was no time for long conferences, and at night we nearly fell to the ground with exhaustion. So I heard Kiernan and Mika's story only piecemeal, during the times when we had to walk the horses or stop to eat or relieve ourselves.

They had fled into the woods that first night, Mika threading her way down animal paths she knew and Kiernan following behind her. There had been a cave some distance from her house, and they had hidden there for over a day, fearful that Melaina's guards would still be searching the woods. After that, it was Kiernan who ventured into March Holdings to buy food and see the lay of the land. The soldiers hadn't been able to see him clearly in the night, he had hoped, but he spent little time in town in case they were looking for strangers. But he managed to glean that a villager, whose house lay closest to the road that led to House Sare, had seen a troop of men heading toward the manor, the baroness with them.

They had held as little hope for me getting out on my own as I had. So they had snuck closer to the house one night, and together formulated the plan to start a fire and try to flush me out.

"I almost refused," Kiernan told me. "What if Melaina had just left you chained up and we ended up killing you? But then I thought that, if she had wanted you dead, she would have killed you outside Mika's house, so she'd protect you from the fire. So we did it. I went into town and bought up a bunch of food for the road, and some oil, supposedly for a lamp. We wrapped up my spavel cloak in a ball and dipped most of it in the oil, set it on fire, and chucked it over the wall toward the stable." He shook his head. "I didn't think the fire would get that big, though. But they opened the gates as soon as they saw how bad it was, and we slipped inside. You know the rest."

I never did ask where they got the horses that Mika and I rode.

It was strange, our flight back to the city. In some ways, I thought of nothing but what would happen when we reached Vivaskari. I needed two plans: one to get into the coronation and the second to convince the people there that they were about to crown the wrong girl. I had neither. It worried me, because I had only two days before we reached the city. And on the third day, the coronation would begin. I thought about it constantly, creating and rejecting ideas with so much concentration that I was glad my horse only had to follow Kiernan's.

But in another way, I treasured those two days. I rode with Kiernan, who had come to find me. When this was over, I was going to have to tell him that we had to forget that he loved me, forget that I loved him, because the world would never let us be together. That, Melaina had been right about. But for now, I could pretend that day would never come, that we would always be as we were now.

And then there was Mika. The princess of Thorvaldor, whom I had found.

My first impressions of her proved to be utterly accurate. She was as wary as a fox, suspicious of most everyone, and quick to lash out with her sharp, often rude tongue. She could also be as prickly as a hedgehog, leaving you full of spikes after what started as a simple conversation. Still, she cared for her horse with surprising tenderness, giving it little treats from her own supper the two nights we camped. She endured the aches and sores that riddled her legs stoically. My own pains were bad enough, but I had ridden regularly once, and so I couldn't imagine how Mika, who had never been on a horse, must have felt. Still, aside from grimacing whenever she mounted or dismounted, she showed no sign of complaint. And she liked Kiernan, joking with him even in the midst of our flight. But she didn't seem sure about me. She had helped rescue me, of course, but she seemed to view me like a wind that had blown her far from her home to a place she wasn't sure she liked.

It was no wonder, I told myself. She had had a hard life, from the few stories she told when we stopped for the first night, all of us unable to sleep. It had been so dismal, in fact, that it made me slightly ashamed to think of how I bemoaned my own change of circumstance. At least I had Philantha, and Kiernan, and even Aunt Varil, whereas the only person who had truly cared for

EILIS O'NEAL

Mika had been the woman Melaina had given her to. I wondered how Melaina had gotten Mika to the woman, and what she had told her. Mika didn't know. The woman had claimed to be her grandmother, and Mika guessed that she had actually thought she was. They had lived together in the tiny house, scraping a living by scavenging the forest and making wood remedies that they were sometimes able to sell in town. The townspeople had mostly looked down on them, and Mika had few friends. It had made her tough, unflinching, willing to look at a situation and speak the truth about it no matter how painful.

Which meant that she rode to Vivaskari with a kind of resigned fatalism. I had warned her about the oracle's prophecy, to which she had snorted and said that she never expected to live much past twenty anyway. In some ways, I was surprised that she agreed to come with us at all. When I asked her about it, though, she only shrugged.

"What's waiting for me at home but a cottage that Melaina'll be watching forever? At least this way, if we win, there'll be something worth doing for the rest of my life." One side of her mouth twisted. "I had time to think about it, while we were waiting to try and free you. There're other people like me out there, people that the king and queen never thought about. Hard workers, but without even a piece of luck to call their own. If you can make me queen, I could help them." Then she narrowed her eyes at me. "They taught you about how to be a queen, right?"

I raised my eyebrows wryly. "For sixteen years. I learned all of it, and I was good at it. Not that it's done me much good since."

She hunched her shoulders. "Well, I suppose you think it's silly. Me going along with you just for that."

I thought about the way the wizards' college took only nobles and people with money. I thought about how the king and queen had picked a common girl to replace the princess, ready to sacrifice her without her consent if need be. I thought about their gift to Aunt Varil, which had been a nice thought, but nothing truly helpful, given without clear understanding of her situation. I had never noticed those sorts of things when I had been the princess. Oh, I had given charity to the poor on certain feast days, had thought I cared for the plight of those living in Two Copper district. But it hadn't really touched me. And I certainly hadn't worried about the people who might not be starving but still weren't really living. Now, though, I had seen the divide between the crown and the people it was supposed to serve. I had, to a small extent, lived in the crack it made.

I shook my head. "No. I don't think it's silly."

We regarded each other silently, as still as a person and her shadow. Finally, Mika tossed her head and laughed. "Not that the diamonds and soft beds and feasts aren't enough reason."

"Of course," I agreed with a laugh of my own.

After that, something eased a little between us. We were on the same mission and, I felt, learning to like each other in the process.

Even avoiding the roads, we reached Vivaskari at the end of the second day, just as the sunset painted the distant city walls orange and yellow. Kiernan went ahead to an inn and livery stable that stood just outside the walls while Mika and I waited behind a hay barn at the edge of one of the last farms. Even though Melaina knew he had come for me, he was the one she would have the most trouble arresting, since he was an earl's son.

"Don't worry about him," Mika said after we had been wait-ing a time. She sprawled on the ground, her back against the side of the hay barn. The horses stood tiredly in its shadow, neither inclined to wander off. "He'll get the lay of the land and then he'll come back."

I picked at a piece of grass, slitting it with my nail. "I can't help it. I think that, if we live though this, I'll sleep for two years, just so I don't have to worry anymore."

Mika's dark eyes glimmered in the dim light. "For two years, hmm? And whose bed'll you pick to sleep away two years in?"

My cheeks went hot. She had sharp eyes, I realized, a way of noticing things while you thought she was paying attention to something else. Good qualities, for a queen. "It's not like that," I mumbled.

Mika arched her eyebrows. "Why not? He watches you, Sinda. Like you're his best treasure, only he can't think of a way to slip you into his pocket. Hasn't he-of-the-throwing-daggers been brave enough to mention it?"

"He did, once," I said. "Right after Melaina sent a storm to try to kill me. He didn't want me to go look for you. He was scared—well, scared I'd get caught, or hurt. I told him I had to try, and I put a spell on him to keep him from betraying our secret. He kissed me, and then he left. Then the king got sick, and I came looking for you." I leaned my head back against the barn's side. "So everything's . . . strange, now. And he hasn't . . . he hasn't said anything about it since he found me. . . ." I trailed off, biting my lip. I had spent so much time worrying about how to tell him he couldn't love me anymore, but it hadn't escaped my notice that he hadn't mentioned the subject since finding me. Maybe the things I had worried about in Melaina's cell were true. Maybe I *had* hurt him too much, using that spell against him. Maybe he had come after me only because we were friends, because he felt guilty about letting me go off alone.

"He hasn't said anything," Mika repeated flatly. "While we've been racing across the countryside with Melaina's guards behind us or in front of us, and me sleeping an arm's length from the both of you each night." She shook her head in disgust. "For a girl who's supposedly got all this learning, you can be sort of stupid, Sinda."

"Excuse me?" I said stiffly.

Mika leaned forward until her face was close to mine, and then she said, slowly, as you would to a child, "He loves you. It's plain for anyone to see. He came after you, didn't he? Admitted he was wrong to abandon you?"

I shrugged. "We've been friends since I was born, or almost."

"He doesn't look at you like he thinks you're just his friend."

"It doesn't matter," I insisted. The doubts that Melaina had stirred up, that I had had so long to contemplate in her cell, flared inside me again. "What can come of him loving me? He's still an earl's son and I'm . . . a scribe girl. His family would never let him marry me. They were lining up girls at court for him to pick through before we left. Girls with titles and land . . . noble girls. It doesn't make any difference if he loves me. We can't be together."

Mika pushed herself back as she blew a breath upward to stir the hair on her forehead. "What makes you think he'll ask their permission?"

I gaped at her. Kiernan, not marry who his family wanted? It wasn't done, not in the noble families of Thorvaldor. You married to create ties to other nobles, to strengthen your family's position. Sometimes you got love as well, but that was just luck thrown into the bargain.

"And you. You're willing to fight an impossible battle to get me on the throne, but you won't fight for him?"

"I never said that," I said, stung. "I just—" But I could go no further, because just then I heard the jingle of horse tack, and then Kiernan rode into view.

He slid down off his horse after glancing around to make sure no one was nearby. "I don't think anyone noticed me," he said. "I had a drink in the inn and got some information from the people there. The king was buried just two days after he died." He paused, his eyes on me.

He hadn't been my father, but he had been the closest thing I had to one. It hurt, to know that I would never see him again. But I didn't have time to mourn him, so I only breathed against the tightness in my chest, motioning for Kiernan to go on.

"They hardly let him lie in state at all. Something about keeping the fever from spreading. And the coronation is tomorrow, just like Melaina said. They're not even waiting for the delegations from Wenth and Farvasee. They'll just pay their respects when they arrive in a few weeks. And the coronation won't be open to everyone—each person entering the palace gates will have to be checked by a palace guard and a wizard from the college. To keep the princess safe."

He sat down on the ground, his legs stretched out in front of him as he tugged off his boots. "Which is all that we knew. But there's more. The city gates are being watched, too, to make sure no 'dangerous elements' enter the city. I think," he said, raking a hand through his hair. "I think that Melaina's people got here before we did and told her you escaped. If a courier took two horses and rode them hard, he could have beaten us. So she'll probably be looking for us at the city gates." He stopped, watching me. He looked as tired as I suddenly felt, as ragged as a torn sail in the wind.

For a long time, none of us said anything. My mind was whirring again, but without results. Finally, though, Mika said, "But you're a wizard. You could . . . disguise us, or turn us invisible. Something to get us in the city and the palace."

"I'm an unpredictable wizard," I countered with a sigh. "I don't know if Kiernan told you, but I'm not exactly in control of my magic. There's too much of it, and it was buried under the spell for too long. Half the time, when I try to use it, it comes roiling out and I blow something up." I shifted, trying without success to get comfortable on the ground. "I might be able to do a spell to get us through the city gates," I admitted finally. "But magic won't work at the palace gates. The wizard will be watching for magic, waiting to sense any whiff of it. They'd notice us if I tried to get us in under magical disguises, and the guards will certainly catch us if we try it without."

"Well, you spent your whole life in that palace. Are you telling me there aren't any secret passages or tunnels that you found? Something no one else knows about."

I shook my head. "There isn't anything—"

I snapped my eyes to Kiernan as ice suddenly formed under my skin, only to find him staring hard at me as well.

"Nameless God, we're stupid," he whispered. "King Kelman's Door."

　　　　　EILIS O'NEAL

"It will open from either side," I said quickly. "And we have her now. It'll be there if she's there. 'Royal blood.' But we need the map—without it, I'm not sure I can find the exact place the door is from the other side of the palace wall."

We were grinning at each other, so wildly we must have looked insane.

"Sorry to interrupt," Mika drawled out of the darkness, "but what's this door you're talking about?"

CHAPTER TWENTY-TWO

I woke before dawn, while stars still spotted the sky and the others still slept. It was too early to attempt the spells of disguise and the gate into the city. My eyes squeezed shut, I tried to force myself back to sleep to no avail. So I finally hauled myself up and, treading quietly so that I wouldn't wake Kiernan and Mika from their places in the hay barn, crept outside to watch the dawn come.

It's already so warm, I thought as I sat with my back against the barn, my knees drawn up to my chest. If the king hadn't fallen ill, the entire court might have journeyed to the lake country for a few weeks to escape the coming summer heat of the city. I imagined what went on at the palace instead. The lower halls would be already bustling as fleets of cooks, maids, and butlers hurried to arrange the last-minute details of the coronation. The nobles would still be asleep, but not for long, as serving men and women came to help them into their finery for the day.

Kiernan would have been among them, if he hadn't come looking for me. I shot a glance toward the door of the barn, as if

I could see him through it. I didn't know what to do about him. One kiss, one declaration of love. Maybe it hadn't been enough to survive how I had pushed him away, used magic against him, chosen Thorvaldor over him. He had come to find me, yes, had said he had been wrong. But he hadn't done anything else, regardless of what Mika said. Maybe he had realized how futile it would be to love me. Though I tried to push it from my mind, I fairly hummed with the knowledge that I might die today. He wouldn't have forgotten. It might be too much, the fear of losing me, so much that he had withdrawn his heart to protect it.

Of course, even if I lived, he must know that we couldn't marry, must know what I would have to tell him. The Earl of Rithia would never let his son marry a commoner, and I wouldn't be able to live with myself if I let him throw off his titles, walk away from his family, for me. Even Melaina had known that well enough to toss it in my face.

I wondered if Melaina was asleep, there in the palace. I doubted it. I had no hope at all that she wouldn't know of my escape. Somehow she would know—be it a message by courier or a spell to let her know if I crossed House Sare's gate. She would be planning, watching, waiting. This was the moment of her triumph, and she wasn't going to let me take it from her easily. My only saving grace was, strangely, the strength of her desire to place Orianne on the throne. She would have to move carefully; it wouldn't do to have any suspicion fall on Orianne now. Perhaps that would be her weakness. Or perhaps she would abandon her careful measures, the covering of her own tracks, in her desperation.

Orianne. Was she asleep? Again, I doubted it. She had lost the man she thought her newly discovered father. And in a few hours, she would be crowned queen. She had had only a few months to become used to the idea of being the princess. I imagined her standing by the window of my old rooms, tall and serene, watching the same dawn I watched. The two of us, the false princesses. What would become of either of us after today?

Mika. What would become of her? Even assuming that we triumphed, her road would be hard, perhaps harder than Orianne's or mine. Her world was about to change, to expand far past the boundaries that she knew. She hadn't shown it, but she must be scared.

I was scared. I might have escaped death at Melaina's hands, but the oracle's prophecy still loomed in my mind. If I continued on this course, it seemed likely that someone would die. Today, perhaps. I picked at a weed growing in the grass. If only I knew which of us was in danger, which side of the triangle needed protecting most. I could prepare better then, take precautions. But as it was, there were no precautions to take, nothing to do but rush into the fray.

But was I doing the right thing? I thought I was doing it for the good of the country, but maybe Kiernan was right. Maybe it was really just for me, to prove to myself that I wasn't a nobody. Was it my sense of duty pushing me on, or my own vanity?

The oracle had seen my path branching away in choices and chances. Was I taking the right way? If Mika died, everything, all of it, would have been for nothing. But would it be worth it if I died? If I bled to death, knowing I had put her on the throne, would I feel it had been a price worth paying?

EILIS O'NEAL

Nameless God, I prayed, *I know that it matters not to you who sits upon the throne. But it was your oracle who helped me on this path. So you must be watching us, if only out of the corner of your eye. Please, hold us in your hands today.*

I barely heard her footsteps before she settled herself down beside me, and it startled me into jumping. "Sorry," Mika said. "Living in the woods, you know. Gran always said I should pretend to be a deer so no one could hear me coming."

Her voice sounded light, but when I turned to look at her, I saw that her face looked tight around her eyes and paler than usual. "Is Kiernan still asleep?" I asked.

"Snoring like a bear. I think I could've danced on his head and it wouldn't have woken him."

We sat silently for a while, and then she said, "So this prophecy of yours. It says that one of us will die today."

The eastern sky was turning gray, tinted with the barest hint of rose. "They don't come true, sometimes."

"That's not a lot of help, from where I'm sitting."

"No," I agreed. "Not a lot. But at least it didn't say we'd lose."

"Winning doesn't mean much if you're dead, Sinda."

Soon there wouldn't be any stars out at all. "This time it might," I said softly.

Mika didn't answer. Instead we sat in silence, our chins in our hands and knees pulled up against our chests, waiting for dawn to come.

A few hours later, I rode toward the city, my back as straight as a sword and my stomach as knotted as an old fishnet. The road leading to the Guildhall district gate was crowded with people trying to get into the city. Few would be allowed into the actual coronation, but all wanted be able to say that they had been in Vivaskari when the princess became the queen. So I had to work to keep my horse under control as people—horsed and unhorsed—pressed around it. I tried to keep my eye on Kiernan, who had gone ahead of me, but I kept losing him in the crowd. Mika was somewhere behind me; we had thought it best to enter one by one, in case the guards were looking for a group of two girls and a young man.

I had managed three spells that, though they didn't transform us entirely, altered our features enough to fool someone who didn't know us well. Working the spells had left me jittery, though; I had accidentally charred a section of grass around my feet before I managed to wrangle the magic back down. *But we should be able to enter the city undetected,* I thought, *and reach Philantha's to retrieve the map.*

Never mind that I still had no plan for afterward, when we reached the palace.

I pushed the thought away—it made my stomach tighten even more to think of it—as Kiernan approached the guard at the gate. The man, a tall and burly fellow, looked harried by the sheer number of people trying to enter the city, and, even though Kiernan's sword hung from his belt, he gave Kiernan only the most cursory of glances before waving him inside.

One down, I thought, while resisting the impulse to look over my shoulder for Mika.

I expected the guard would surely notice that something was wrong with me. I felt so weak and nervous that I had to grip the saddle with one hand as the family in front of me was examined. But the guard merely flicked his eyes over me. If the spell still held, he would see a young girl with dark blonde hair, wearing a dress with the emblem of the shoemakers' guild. I didn't have the skill to make them last very long. An hour maybe, from the time I cast them. Mine must have still held, though, because he let me pass.

Inside, Kiernan had waited for me a short distance from the gate, though close enough that we could still reach it quickly if we had to. We both turned our horses to watch, hands clenched on the reins, as Mika neared the gate.

Mika was having some trouble controlling her animal; a screaming baby behind her made it prance nervously, but she managed to calm it as she reach the guard. He looked at her, then nodded, and I heard Kiernan's sigh of relief.

Her horse had taken only a few steps past the gate when the guard whipped around, raising his hand. "You!" he cried. "Stop!"

Kiernan kneed his horse forward just as I swung from my saddle. If I had to do magic, better that I didn't have to control a horse at the same time. As I dropped to the ground, I heard Kiernan swear as a cart pulled in front of him, its driver peering at the cross street in confusion, as if he didn't quite know where he was going. Kiernan wouldn't reach Mika in time.

Mika turned slowly, her face revealing nothing. The guard strode toward her, reaching up to take hold of her reins. He said something to her, then handed her something. She nodded and the man wheeled around to return to the gate.

"An apple," she said when she reached us. A fine sheen of sweat had broken out on her forehead. "Fell out of my saddlebag."

"An apple," Kiernan repeated, then let out a whoosh of breath that turned into a frantic laugh.

"Enough," I interrupted. "The coronation starts in two hours. We have to get to Philantha's."

It took longer than usual to thread our way through Guild-hall into Goldhorn. The city had swelled with outsiders, and it seemed that every city resident had decided to go out into the streets. I considered abandoning the horses and continuing on foot, but Kiernan's mount was his own, and I doubted that he would want to leave it in the street. By the time we reached Philantha's stable, though, I almost threw myself from the saddle in my haste to get down.

I had taken only a few steps toward the door when I slowed in confusion. It was quiet in the tiny stable yard behind the house, even considering the noise in the street. Where was the sound of Gemalind humming through the kitchen window? Where was Tarion, who usually would have scrambled out to take our horses?

I heard Mika and Kiernan slide off their horses and then hurry toward me. "Where is everyone?" I asked.

Kiernan surveyed the silent house. "Could she have given them the day off? Gone to the coronation herself?"

I licked my lips. "The first—maybe. The second—" I shrugged. "She doesn't like spectacle. She might go, as a college wizard, but not so early. She'd wait until the last minute, then slip in the back. Kiernan . . ." I trailed off. There was no need to put my worry into words; I could see the same thoughts on their faces.

"We still need the map," Kiernan said. "And some different

clothes wouldn't be bad. Something to make it look a little more like you two belong at the coronation." Kiernan himself, though not dressed as he normally would be for a coronation, had at least changed into clean clothes from his saddlebags that morning. My own change of clothes had been lost, along with the nag I rented, in March Holdings. "Mika's smaller than you, but not by much."

"They kept most of my nice dresses, but anything's better than this," I said, grabbing my travel- and prison-dirtied clothes. We wouldn't fit in, even in my best, but we wouldn't look like street urchins either.

My neck prickled as I stared up at the house, but then I shook my head. We couldn't afford to delay any longer. "We have to go."

The house was even quieter inside. I shivered as we made our way to the grand staircase without seeing anyone. Though my shoulders ached with tension, I tried to tell myself that nothing was wrong, that the feeling of eyes on my back was my own imagination. I had almost convinced myself when we reached the second floor, and I heard the moan.

The three of us froze for an instant, and then I dashed down the hall toward the crumpled form lying two doors down from Philantha's study.

It was Gemalind, the cook. Swallowing hard, I rolled her over as gently as I could, only to find a massive black-and-purple bruise spreading across the side of her face. I raised a trembling hand toward her nose, and felt a faint breath stir against my fingers.

"Philantha," I gasped as I staggered upright. "Her study." I stumbled the few feet toward the door, blood rushing in my ears.

The door to the study was slightly ajar, and I flung it the rest of the way open so violently that it banged against the inside wall.

Most of the room was undisturbed. The table covered with open bottles of liquid, none so much as overturned, still stood near the door. The snakeskins, feathers, bird nests, and animal claws lay in the corner where Philantha kept them. Books lay scattered across the room, but only in a laid-down-while-reading-them sort of way. At first glance, nothing was wrong.

I took a step into the room, and glass crunched under my boot. I looked down to see a line of broken shards, as if someone had thrown several of the glass scrying balls toward someone near the door. As my eyes followed the trail, I saw one of the tables lying on its side, a puddle of blue potion mixed with wet sand spreading around it.

I rushed forward, and on the other side of the overturned table lay Philantha.

She was pale, so pale that the lines of blood that had trickled from her nose and mouth stood out like red spiderwebs. She lay on her side, one arm bent up under her, as if someone had pushed her down and then left her. I could see the dark bruises that hands had left around her neck.

"No," I whispered as I dropped to her side. I reached out to grasp her shoulders, unhook her arm from behind her back. I couldn't bring myself to check for her breath, as I had for Gemalind.

"I should have told you." I had stood in this very room before I left and had almost, almost told her where I was going. But I had been blinded by my own protestations that there wasn't enough proof. I had convinced myself that I would put her in danger by telling her. But those weren't the real, final reason. As Kiernan had said, I had wanted, secretly, in my heart of hearts, to find Mika myself. So I had left in silence. Instead of protecting her, I had left her vulnerable to the very thing I had feared. She would have had no warning, no idea that someone might come to hurt her.

Tears were forming in my eyes, and my shoulders had started shaking. "This is all my fault," I mumbled. "I should have told you."

I reached out to brush a strand of her hair off her forehead, and as I touched her face, she coughed.

"Philantha," I breathed. Then, over my shoulder, "Kiernan, Mika! In here!" Turning back to her, I grasped her hand in mine. "Philantha, can you hear me?"

Her eyelids fluttered, then opened to pained slits. "Sinda?" she rasped.

"It's me," I confirmed. "Are you—" It seemed absurd to ask if she was all right. "What happened?"

"Men," she said weakly. "Two of them. They had . . . wards. My spells just glanced off them." She closed her eyes as a wave of pain seemed to grip her. "Gemalind?" she said through gritted teeth. "I heard her . . . in the hall."

"Alive," I said. "Hurt—not so badly as you—but alive. Where are the others?"

"Told them to go, enjoy the day. They all left early. All but her." She forced her eyes open. "They wanted you, Sinda. Kept asking where you were, if you'd come back."

"I know," I said. "I'm sorry. I should have . . ." I heard Kiernan and Mika behind me. "We need to call a healer," I told them.

"I'll find someone to send," Kiernan said before hurrying out of the room.

"I don't have much time," I told Philantha. "I can't explain now, but we have to get to the palace before the coronation."

Philantha's eyes, hazy with shock and hurt, had been flicking between Mika and me. "Spell. I feel it . . . between you two. Strong. Something connecting . . ."

I nodded. "She's the princess, Philantha. The real princess. And they're about to crown the wrong girl. We have to stop them, but we have to get there first, and then . . ." I floundered again, still unsure of what I would do once we got there.

Philantha laid her head back against the floor. "Like I thought," she murmured. "Her essence, still in you. Almost see it. That's . . . connection."

"You were right," I said. The door creaked as Kiernan entered.

"I paid a boy to run to the college," he said. "There should be some healers still there."

I squeezed Philantha's hand. "I have to go. We have to get something from my room, and then we have to go. I'm sorry."

Her eyes had closed; she seemed to be falling back into sleep. "In both of you," she mumbled, and lay still.

"Can you stay with her for a moment?" I asked Kiernan, who immediately came around the table and knelt down by Philantha. "Come on," I said to Mika. "We can change clothes in my room, and get the map."

Kiernan and Mika had arranged Gemalind more comfortably, I saw as we hurried down the hall. I didn't stop to look at her again; the healer would help her when one arrived. In my room, Mika and I pulled off our clothes, with no thought of modesty, to

EILIS O'NEAL

don two of my best dresses. Mika's was a bit too large, and neither was nearly grand enough for a coronation, but they would do.

"Which board was it?" I muttered to myself as soon as I was dressed. Mika flashed me an inquiring look, so I explained. "Before I left, I hid King Kelman's map under one of the floorboards. I didn't want anyone to find it, but I couldn't think of a better place. Ah!" That one, half hidden under the bed, with a dark knot at its end. "There a comb on the table," I said. "Toss it to me."

The handle of the comb was just thin enough to slip between the boards, which creaked as I wrenched between them. But the loose one came up and under it, safe and undamaged, I found the gently rolled-up map. The genealogies and the oracle's confession, also there under the floorboard, I stuffed into the pocket of my dress.

"Let's go," I said. "The coronation will be starting soon."

Mika nodded and followed me out the door and down the stairs. As we entered the second-floor hall, however, I ran headlong into Kiernan, who grabbed my shoulders to keep me upright.

"Shh!" he hissed, a finger over his lips. "I heard something downstairs."

Creeping across the floor, we snuck to the railing that looked out over the entrance hall. Sure enough, two men armed with long daggers were slowly soft-footing it up the stairs. Melaina's men may have left Philantha for dead in the study, but they had been watching the house from outside, waiting for anyone to come back.

We flattened our backs against the wall so that they wouldn't see us. "Is there another way out?" Mika whispered.

I pointed. "Down the servants' stairs. We could make it to

the door to the garden, and out from there. Unless they've left more men outside."

"We have to try," Kiernan agreed, his hand hovering over his own sword. "But we have to go now."

"But Philantha," I said. "And Gemalind. They might hurt them more. And the healer's coming."

Kiernan's expression was stricken, and Mika had balled her fists up so tightly that her knuckles were white. But he shook his head. "If they catch us, that'll be it, Sinda. No more chances. Orianne crowned queen."

"I can't leave her! It's my fault that she got hurt!" I should go, I knew it. The coronation would be starting soon, and if we were to be in the Hall of Thorvaldor to get everyone's attention— somehow—we had to leave now. But I couldn't seem to move; I felt like my legs were locked to the floor by manacles.

I had sacrificed so much to find Mika, had walked through danger I hadn't known I could face. I had put her and Kiernan in danger and we had only narrowly escaped. To be caught now, to let it all be for nothing . . . the idea was unendurable. But Philantha had taken me in when I had been alone. She had believed in me when the wizards' college turned me away. She was my friend, and hurt, and I couldn't go.

"She'd want us to go!" Kiernan was arguing.

"I can't—" I cried, but it was too late. The men stepped onto the second-floor hallway and saw us.

"Seems you were right," the taller one said to the other. "Two little sparrows, and a popinjay with a sword to protect them."

The second man smiled, a leering, ugly thing. "Come here, sparrows," he called. "We won't hurt you—much."

"Stay back!" I yelled, and then, reaching deep for the magic, tried a spell that would let me toss a ball of fire to the floor at their feet.

I couldn't do it. The ball sputtered in my hands, then died.

"Not very good at that, are you, sparrow?" The first man waggled his knife at us as he stalked down the hall.

Sucking in a breath, I tried again, and this time the ball of fire glowed between my hands. I lobbed it toward them, then flung out my arms, trying to push Kiernan and Mika back away from the blast.

It should have exploded; I had seen Philantha set a straw doll aflame in seconds. But it seemed to bounce off them, sliding away as if a glass wall surrounded them, and then vanished into the air.

The second man grinned again. "Wards, my dear," he said. "Powerful ones. Yon wizard"—he jerked his head in the direction of Philantha's study—"her spells didn't work either."

"Run," I whispered. And then more loudly: "Run!"

Mika and I turned in the same instant, pounding down the hall toward the servants' stairs. I heard a gasp, the clatter of a dagger skidding down the hall, and looked back to see one of the toughs clutching at his arm while the other stared at him in horror. Kiernan wore a fierce grin as he whipped around to follow us.

He had surprised them; they looked like street fighters and hadn't expected a noble like Kiernan to actually know how to fight. But they were professionals, and as we reached the stairs I heard them coming in pursuit. We nearly fell down the stairs, as we raced down the hall and burst through the back door into the walled garden. Kiernan slammed the door behind us as he came through, and I heard it knock into one of the men. We ran through the garden door and down the alley toward the street.

"The northeast wall," I gasped to Kiernan. "What's the fastest way there?"

"Follow me," he yelled, and we plunged into the crowds moving toward the palace to await the announcement that the princess had been crowned.

I didn't know how far behind us the men were, so we ran as if they were only a few steps away. My side ached before we had gone a few blocks, and I could hear Mika panting beside me. Sweat trickled down the side of my face, and I heard my gown's hem rip at least once. While the crowds slowed us, they also hid us, disguising us in the mass of people milling in the streets. But we needed a good head start because, though I knew generally where we should go, I would need a moment with the map to locate the exact spot.

We had reached Sapphire when I reached out to yank Kiernan back. The crowds were thinner here; many of the residents of Sapphire would actually attend the coronation. So we huddled in the shadow of a huge tree, Mika watching for our pursuers as Kiernan and I studied the map.

"Look," I said, touching the map gently. "It's right where we thought it was."

"We'll be able to see that big tree over the wall, the one by the benches where we were sitting when . . . when they came for you," Kiernan agreed. "You're sure it'll work?"

I nodded, ignoring the twinge of doubt inside me. "It has to."

"Well, we're about to find out," Mika said suddenly. "They're at the bottom of the hill."

They had seen us but, thinking that there were few places for us to hide, they came more slowly, obviously as winded as we were. I grimaced at the thought of more running, but as Mika and Kiernan dashed from behind the tree, I followed, the map in my hand.

Up the road and around the corner, and we were there. The palace wall stretched in both directions, west toward the palace gate and east toward the spot where it would meet the city walls. We jogged, Kiernan and I glancing overhead to look for the tree inside the wall that would mark the door. I stumbled from looking up, almost going to my knees, but Mika grabbed my arm and pulled me onward. And then, suddenly, I saw it. Green leaves swayed in the breeze, visible even over the wall.

"There," I wheezed, and we stumbled to a stop. Melaina's men would be on us at any minute.

"Where is it?" Mika demanded.

"It should be here," I cried, pulling the map open. Yes, we were standing just outside the place Kiernan and I had found so many months ago. "It should be here!"

"Maybe she has to touch the wall," Kiernan said. Mika ran her hands over the wall, patting it down like a horse, but nothing happened.

"She's here! It should appear for her," I moaned, afraid to look back over my shoulder for the men. "See?" I ran my finger under the runes. "'Take heed, all who would attempt the Door of the King. Let it be known that only for one with royal blood and royal words will the Door appear.'"

"What about that part at the end?" Kiernan asked.

I shook my head. "They're just gibberish. The mapmaker's name or something."

"No, they're not," Mika said from over my shoulder in a odd, tight voice.

"What?" I gasped, just as Kiernan said, "You can read those?"

She nodded, eyes wide.

"But I couldn't translate them," I said. "Can you read ancient runes?"

She shook her head. "But I can read that."

Royal blood, I thought. *Royal blood and . . . royal words. Words spelled so that only someone of royal blood would be able to read them at all.*

"Quick! What do they say?"

Mika stared at me, an unreadable expression on her face. "I am Thorvaldor," she whispered.

Light flared from the palace wall, so bright that I had to put up a hand to shield my eyes before it died away.

As the light dimmed, I felt Kiernan grab my hand and squeeze it tight. Because there, set where a blank wall had stood only a moment before, was a small, wooden door.

CHAPTER TWENTY-THREE

Booted footsteps echoed down the street as Melaina's men saw us standing there. They put on speed. "Go through, go through," I shouted, and we tumbled over one another through the door. Kiernan slammed it behind him as I glanced around wildly, expecting someone to have seen us fall into the palace gardens and called the guard. But there were no pleasure walkers out today; everyone was inside, awaiting the start of the coronation.

"They'll be able to come through, too," Kiernan said as he hefted his sword out of its sheath. "You two, go! I'll hold them—"

But Mika only took a step back from the door, and, with her royal blood and words withdrawing, it vanished, leaving nothing but the wall behind.

I let out the breath I'd been holding at the exact moment that Kiernan and Mika did the same. Our eyes met, and there, in the middle of the palace garden, we began to laugh.

But we couldn't laugh for long. When our giggling had died away, I scanned the garden as I chewed on my lip, thinking.

"Will they be able to get in?" Mika was asking Kiernan, who shook his head.

"I don't think so. The coronation will start soon, if it hasn't already, and Melaina made sure that no strange people could get in. Unfortunately for her, that'll include her ruffians. I think we'll be safe."

Mika snorted. "Of course. Perfectly safe."

I ignored them. In my mind I was traversing the halls of the palace, deciding which ones would take us to the Hall of Thorvaldor with as little notice as possible. I had to push back the memories that were threatening to overwhelm me: the smell of the gardens in summer, the way the sun shone on the buildings of the palace. I couldn't slip back into those feelings, those longings for things that were past. I had to focus, but it was hard, because I felt so tired and scared. . . .

Somewhere in the palace, bells began to ring. The coronation was beginning.

Yanking myself free of the memories, I reached out to grab Mika's hand. "Follow me," I told her. "Whatever happens, however anyone tries to stop us, just follow me. If I'm taken, follow Kiernan. You both know the story—you can tell them."

"So that's our plan?" she asked. "Just waltz in and just tell them?"

I nodded with a shrug. "I can't think of anything else. We just have to get into the hall and make it to the front. We should be able to get enough out that they'll want to listen."

"When you're telling the story," Kiernan put in, "just make sure that they know Orianne didn't have anything to do with it. That she didn't know. The last thing we need is a mob attacking her or something."

"Agreed." I took a deep breath, though it didn't steady me as much as I would have liked. "Let's go."

Because of the bells, we took the most direct way possible. The very route, I realized, that I had taken with Cornalus the day they had told me who I really was. Now, though, no nobles strolled the halls, no servants scurried to do their bidding. Everyone was either in the Hall of Thorvaldor or in the feasting rooms, making them ready for the celebrations to follow the crowning.

Still, two guards stood at one of the side doors into the hall, just as they always did. One held out an arm as we approached, but Kiernan slid smoothly to the front of our group. "You won't tell my father we were late, will you?" he asked with a rueful smile. "He threatened to banish me back to Rithia if I couldn't be on time today. But it was my cousins, truly. They're overwhelmed with being in the city—couldn't seem to get dressed this morning."

The guard glanced over Kiernan's shoulder at us. Mika and I smiled the same tight smile. *He'll know,* I thought. *He'll recognize me, or realize how alike we look. He'll know something's wrong.*

But the guard only grinned at Kiernan, promising not a word to the Earl of Rithia. I could hear voices indoors, and the murmur of hundreds of people as he pushed the door open a crack to let us slip inside.

I had no idea what was occurring at the front of the room. Though chairs had been set in rows to cover the entire floor of the hall, the crowd was still standing, blocking my view; only the white columns were visible where they reared to hold up the ceiling. I could hear shuffling in the balcony above, and knew that it, too, had been filled. A single aisle had been created in the center of the room. I pushed and clawed my way through the chairs to reach it, Mika and Kiernan behind me. Offended muttering rose up as we shoved past people, but I paid it no mind. I practically fell into the open aisle, knocked forward again as the others skidded after me.

No one noticed. All eyes were locked on the front of the room where Orianne was kneeling on a short platform in front of the throne. Her dark hair fell in shining waves down her back, and she wore a long red robe trimmed with ermine, which fanned out around her where she knelt. A priest of the Nameless God held his hands over her head, blessing her. Even from behind, she looked regal, elegant, everything that a princess—a queen—should be.

There was a moment, a second when I could have hesitated, when I could have turned around and left. She had been trained, after all, almost as well as I had in the things a ruler should know. And she looked the part, much more than Mika or I did. No one had truly seen us yet; we could have gone without anyone ever realizing we had been there.

I didn't even pause.

"Stop!" I shouted, striding forward with my head raised. I had never walked so straight, so purposefully when I had been the princess. The old queen sitting on a chair beside the throne on the dais, looking sad and proud at the same time, saw me first. Her hand went to her chest, as if she felt faint.

"Stop!" I cried again as heads turned to look at me. The priest's hands faltered over Orianne's head. "She isn't who you think she is."

I had reached the front of the room, mere steps from where Orianne now rose and turned to see me. Her eyes widened, and

EILIS O'NEAL

I saw her throat flash before a figure peeled away from the first row of chairs, where Cornalus and the other members of the council sat.

Melaina stepped out in front of me, forcing me to stop.

Her own dark hair, the exact color of Orianne's, I now saw, was coiled about her head in crownlike braids. She wore a red gown piped with the black of a Master wizard. She was beautiful, queenly, and her eyes flashed as she saw me, then widened even more as her gaze flicked behind me to see Kiernan and Mika.

"What is this?" she asked in that velvet voice, which nevertheless carried to the very back of the balcony.

"You know what it is, Melaina," I said in a low voice. Then, shifting my gaze to Orianne, I said softly, "I'm sorry."

Then I spun to face the noble ranks of Thorvaldor and cried, "You have been deceived! My lords and ladies, you have been betrayed by one of your own."

I heard a rustle from behind me, and then the queen called, "Nal— Sinda Azaway. What is the meaning of this?"

Looking around at her, I felt my heart thump painfully. No matter what Melaina said, no matter how the queen had let them treat me, she had been my mother, once. "You were deceived," I repeated more softly. "We all were. By Melaina Harandron."

"This is ridiculous," Melaina began, but Orianne raised a quick hand.

"Let her speak," was all she said, but Melaina had to fall back, a dangerous look on her face.

"She conspired against you, Your Highness," I said. "She worked with the oracle of Isidros—her sister—to make a false prophecy, one that would make you think that Nalia was in danger. She convinced you to switch your daughter with another girl to protect her, but when you did, she switched her again, for her own daughter." I raised a hand to point an Orianne, standing so straight and rigid on the little platform. "She gave Nalia to a poor woman in Saremarch, where she would always know where she was. She killed her own sister so that she wouldn't have a change of heart and tell. She sent redvein fever to Neomar so he would have to leave the city, so he wouldn't notice that Orianne had the spell on her, too. She killed the king with that same illness!"

A gasp from behind me, and then the queen was on her feet. "What?" she cried. "What did you say?" Her face, already pale and tired looking, had gone whiter still, and her hands clenched her skirts.

"She killed the king," I said quietly. "She told me she did."

The queen pressed her lips into a thin, tight line. "Why would she do that? Melaina has been loyal to our family, one of our best advisors. Why would she do any of that?"

I wanted to go to the queen, to take her hand, but I made myself stand very still. "It wasn't just for herself. It was vengeance. She hid it, but she's a Feidhelm, and she wanted the throne for her own family."

It was an old story, that of the Feidhelms, but the queen knew it. I could see her eyes flick to Melaina, considering. A murmuring rose in the crowd as the few people who remembered the Feidhelms whispered to their neighbors, and those to their neighbors as well.

"A fine story." Melaina's voice cut through the tumult, clear and sharp, and I jerked around to see that she had turned to

EILIS O'NEAL

face the crowd. "But just that—a story made up by the girl set up to replace the true princess so that she might grow up out of danger." The muttering began again as people realized for a certainty who I was. Melaina shook her head, a graceful, smooth motion. "It has been hard for you, hasn't it, Sinda? Getting used to your real life? Hard enough that you've come here with this wild tale, hoping to bring down the true princess?"

"That's not true," I cried, but Melaina was speaking again, her midnight voice so seductively calm.

"Your Highness," she said, inclining her head to the old queen. A look at Orianne: "My princess. My fellow Thorvaldians. What is more credible? A sixteen-year-old plot concocted by me? One in which I killed my own sister, faked the death of my own child. One that I set in motion all alone, without the knowledge of a single other soul." She smiled. "My fellow wizards at the college will tell you I am clever. But I am not that clever.

"So . . . which is more credible? This strange story, or another answer? That this girl, half crazed by the upending of her world—a sad thing, true, but one done for the good of this country—should come here and try to disrupt the coronation?"

The muttering grew louder as people craned their necks to get a better look at me. "I've been to Isidros," I shouted over the noise. "I've seen the oracle's own writings. I have her confession with me now." It did no good. Hardly anyone seemed to be listening to me. "We came in through King Kelman's Door. Only the true princess could do that!"

"More fantasies," shot back Melaina. "You came in with Kiernan Dulchessy, who will apparently do anything for you, as he's been caught in your wiles for years."

"She has the birthmark," I cried, lunging forward to drag Mika to the front; I grabbed her arm and forced it into the air. "The princess's birthmark."

"A trick," Melaina said easily. "One *you* have concocted, Sinda."

"It's true," I tried again, but my voice cracked with strain, and no one heard me. The councillors in the first row were looking at me and shaking their heads while the noise from the crowd increased. Fingers were jabbed in the air as the sound grew; people glared at me, at Kiernan and Mika, from their places. Dropping Mika's arm, I took a step toward the queen, thinking that perhaps I could persuade her, but she had retreated toward her chair again. Kiernan was trying to reach Cornalus, but two noblemen had reached out to grab his arms; he struggled in their grasp, trying to reason with them. Mika stood alone, just a few steps from the platform where Orianne had wrapped her arms around herself. Melaina took a step toward Mika, who backed up and tripped against the platform. I whipped around and saw the queen still standing by her chair, a pained look on her face as she stared at me. But she did not come forward to help me.

They don't want to believe, I thought in despair. *It's too much, too hard, and she's too good.*

We had failed, I realized. In just a moment, someone would call the guard, who would arrest us for treason. I had to do something, but what? No one could hear me over the shouting now—no one wanted to hear me. I had run out of options.

I looked from Mika, who was scrambling onto the platform to escape Melaina's advance, to Orianne, who seemed frozen in her place. Three men held on to Kiernan now, and he was flailing

EILIS O'NEAL

as he tried to free himself, his eyes swinging wildly from Mika to Orianne to me. Kiernan, who should have been standing among the nobles, dressed in his best finery, ready to make mischief at the coming feast. Where he *would* have been standing, if not for me. Instead, he stood on my side, inside the strange triangle of Orianne and Mika and me. Fighting against Orianne, who was his friend. Fighting for me, his best friend, and a girl named Mika whom he had only just met, but liked immediately.

A mirthless laugh escaped my lips. He had loved all of us in different ways, for all the good it had done him.

And then something inside me shifted, as if a piece of broken roof had fallen to let the light into a dark room.

Kiernan had loved us. All of us, in different ways. He had seen something in each of us that he could cling to, that he could love. Was it the piece of soul we all shared? Though Mika's by right, some part of her lived in Orianne, and somewhere, the tiniest bit still hid inside me. Even Melaina had said it, that they had not been able to get it all out.

What had Philantha said? *Spell. I feel it—between you two. Something connecting . . .*

The spell still bound us, three sides of a triangle, holding our souls together. It was the spell that still made Orianne appear to be the princess. If only there were some way to make Melaina remove it, or to call Neomar to the city. But that was foolish, more than foolish—absurd. Melaina would never remove the spell, and Neomar was sick or dying, and too far away to help. There was no one, no one who could—

I froze, my heart beating so quickly it hurt. In my head, Philantha's silly, jumbled voice said: *It's easiest, of course, to cast a spell on yourself. You know yourself, inside and out, even if you don't know that you do. It's other people, of course, always other people who make it hard, because you don't know them, not the way you know yourself.*

Mika's soul was still inside me, part of me. And it was inside her, too, and Orianne. A true triangle, those bits of soul forming the sides that connected us. It was a powerful spell, built to fool anyone who thought to look for it, made by the most powerful wizards of the age. But it was inside me. I might not have Melaina's training, but I had power, power I had never let fully free. And I knew, finally, who I was. I had been finding it out ever since I had left my old identity behind that spring, even if I had resisted it and cursed it at times. In the last few weeks, I had been tested and tried, and I had made it through, though not without cost. I could finally see myself as I really was, the good and the bad, the parts of me that were strong and the parts that were weak. I knew who I was.

I was Sinda Azaway, and I could do this.

Kiernan shouted; Mika cried out as Melaina reached for her. I didn't have time to think, or consider, or worry.

Find it, I thought. *Find her soul in me, and Orianne, and give it back to Mika.*

Throwing my head back, I flung my hands upward and unleashed magic.

Control. I had wanted it so badly, needed it so badly. I hadn't ever wanted to really let my magic out, had felt I couldn't unless I had a strangle grip on it. I had worried that it would overtake me, burn me up from the inside out, and everything around me.

EILIS O'NEAL

Now the magic raged up and out, racing from me to Orianne and Mika. *Control*, I thought as I fought to hang on to the magic, to direct it as I wanted. But there was no control; the magic streamed toward them, enveloping them in its power as it had enveloped me. I heard Orianne scream; my own insides felt like they were on fire, but I couldn't stop it. *Control*, my body cried out.

I felt the magic dwindle as I sought to regain my grip on it, felt it grow sluggish and start to die. The spell would fail; I knew it, could feel it starting to collapse around me. But if I didn't do this now, there would never be another chance.

Just find it, I thought, and let go.

And suddenly, everything slowed down. It was like the magic, which had been pouring from me, paused and looked back, consideringly. As if it were asking me what to do. As if, once I had stopped trying so desperately to control it, it could work with me.

Her soul, I thought. *It's in us and it shouldn't be. Give it back to her.*

A golden haze blossomed around me, obscuring the hall and the people in it, but not before I had seen similar hazes rise up around Mika and Orianne. I was dimly aware that the noise coming from the crowd had quieted as the people realized that some spell was occurring, and I heard the tiniest of gasps from where the queen stood. *Good*, a small part of me thought. *She's seen this before. She'll know what it means.* But the larger part of me had no care for the queen, or the crowd, or even Melaina standing only a few paces from Mika. I saw only the haze, I concentrated only on the magic ferreting around inside me, looking for the part that didn't belong.

I felt it when it went. Not as big as the last time, but an emptiness nonetheless, a place where there had been something, and now there wasn't. Before I had wanted to claw that piece of soul back to me, stopper it back into the hole it had left inside me. *Take it,* I thought this time. *It wasn't ever really mine to begin with. And besides, I don't need it now.*

Slowly, slowly, the golden haze faded, so that I stood blinking and shaky in the hall. That expenditure of magic—more than I had ever used before—combined with the taking of Mika's soul, was going to catch up with me in mere moments, I knew. Still, I couldn't bring myself to say anything; I could only look toward Orianne and Mika.

Mika had doubled over to clutch her stomach, overwhelmed by the feeling of her soul coming back together. Orianne stood more straightly, but with a hand pressed over her heart, her face pale and quiet, her eyes on me. With what looked like great effort, she lowered her arm and touched a spot just below her elbow with her other hand.

"It's gone," she said quietly. "I felt it. I felt it go out of me. Something . . ."

"Her soul," I said with a glance at Mika. Twice now, Orianne had been told who she was, only to have it taken from her. It had been almost unendurable for me the first time; I couldn't imagine what a second time would feel like.

"I'm sorry," I told her, knowing it wasn't enough.

Whispers had started in the first rows, where many of the college wizards sat. By now they would have sent probing spells at all three of us. They would be realizing who the princess was, and who she wasn't.

EILIS O'NEAL

I didn't sense the slightest buildup of magic before the blow hit me. One minute I was standing there, and the next I was sprawled on the ground, feeling like a battering ram had pounded into me. A second later invisible hands gripped my throat, so that I gagged, scrabbling at my neck, and tried, without success, to suck in breath before more magic pinned me, frozen, in place.

"Stupid, meddlesome girl," Melaina hissed. From my position on the floor she seemed to tower to the ceiling, and the air around her crackled with magic. The nobles holding Kiernan stumbled backward. He wrenched free and drew his sword. A flick of Melaina's hand caught him in a spell so that, though he strained and pulled against it, he couldn't move at all.

I heard movement from the area where the college wizards sat, but Melaina threw a hand up toward them, shouting, "Any spells and I'll bring this whole room down."

The sounds of movement stopped as the wizards hesitated, unsure whether to risk Melaina's sending a magical jolt through the foundations of the room before they could disable her.

"You could have been powerful," she continued to me. Her beautiful face was contorted with rage. "I gave you the chance. Now, you'll just get to watch *her* die before you do."

She whirled, arm outstretched, and what looked like a bolt of lightning arced from her fingertips toward Mika. I couldn't move; I couldn't scream. I couldn't even close my eyes.

A triangle, set in a storm. One of its sides crumbled and fell away, leaving only two.

No, I tried to cry. *No!*

Orianne leaped.

She tumbled in front of the bolt, her ermine-trimmed robes

flying behind her. It hit her squarely in the chest, and she dropped like a stone at Mika's feet and didn't move.

Silence, and then a collective gasp. Melaina staggered, her hands clutching her arms. The spells on me lessened so that I could breathe, could move.

"No," I heard her whisper.

And then Kiernan struck her from behind, ramming his sword through her back and into her heart. She didn't even cry out. She only lifted one arm toward Orianne, and fell.

With her death, the last vestige of her magic washed off me. I scrambled to my feet, lurching over the space between us, and dropped to my knees beside Orianne. Mika had done the same; she cradled Orianne's head on her lap. A thin line of blood ran from one corner of Orianne's mouth, but her eyes blinked when she saw me.

"I'm sorry." My tears fell onto the neckline of her gown, and I futilely tried to brush them away. "Orianne, I'm so sorry."

The barest of smiles curved her lips. "Orianne," she whispered. "No one calls me that anymore. You remembered."

She drew in one rasping breath, and then her eyes slid to the side, locking in place, and her chest stilled.

I looked from Orianne's still form to Melaina's, and then to Mika's anguished face. Kiernan had wrenched his sword free of her body, but he made no move to approach us. People were moving around us, talking and scurrying about, but I could barely hear them. Mika and I sat without moving, Orianne still across Mika's lap—the three princesses, what had once been a triangle, and now was broken.

CHAPTER TWENTY-FOUR

When it was all over, I went home to Philantha.

They would have made room for me at the palace, given me a whole wing if I had asked for it, but it didn't feel right to stay. I wanted to make sure the healer had come, to explain to my teacher what had happened. Besides, in the hubbub that followed the almost-coronation, only a few people really noticed that I had gone. The queen, who pressed my hand without speaking. Mika, who broke away from the wizards and nobles and councillors to stand in front of me.

"Didn't say you were going to spell me," she huffed.

"I didn't know I was. I didn't know I could, until right then."

She raised her eyebrows. "Big magic, for someone who could barely disguise us this morning."

I shrugged tiredly. Having spent so much magic, I felt ready to drop. "It was in me. That piece of your soul. So it *was* me. And that means that in some ways, you and—" I swallowed. "You and Orianne, you were both me, too. We were all the same. It would have been almost impossible for anyone else, anyone besides Melaina or Neomar. But it's always easiest to work a spell on yourself. And I thought . . . well, I thought I had nothing to lose."

We looked at each other, consciously not looking at the dais where Orianne had fallen. Neither of us said that I had been wrong, that there had been something to lose.

"I'll come for you," she said before she was called away. "Don't think I won't."

No one else noticed me leaving. Only Kiernan, who hugged me close in silence, and then let me go. He had always known what I needed, even more than I had.

Back at Philantha's house, I found her ensconced in her bed, layered in healing salves and spells. Gemalind had received similar but less intensive treatment, and she was recounting the events to the maids and butler, who had returned to the house. I checked on both of them, told the butler to alert the city guard to the presence of two toughs who might still be watching the house, and went to bed.

A day passed, then two, then several. No one from the palace came to seek me out. I had told the story, given them the genealogies and the oracle's confession from my pocket, told them where to look to find more evidence. Not that anyone really felt the need to go looking, not after what had happened. There had been talk of a reward, for my service, but I had only shaken my head. It felt too much like blood money, and I had tasted enough blood to last a lifetime.

Philantha, in her true, stubborn form, was up after the second day, swaddled in blankets in one of her study's chairs and directing the cleaning of the room. She had sniffed when she first saw me, then smiled.

"Something's changed," she had said. "I can feel it, and I'm never wrong about such things, you know."

"I know," I replied with a small smile. "And it has."

"Good," was all she said. Then she made me help clean the study with magic, and not my hands.

She was right. Something had changed. I felt . . . looser, more at ease in my own skin. The magic that I had tried to hold in for so long, only to have it come bubbling out in frantic ways, seemed to settle inside me. It was there, and sometimes insistent to be used, but more peaceful. Or maybe I was more peaceful, at least with it. I didn't feel scared before I started a spell anymore; I just tried it, and if it worked it worked, and if it didn't, at least nothing exploded. The control I had sought I relinquished, in favor of a sort of joining, an acceptance between the magic and me.

Other things, though, weren't as easy.

I spent a lot of time wandering the city. For days, all the talk was of what had occurred at the coronation, though less and less of it resembled the truth as the stories spun wilder. People also talked of what had occurred afterward, which I heard with some skepticism. Some things, though, I took to be true.

They had interred Orianne in the Harandron tombs at Saremarch. She had, after all, been the baron's daughter, and innocent in this, no matter what her mother had been. The caravan that moved her body had been seen off by the old queen and the new princess, who stood watching it from the palace gates until it could no longer be seen.

Melaina had been buried on a hillside outside the city, a point called Traitor's End. No one but the grave digger had seen her laid into the ground.

The wizards' college was in an uproar, it seemed, to have had one of their own turn so violently against the crown. Luckily, they were no longer without a leader. The fever that had stricken Neomar had lifted the very day of the coronation, and he had returned, weaker but still sharp, to his duties.

I heard about myself, too. This time, my name didn't fade away into distant memory but remained clear in people's minds. I was described as clever, brave, sacrificing, even beautiful. Luckily, with such words being bandied about, no one looked twice at the scribe girl pacing the streets of Vivaskari at all hours.

I had a lot to think about.

Had it been worth it? I thought, standing outside the palace wall in the spot where, should Mika decide to stroll, a door would open for her. We had won, yes, but at what cost? Philantha would walk with a limp for the rest of her life because I had been too prideful to tell her what I knew, and Gemalind still spooked if you entered the kitchen too quickly. The house of Harandron had fallen, with no heir to assume its mantle. The king had died long before he ought to have, leaving the queen alone and, if the rumors were true, frail.

Orianne had died, just as the oracle had prophesied.

She had given up her life herself, I tried to tell myself as I wandered the streets or practiced spells for Philantha. In that split second, she had chosen. I told myself that, but it didn't help. She had been kind, and gentle, and unaware of the mechanisms that had ordered her life. As Kiernan had once said, she would have made a fine queen. Just not the rightful one.

　　　　　　　　　　EILIS O'NEAL

Without me, she would have been alive.

It was a weight that made my steps heavy, a thought that haunted me when I tried to sleep at night. When I had thought of the oracle's prophecy, I had, somehow, always assumed it would be me dying, or Mika. I had considered Orianne only as an afterthought. But she had been the one to pay the price of the events I set in motion.

Would things have been different if I had acted differently? If I had told someone, as Kiernan had wanted? Would Philantha have been prepared for the attack? Would the wizards and healers attending the king have known his fever was brought on by magic and been able to save him? Would Orianne be alive? I didn't know; I would never know. Maybe everything would have played out as it had, and maybe not. Whatever might have been, I kept telling myself, I am the one who helped set these events in motion, and I have to accept the consequences of my own actions.

But had it been worth it? I wasn't sure.

I was sitting in the garden the day she came, my fingers idling in the little fountain. It was a bright day, and I had almost decided to go inside when the gate in the back opened, and Mika walked in.

"Told you I would come for you," she said at my surprised look. "You think I'd forget?"

She sat down beside me on the fountain's rim. She wore a long dress of dark green, and her hair looked as if it had been pinned neatly around her head that morning. But she kept pulling at the neckline of the dress, stretching it away from her skin, and several strands of hair had fallen loose around her face. Her eyes flicked back and forth a few times as she looked around the garden, a fox still.

"They keep calling me Nalia," she said finally. "I can't get used to it."

"You may not," I said.

She shrugged. "At least Kiernan doesn't. And they have so many things I'm supposed to learn, and double-quick, like my gran used to say. Places and people and treaties and . . . everything. I fall asleep with it running in my head."

"I'm sure you'll be able to learn it all," I started, but she raised a hand to interrupt.

"What are you going to do, Sinda?"

I scrunched my face in confusion. "What? When?"

"For your life. What're you planning to do?"

I swallowed, my mouth suddenly dry. "I . . . I don't know, exactly. I'm going to keep learning from Philantha. I want to visit my aunt in Treb, to see if . . . if we can get along better. I think I'll . . ." I faltered, unsure. I had spent so much time thinking about getting Mika on the throne that I had never thought much about afterward. Though I had finally had the time to think about my own life in the long days that had passed since the aborted coronation, my mind had been filled with other things. Now, though, reality seemed to press on me with Mika's words. What was I going to do, now that I no longer had a country to save? Now that I knew myself a little more, knew what I was capable of. My life, I realized, had gone still, like an unfinished painting. It was as if I hovered above it with a brush, unsure where to go from here. I had achieved my goal, completed my quest, and I had no idea of what to do with myself.

"Thought you wouldn't have much of a plan. Which is good, because I need you," Mika said shortly.

It was not what I had been expecting. "What?"

She turned to face me fully, a line of tension appearing between her eyebrows. "You know it all, Sinda. All the things they want me to learn. You could be my . . . my chief councillor. You could come live in the palace, or you could stay here, keep learning from Philantha. It'd be good to have a wizard I knew I could trust. I just . . ." For a moment she lost the wary, tough expression that was always on her face. She looked young, and scared. "They keep calling me the princess—they want to crown me queen sometime soon. She exhaled through her nose. "Well, most of them. There are a few who keep grumbling about my 'upbringing,' and whispering about whether or not I can read. I guess they're not sure if someone who grew up in a hut in the woods is really fit to be queen."

I goggled at her. All that we went through, and still it wasn't good enough for some of the nobles? "Who else do they think they're going to get for the job?" I asked in confusion. "Your closest relatives are two third cousins—which means they both have an equal claim to the throne. It would be chaos if they tried to pick between them, never mind ridiculous. *You're* the princess, the real thing."

Mike lifted one shoulder in a shrug. "That's what the queen—I mean"—she stumbled a bit on the words—"my mother keeps saying. That they'll come around, because I'm the true princess and rightful queen. Honestly, though, I don't feel like either of those things. But I might, I think, someday, if you helped me."

"And afterward?" I asked ruefully. "You won't need me like that forever. And then I'll still be here, without a plan."

A sly look stole across her face. "I've been thinking. It's like we were saying, out there on the road. Something's wrong here, in Thorvaldor, under all the things that are right. Lots of people who don't have a wet cat's chance at changing their lives. People like my gran, and us. And I've been thinking, maybe this, all this, maybe it happened so I'd know it. 'Cause I wouldn't have, if I'd grown up like I was supposed to. Maybe it happened so I could start to change it." She sneaked a glance at me then, her face caught between defensiveness and honest question. "Do you think that's silly? That I'm just looking for ways to make sense of it?"

The God cares naught for such earthly things as thrones, and who sits upon them. The oracle's words hovered in the back of my throat, but then stuck there. Perhaps, for once, the God had cared, at least a little.

"No," I said, as I had on the road. "I don't think it's silly."

Mika sighed, like a load had been lifted from her, before saying, "Anyway, it's what I've been thinking. As for afterward, once I know what I ought to, I figure there must be other people like you. People too poor to get into the wizards' college, but with magic inside them. They could use a school of their own. Course, there'd have to be someone to run it. If you learned enough from Philantha . . ."

A grin was spreading across my face. *Yes,* a voice inside me whispered. Whether it was my own, or someone else's, I wasn't sure. I looked at Mika, who was staring off into the distance at some future inside her head.

The cost had been high, and even higher for some than for me. But looking at Mika, I felt sure of one thing.

Whatever the cost, I had made the right choice.

"All right," I said. "I'll do it."

EILIS O'NEAL

Mika grinned back at me and hopped up. "Good. I have to go now, though. I had to threaten to demote the guards to get them to let me out of the gates alone. You'll come tomorrow, then?"

I felt a little lightheaded. Strange, how quickly things could change. That morning I had felt conflicted, unsure about my course. But I had a path now, a way to do what I had been trained to do, to aid Thorvaldor. "I could come now," I said. "Philantha doesn't need me right now. I could tell her what we've talked about and—"

But Mika only shook her head. "No. You have something else to do now."

I shook mine back at her, perplexed. "No, I don't."

Mika fixed me with a look that said, for all my knowing what a princess should know, I was really and truly stupid. "He's been waiting for you," she said.

My heart did a tiny flip. "Kiernan?"

"Who else?" Mika snorted.

I had been thinking about him constantly; he intruded into every other thought, even my sadness over Orianne. But I hadn't seen him, not since the coronation. Maybe I had been right, I had begun to think when he never appeared on Philantha's doorstep: he had given up on me.

"Are you still worried about what his parents will think? You're the princess's chief advisor now," Mika scolded. "You can hold your head up in any room in the country. But if you're worried about it, I suppose I could grant you a title. . . ."

I laughed without meaning to, shaking my head. "No, no," I said. And then, more seriously: "I don't think I'm worried about that anymore. I saved the country, didn't I? Surely that counts for something." But then, doubt crept in again. "But he hasn't come," I said plaintively.

Mika put a hand on the gate, as if she would leave, but then she turned and sighed. "He's letting you make up your own mind, because that's the only way you'll ever really let him in. This time," she said, "you're going to have to go to him."

I found him, with a little hint from Mika, in the gardens where we had met when I first came back to the city. "He goes there every day," she had said. "Waiting."

He was standing with his back to me, as if regarding a particularly elaborate section of flowers. But he didn't move when I crunched across the gravel path, and I realized he wasn't seeing the flowers at all.

Still, he didn't jump when I tapped his shoulder and said, "I'm here."

Kiernan turned slowly, one arm twitching like he wanted to hug me. But he didn't move.

"I'm sorry it took so long," I said. "But I had so much to think about, and I didn't . . . I didn't know . . ."

Still, he waited.

I blew out an impatient breath. "She's made me her councillor, you know. I'm to help her learn how to be queen, be the voice whispering advice behind her throne. And then she's going to help me open a school for magic."

He only gazed at me, not helping in the slightest.

I jigged up and down a little where I stood, scowling at him. Once, I might have given in to the worries that had plagued me since that first kiss. That he might have loved me once, but had decided it was too much trouble. That he was too angry over the spell I cast over him to forgive me. That our stations were so different that his family would never allow us to be together. I might have faltered when faced with the doubt that nettled me as he continued to stare at me so implacably. I might have turned red and slunk away, rather than stand firm before him. Once, back when I had left my life behind without a fight. But not now. I was stronger now, braver. I had faced my worst fears, and survived them.

"So I really think that your parents should let you marry me. Not right now—I have so much to do, with Mika and Philantha and the magic—but someday. Someday not too far away. I did save Thorvaldor, after all, and I expect that Mika will pay me well in exchange for my years of knowledge. She even threatened to title me—it would be just like her to want to rub everyone's noses in my commonness. And I think that, if they have any objections, you should just—"

"Break with them?" he asked. He was trying to be serious, but one corner of his mouth kept twitching.

"Well, yes," I admitted.

"I already did," he said, and my mouth fell open. "Or at least, I threatened to, if they wouldn't give me their blessing." A thin line worked its way between his eyebrows, and his smile dimmed a little. "I think they knew it was coming, but it didn't make my father happy. He stormed around shouting about duty, and for a while I thought I might really have to go through with it."

The line deepened, and he glanced away from me. "That was frightening. It was my choice—*is* my choice—but practically it would have been . . . difficult. You aren't the only person who was trained for just one thing; I don't know if I know how to be anything but the future Earl of Rithia. I kept telling myself I could do it, become someone else if they disinherited me, but I didn't want to break with them. I would have, but I didn't want to."

My heart clenched a little, seeing the glimmer of tension around his eyes.

Suddenly, the tiny grin flickered at his mouth again. "But then my father started thinking about the advantages of my marrying someone who had done the future queen such a service. After that, he was happy to give his blessing."

I shook my head as if to clear it. I had come here asking him to do just that, but hearing it out loud seemed like something from a dream. "You really told them you wanted to marry me?" I asked.

The smile had taken over his whole face now. "I told you before: I fell under your spell before you even knew you had magic, before you saved a kingdom, back when there was no chance *you* would be allowed to marry *me*. Nothing's really changed since then, except that now any children we have might be wizards themselves, and I'll be hopelessly outnumbered.

"So, yes, I want to marry you. Someday. If you'll have me," he said modestly.

"Of course I will, you idiot," I said with a shriek, and threw myself into his arms. Some things, though, never change, regardless of how many countries you save. I tripped at the last moment, and we both went down in a laughing heap. It didn't stop me from kissing him for so long that we both were gasping by the time it ended.

"So what should I call you now?" he said when we had our

EILIS O'NEAL

breath back. "Savior of Thorvaldor? Soon-to-Be Master Wizard? Chief Councillor of Wise Words? My own love?"

"Sinda," I said, without the slightest twinge of old memories, or something lost, or regret. "Just Sinda. Though I like that last one almost as much."

Kiernan reached out and tucked a strand of escaping hair behind my ear. "I think I like Sinda best myself," he said.

We hauled ourselves up and, still laughing, brushed grass and sticks from our clothes. Then, arms around each other, we began the walk back to Philantha's house to tell her that her scribe had just gotten a new job and become engaged in the same afternoon. I looked back up the hill once, toward the palace, and then turned away. I would go there tomorrow, but right now, it didn't matter. Today I only had to walk with Kiernan, to visit Philantha, to finally be just myself.

For once, for the first time, it was enough.

ACKNOWLEDGMENTS

I've been waiting for this book, my first book, since I was about three. But without a great many people, I could never have written and whipped it into good enough shape for you to hold now.

Thanks to many teachers over the years, including Mrs. Waleska, Mrs. Scribner, Mrs. Victor, and Mrs. Sellers, all of whom encouraged a shy girl to write. Thanks to the Tulsa City-County Library, for hosting a young writers' contest that gave me confidence. Thanks to Fran Ringold, the best boss imaginable, who encourages me in all ways. Thanks to my friend, Quin Swiney, who faithfully listened to everything I ever wrote as a teenager.

Thanks to my agent, Craig Tenney, and the folks at Egmont USA, especially Elizabeth Law, for taking on and believing in a new writer.

And finally, thanks to my first readers: punctuation goddess Diane Burton; continuity stickler Lisa Wellinghoff; my unfailingly supportive parents, Helen Beth and Johnie O'Neal; and my wonderful husband, Matt Smith. I mean it when I say that, without your ideas, sharp proofreading eyes, and support—even when I'm being neurotic—this book would not have happened.

EILIS O'NEAL (her first name is pronounced "A-lish") is the managing editor of the literary magazine *Nimrod International Journal*. She started writing at the age of three (though the story was only four sentences long). She lives in Tulsa, Oklahoma, with her husband, Matt, and two dogs, Nemo and Zuul. *The False Princess* is her first novel. You can visit her online at www.eilisoneal.com.